THE
SEARCH
FOR US

Also by Susan Azim Boyer

Jasmine Zumideh Needs a Win

THE
SEARCH
FOR US

A Novel

SUSAN AZIM BOYER

WEDNESDAY BOOKS
NEW YORK

First published in the United States by Wednesday Books, an imprint of St. Martin's Publishing Group

THE SEARCH FOR US. Copyright © 2023 by Susan Azim Boyer. All rights reserved. Printed in the United States of America. For information, address St. Martin's Publishing Group, 120 Broadway, New York, NY 10271.

www.wednesdaybooks.com

Designed by Donna Sinisgalli Noetzel

Library of Congress Cataloging-in-Publication Data

Names: Boyer, Susan Azim, author.
Title: The search for us : a novel / Susan Azim Boyer.
Description: First edition. | New York : Wednesday Books, 2023. | Audience: Ages 12–18.
Identifiers: LCCN 2023017158 | ISBN 9781250833709 (hardcover) | ISBN 9781250833716 (ebook)
Subjects: CYAC: Family life—Fiction. | Siblings—Fiction. | Iranian Americans—Fiction. | Fathers—Fiction. | LCGFT: Novels.
Classification: LCC PZ7.1.B6955 Se 2023 | DDC [Fic]—dc23
LC record available at https://lccn.loc.gov/2023017158

Our books may be purchased in bulk for promotional, educational, or business use. Please contact your local bookseller or the Macmillan Corporate and Premium Sales Department at 1-800-221-7945, extension 5442, or by email at MacmillanSpecialMarkets@macmillan.com.

First Edition: 2023

10 9 8 7 6 5 4 3 2 1

To Wayne and Mitzi, who inspired it ♥

THE
SEARCH
FOR US

CHAPTER ONE

Samira

Samira Murphy was the first to admit, she was an OF: an over-functioner. If shit hit the fan, she could be counted on to clean it up. She didn't need help. She helped.

Yet, here was her guidance counselor, Mrs. Sandoval, peering at her with wide, sad eyes over her pink-rimmed reading glasses as if Samira were as helpless as a newborn kitten.

"I know your grandfather passed, suddenly and unexpectedly, this year," she said in a low, mournful tone. "As I said before, I'm so deeply sorry for your loss."

It wasn't *that* sudden or unexpected. The doctors had warned that Grandad's abdominal aortic aneurysm would burst. The advance notice didn't make it any less of a gut punch.

Mrs. Sandoval adjusted her glasses. "You've had twenty-two absences this year. More than the student handbook allows."

Well, yes. Between hospital visits, Grandad's funeral, worrying about her brother, Kamron, and bad cramps, she had missed a few days of school here and there.

Samira gathered up her long, dark hair and twirled it around her finger. "Mrs. Sandoval, didn't the pandemic prove attendance was optional when we could have done our work from a smartphone on a desert island?"

Mrs. Sandoval tapped Samira's transcript with her glasses. "If you have another unexcused absence between now and the end of the year, you may not walk at graduation. You'll have to go to summer school. And that could derail your admission to Lewis & Clark."

What felt like little invisible mosquitos zinged her abdomen and the inside of Samira's left knee, her autoimmune disorder going into overdrive.

Derailing her admission to Lewis & Clark would derail Samira's dream of starting her own business, which her econ teacher had ignited after he said she had a flair for entrepreneurship.

Actually, he said she didn't take direction well and would probably be better off starting her own business. But he had already inspired her million-dollar idea.

"I added my admissions deadlines to iCal and set up Siri with reminders. I uploaded my ACT scores to the College Board. I'm still on track to make the Dean's List." Samira nodded to the wall behind Mrs. Sandoval, on which a bright blue YOU ARE RESPONSIBLE FOR YOU banner hung. "Don't worry. I'm responsible for me."

She flashed a smile Grandad had labeled "the chomper," wide and broad with a mouth full of blindingly bright teeth she had whitened at the mall kiosk with a half-price Groupon.

Just as her mouth began to tremble from the tension of maintaining that smile, a photo of Mrs. Sandoval's Jack Russell terriers sporting San Francisco Giants kerchiefs caught her eye. Mom had taken her and her brother to a game a million years ago, back when they felt like a family.

Mrs. Sandoval let out a deep exhale. "I'll let you slide for now. But again, no more unexcused absences." She softened. "My door is always open, Samira."

Samira's face got warm and itchy with embarrassment when people—adults, especially—took pity on her. She stood up. "I have everything sorted. Really."

Mrs. Sandoval looked at her with a cross between pursed lips and a half smile. She would have continued the conversation, stayed till the bottom of the ninth. But Samira was already halfway out of the ballpark.

⌖

Samira sat on the cool metal bench in the bus shelter at Old Redwood Highway and Third Street in downtown Santa Rosa waiting for the 44 South. Her head was pounding and her stomach gurgling. There wasn't time to run across the railroad tracks to Aroma Roasters or even across the square to Starbucks for a snack.

She texted Tara: meet at my house for homework?? 20 mins, bring Larabars cherry pie

Within seconds, Tara texted back: omg yes, yes!!! 🙂 💙 🎏 see you there!!!! 🖤 💕 🎉

The nose of the bus shimmered in the distance. Samira wasn't wasting the money she had earned making acai bowls at Juice World over the summer on a car payment, gas, or insurance. She would need every penny—plus the $10,000 bond Grandad had left her *and* a student loan—for college. Her scholarship was generous, but it didn't cover everything.

She had three weeks to cash in the savings bond, accept the student loan, and pay the $1,000 Lewis & Clark deposit before the first of May—as soon as she was certain Gran could get along without her.

If only Gran could master the banking app. Samira had set up all the bills to be auto-paid every month after Grandad's pension and social security had auto-deposited. *This damn thing,* Gran said every time she could not seem to open the app or navigate to the bill-pay screen.

Then, of course, there was Kamron.

The Chihuahua on the corner of Victoria Lane yapped at Samira as she walked to the one-story ranch house Grandad had built fifty years earlier with its peeling avocado-green paint and white trim. "Gran, I'm home," she called out. "Is Kamron home yet?"

Now that she had helped get her brother back into AA, Samira had to make sure he went to his meetings. Yes, she had taken on lots of adult responsibilities since Grandad passed, but she would rather take charge than leave an item on her to-do list undone.

She padded into the kitchen whose country wallpaper was covered in absurdly cheerful gingham bows and peony-filled flowerpots.

Gran was standing over a Crock-Pot. "No, he's not home yet."

Samira greeted her with a kiss on the cheek. "He has an AA meeting tonight."

"Do you want some chili?" Gran asked. "It's the one with my secret ingredient."

Her "secret ingredient" recipes were . . . weird: crumbled goat cheese in her oatmeal, grated zucchini in her chocolate-chip cookies. Dr Pepper and soy sauce in her chili. But one of her strangest concoctions had hit #1 on Samira's million-dollar-idea list: Tangy Tequila Lime Fudge, which Gran had accidentally invented when she mixed up the recipe for vanilla fudge with a boozy cupcake. Grandad said Samira would *knock Mr.*

Wonderful's socks off once she got on *Shark Tank* like her idol Tracey Noonan, the founder of Wicked Good Cupcakes, who had just sold her company for millions of dollars. Imagine what millions of dollars could do for their family.

The rice-paper skin around Gran's cornflower-blue eyes was even more crinkled. Silver-gray roots were visible under her auburn rinse. She had aged ten years in the last year, after Grandad "croaked," as he put it (*Sami, when I croak, be sure to call the tree trimmers so the elms don't get overgrown*). If Mom had known he was going to die, she probably wouldn't have left for her dream job teaching art up in Oregon, but now that she was there, Gran would never ask her to come back.

"Where did Kamron say he was?" Samira asked, her eyes narrowing with concern.

"I think he's on a job today," Gran said distractedly. "Somewhere in Windsor."

If Kamron could hang on to his IT consulting jobs for more than a couple of months at a time, Samira wouldn't feel so guilty about leaving.

"I'll be in my room," she said. "Send Tara back when she gets here."

She stopped by the bathroom for her giant bottle of calamine lotion. A Benadryl would be better to battle back the invisible mosquitoes, but then she would sleep through her Spanish IV homework.

When she got stressed, they attacked, lying in wait for the opportunity to sting her forearms or calves. The little red welts itched for days afterward.

She had begged her mother to put her on steroids back in middle school when the doctor had first diagnosed her with an autoimmune disorder. Instead, Mom insisted that she see an acupuncturist. No way was anyone putting hundreds of needles all over her body. The Benadryl, at least, relieved the itch.

She *had* been under a lot of stress lately. In Social Dynamics class, where she had learned all about over- and underfunctioners, her teacher had cautioned OFs against "fixing everything around them" to avoid looking inward. As far as Samira was concerned, life as an OF was working out just fine. It was the underfunctioners around her she had to worry about.

u at work? she texted Kamron and set her phone down on her nightstand. She would not watch the home screen obsessively. If he didn't text back right away, it didn't mean anything. Necessarily. He could be in a meeting. Or on an important call.

Or in a bar.

She scratched the welt that had appeared on the inside of her forearm and managed to occupy herself for the next half hour studying future tense for her Spanish quiz; she didn't look at her phone once until Tara pulled up outside.

No reply from Kamron yet.

Samira seized her phone, tapped Find My Friends, and pinpointed Kamron somewhere along Old Redwood Highway near Mark West Springs Road, which *could* be his job site.

Or could be Tommy's Tavern.

And the invisible mosquitoes swarmed.

CHAPTER TWO

Henry

Henry Owen scanned the ice, tracking the puck like a drone paired with its target. He checked the Mariners' winger into the boards hard, slamming him up against the plexiglass. Their hockey sticks tangoed.

He gained control of the puck and circled around the back of the net, then fired toward his winger, Daniel, who was blasting down center ice in perfect position to receive Henry's pass. Daniel sped toward the goal, got a slap shot off above the goalie's left shoulder, and scored.

Henry's stick shot up into the air. He would get the assist. There were only six more end-of-regular-season home games to boost his stats with his club team, the Ice Devils, and have a shot at freshman starter for the University of Denver.

Robert and Jeannie clapped politely, as if they were at a golf tournament. *Mom and Dad, Mom and Dad.* They had raised him since he was two years old. Why was it so hard to think of them as his parents instead of his aunt and uncle?

For starters, he looked nothing like them. Then again, he didn't look like his bio-mom, Nancy, either, who sat two rows behind them, on her feet shouting, "That's my boy!" She said

Henry got his brown skin, hazel eyes, tousled hair, and the dimple in his chin from his dad. His bio-dad.

Most days, Henry thought about him at least once. Where was he? Why had he disappeared? And, most important, did he ever think about Henry?

If he passed a brown-skinned man with tousled hair who looked to be about his bio-dad's age at, say, Sprouts, he had to resist the urge to follow him around like a lost puppy.

His girlfriend, Linh, sat next to Mama. She got the whole Mom/Mama thing right away, maybe because she had been adopted. Nancy, whom Henry called Mama, was his biological mom. Nancy's older sister, Jeannie, whom he called Mom, and Robert were raising him.

Linh's face was all sharp angles softened by a crooked smile. Her hair smelled like oranges because her mom stocked her bathroom with products made only from natural essential oils. Mama was probably talking her ear off, but she didn't seem to mind. She was good with parents.

The coach signaled a line change. Henry skated to the boards and collapsed on the players' bench next to Daniel, who squirted water straight to the back of his throat and fist-bumped Henry. "That pass was golden."

"Thanks, man." Henry mainlined his own water bottle.

Daniel removed his mouth guard, doused it with water, and stuck it back in. "You'll make freshman starter for sure."

"Or my dad will disown me," Henry said with a half laugh.

When he was in juniors, he would have been psyched at the possibility of making freshman starter for a college team. But Robert had hounded him about it so much that Henry hadn't even accepted admission to the University of Denver yet. He would. He just hadn't gotten around to it.

Coach signaled another line change. The Devils were up four to three with two minutes and thirty seconds left to go in the third period.

Henry got the puck into the neutral zone. The Mariner he had shoved into the boards earlier made a run for the net. Henry skated after him, when suddenly, a stick crashed into his shoulder blades. He lurched forward right as the ref blew the whistle.

Cross-checking from behind was for bullies and cowards, Coach had said. Doesn't give your opponent the opportunity to brace for impact. If there was anything Henry hated, it was a bully.

He spun around and slashed the Mariner across the waist with his stick. In an instant, they had both dropped their gloves. Henry grabbed the Mariner's jersey with one hand while trying to knock his helmet off with the other.

Coach had warned him not to fight after the whistle. But at times like these, he wasn't thinking about what Coach had said; he wasn't *thinking* about anything, really. He was *feeling*. Adrenaline. Anger. Intensity. Something more than the nothingness that usually surrounded him.

He was now on top of the Mariner, pounding him through his pads. The refs tried to pull him off. All he could hear were his own muffled grunts until a voice finally broke through.

"Henry. *Henry*."

Henry immediately stopped swinging and allowed Daniel to lift him up. The Mariners' coach escorted the other player to his feet and off the ice.

"I . . . sorry," Henry called after him.

"*Dude*," Daniel said as Henry skated toward the penalty box. "They've called me the N-word out there, and I don't do that shit."

He shouldn't have done it. The problem was, once it got started, he couldn't stop.

Henry bumped open the door to the penalty box when the head ref grabbed his arm. "Number eighty-eight, *game misconduct*," he shouted.

Linh was looking at him with arched eyebrows like, "Really?"

Mom's lips were pursed. Dad was frowning.

Mama was on her feet yelling, "You suck!" at the ref.

Henry peeled off his jersey and threw it into his hockey bag on the locker room floor. No one ever kept anything in the lockers at the rink, which reeked of salt and sweat.

The goalie fist-bumped him on the way to his locker. "You're a beast, man."

"Shouldn't have dropped my gloves." Henry would need to apologize to Coach Nielson.

"Anger management, bro," Daniel said. As the only Black player in a pretty white sport, Daniel Stewart's dad had said he had better never start a fight or escalate one. *You don't need any of those hard-core hockey moms complaining to the coach or calling the cops on you.* And he *was* a cop, a Ventura County sheriff. He also insisted Daniel keep his hair close-cropped even though Daniel's mom wanted it natural.

It wasn't like Henry was proud of dropping his gloves. But smack in the middle of the haze of nothingness that often surrounded him was a small, burning red core of anger that needed an outlet from time to time.

"Henry," Coach Nielsen said, peeking into the locker room. "See me in my office."

"Yes, Coach," said Henry.

"Beg for mercy," Daniel teased.

∞

A freshly showered Henry sat across from Coach Nielsen, who had the surprisingly gentle air of a youth pastor, in a cramped, windowless office. "Henry, you're suspended for the next game," he said.

Henry's breath got caught in his lungs. *Suspended?* That would ruin his stats and jeopardize the scholarship Dad had pushed him so hard to get.

"Coach, he hit me first," Henry said defensively.

Coach held up his hand. "You dropped your gloves. It's your second game misconduct of the season. No one's looking for brawlers anymore. It's a finesse game now. You know that. You could get kicked out of the league."

Henry sank into his seat.

"If you got a league suspension, Denver might withdraw its scholarship."

Dad would be furious. The red core throbbed. Henry was not allowed a single misstep.

Coach leaned forward and clasped his hands on the desk in front of him. "Henry, I mean . . . I gotta ask, do you really want to play college hockey? Because it's starting to seem like you're sabotaging yourself."

Henry squirmed. Mom and Dad had enrolled him in youth hockey when he was eight years old. To keep him out of trouble, Dad had said, even though Henry had never gotten into trouble.

"My dad says it makes the most sense financially for me to play for Denver. Get a full ride all four years if I can."

"I'm asking, what do *you* want?"

What Henry wanted was usually beside the point.

What popped into his head was a gap year. A whole year to slow things down, sort them out. If he said that, Coach might tell Dad, and Dad and Mom would blame Mama.

Mama, who'd had ten different jobs over the last ten years (cocktail waitress, Home Depot cashier, data entry operator, background extra for movies and TV, contact tracer for "the plague," and more), while Henry's dad—his real dad—had been a security guard who "never took responsibility" for him. Mom said he got kicked out of the military.

They would make it sound like Henry was drifting, doomed to follow in Mama's footsteps without the much-needed focus and discipline they provided.

"I want to go to the University of Denver and play for the Pioneers, Coach. Honest, I do."

If he said it enough times, it might start to feel comfortable, like a new pair of Bauer skates that took weeks to break in, instead of pinched and cramped.

"Then keep your temper in check." Coach stood up. "You're still coming to every practice and suiting up for the game."

"Yes, sir," Henry said, rising. "Thank you, Coach. I won't let you down, Coach."

Just as they got to the door, Coach Nielsen said, "Henry, the first year of college is tough. The competition is brutal. If you're not ready, it'll be a disaster."

Henry hesitated a beat before insisting: "I'll be ready, Coach, I will."

CHAPTER THREE

Samira

Mr. McGregor. The new freshman English teacher? *Seriously?"* Samira alternated bites of fizzy Dr Pepper/soy sauce chili and the cherry pie Larabar Tara had brought while on high alert, keeping one ear on the front door, listening for Kamron.

"He's a low-key hottie," Tara said, giggling. "But wait, wait, wait. Let me tell you why."

They were leaning up against Samira's bed, sitting on the hardwood floor all scratched and discolored from years of wear, in the room Samira had shared with Mom from the time they moved back in with Gran and Grandad after her father had . . .

It wasn't exactly clear where her father was or what he had done. Anyway, Samira had the room all to herself now.

The orange-and-khaki coverlet Gran had crocheted for her lay across the bed. Tara had talked her into a bunch of daisy decals on the wall Samira had immediately regretted.

"He looks like Young Santa." Tara was now snorting with laughter. "Like, *literally.* Twinkling blue eyes, a brown beard, and a mustache. A little belly. He's *adorable.*"

Tara was maddeningly carefree. Why wouldn't she be? Tech millionaire dad and doting mom who bought Tara her heart's desires, paid for a Farsi tutor, let her "thin out her Persian nose"—the original was just fine—and hired Kim Kardashian's makeup artist for her sixteenth birthday to show Tara how to accentuate her cheekbones and draw attention to her eyes.

Mrs. Asghari was always fussing over her. Which might be nice—but by now scar tissue had formed over the shock of Mom leaving and Granddad croaking, and Samira had grown accustomed to her independence.

"You're saying you'd want to *date* Young Santa? I thought you were in a 'girl cycle.'" Samira played along while keeping half an ear on the front door. If Kamron had been drinking, she would hear him fumbling for his keys in the lock.

"I am, but . . . oh my God." Tara squealed as if she had seen a baby seal. "Wouldn't that make the cutest Hallmark Christmas movie? A rom-com featuring Mr. and Mrs. Claus. Think about it. What was their meet-cute? But wait . . . we *do* need more queer Hallmark rom-coms." She preened. "And the hottie at Aroma's said my Chanel lipstick was 'fuego.'"

Tara loved obsessing over new crushes, whether it was the girl with the pierced eyebrow at Aroma Roasters or their "low-key hottie" English teacher. Of course, as soon as she came out as bisexual to her parents, Mr. Asghari—who'd been raised as a devout Muslim—put a LOVE IS LOVE sticker on his Audi.

"Hmm, Mr. and Mrs. Claus's meet-cute. A coffee date at the North Pole Starbucks." Samira popped the last bite of Larabar in her mouth and stood up. "BRB. You want anything?"

"No." Tara's forehead wrinkled. "Do the Clauses have kids? Is Santa Claus even a dad?"

She said something else, but Samira was already tiptoeing up to Kamron's bedroom. How many times had she found him passed out on the bed? She held her breath and opened the door.

Empty. Relief cascaded through her. Maybe he *was* at work.

She headed to the kitchen and rinsed out her mug. When she got back to her room, Tara was holding the small framed photo of Samira's dad: his United States Army portrait from twenty years earlier. She was fascinated by it. "Sami, I know it sounds weird, but your dad was super hot."

"You're right. It's weird," Samira said.

She sat down, cross-legged, and took the photo from her. The man in the picture was compact and muscular with brown skin, chiseled features, a dimple in his chin, and tousled, dark hair—what little sprouted out of the crown of his head. Kamron looked just like him. His expression was pained, but then, no one probably grinned in their military portraits. When Samira looked at him, all she saw was a soldier.

And a deserter. *A deadbeat* is what Grandad had called him since he disappeared and stopped paying child support. "I don't. Think about him," she said. *That often,* she didn't say.

She had not seen him since she was a toddler. Something bad had happened, but no one would tell her exactly what. It was like growing up in a war zone—only the war was over, and all the survivors were too shell-shocked to talk about the battle.

Sure, she missed her dad, especially when she was little, which led to embarrassing behavior like clinging to Kamron's Little League coach after practice, the one who looked like that picture of her father. But she'd wised up quickly. Her father was gone. He wasn't coming back.

Tara took the picture. "I mean, *why* would someone named Mohammed Safavi join the *US Army* after 9/11?"

"T, I told you, I don't know anything about him," Samira said with a sigh. "I *do* know that if he paid all the back child support he owes us, I wouldn't have to take out any student loans," she added bitterly.

"Why don't you try and find him?" Tara had been asking this question for ages.

Samira took the portrait and placed it on her nightstand next to Grandad's military portrait. "I wouldn't even know where to begin."

The only reason she kept her father's portrait on her nightstand was because her grandad had asked her to. And the only reason Grandad had asked her was because he was a First Gulf War vet who had sympathy for a fellow veteran.

She had put the portrait of her father away after her grandfather died but took it out again a few days later because Grandad looked lonely up there on her nightstand all by himself.

"You don't know *anything* about your Iranian heritage." Tara clucked.

"So?" Samira laughed. "I don't know anything about my Irish heritage, either."

"Yes, you do. You celebrate St. Patrick's Day every year, your gran makes corned beef and cabbage. You said your grandad gave you his book of Irish poems and told you all about your great-great-grandfather coming to America from some quaint little Irish village. Meanwhile, you know nothing about your Persian heritage." Her thumbs were going a mile a minute on her iPhone. "Your gran made *fesenjoon*—walnut pomegranate stew—with Maraschino cherry juice instead of pomegranate syrup and served it with *steamed* rice, like from Panda Express. It's so wrong."

"Gran said Persian rice takes forever. What are you doing?"

Tara grinned. "It does; let's take one of those genetic tests and see if we can find your dad. I've always wanted to take one."

Samira wrestled Tara's phone from her. "No way. Those things are a hundred bucks."

Tara snatched it back. "I'll put it on my mom's Amazon card." She nudged Samira. "C'mon, it'll be fun. This will be our chance to find out where our relatives are from, whether we have that cilantro gene."

"Yours are all in San Francisco, and I don't need a genetic test to tell me I hate cilantro."

Tara was careening toward the shopping cart.

Samira put a hand on her arm. "T. Seriously. No. I—"

Shit. Kamron was suddenly in the hallway, hollering at Gran, his voice slowed down like a podcast on half speed.

"Is that Kamron?" Tara asked, grim-faced. "I thought he was in . . . AA."

"You have to go," Samira whispered apologetically. They stood up.

"You sure you don't want me to stay?" Tara whispered back. Samira shook her head and led the way down the hall. Tara peeled off for the front door.

Samira crept toward the kitchen. Grandad had cautioned her not to come in "guns a-blazing," but to materialize like a friendly spirit and guide Kamron to his room so he could sleep it off.

That was back when he was only occasionally binge-drinking after Mom left. Which was after he had gotten a DUI four years earlier. Everything got worse after Grandad died; he wasn't there to talk sense into him. Or listen.

"You'll find another job, you always do," Gran was saying. "You know computers better than anybody."

He did. He had been accepted to UC Berkeley's computer science program but couldn't go after he got the DUI; he got the same degree online in two years instead of four.

Samira stood in the doorway without saying a word.

He popped the top on a can of Coke. "No, I won't. Even if I got an interview, my old supervisor would cockblock me."

Total underfunctioner:

- Assumed less responsibility than anyone else
- Was labeled as "fragile" or "irresponsible"
- Became the focus of family worry
- Became less competent under stress

Which meant Samira had to compensate for him. "Kamron, let's call your sponsor," she said gently.

"Why? I'm fine," Kamron said, tossing back the can.

Gran put her hand on his shoulder. "He's been working very hard lately. Are you hungry, honey? Don't you want some chili?"

Samira wanted to scream. Gran never confronted Kamron about his drinking. She made excuses for it. Then it fell to Samira to clean up after him and hide the keys from him so he wouldn't drive drunk.

Shit. Gran's car keys were *right there* on the kitchen counter.

"I'm going to Molsberry," he said. "We need groceries."

Molsberry Market, *for groceries*. Sure he was.

He was probably going to Wheelers, the dive bar next door.

He looked around, bleary-eyed.

The keys. She had to get the keys. Samira inched closer and plucked them off the kitchen counter when he looked away.

He turned back. "Where are Gran's keys?"

Samira gave him an exaggerated shrug.

He moved toward her. "Gimme the keys, Sami," he said. His breath could ignite a torch.

Samira held her ground. "I don't have them," she said.

For a moment, it looked like he might rage at her. The big

brother who gave her piggyback rides and played with her on the Slip 'N Slide and let her win at Battleship, which was ridiculous since he was four years older, and Samira barely understood the game. But that Kamron disappeared every night into a six-pack of Lagunitas.

Instead, Kamron tickled her, right above her ribs, coaxing, "Gimme the keys."

Samira would have been irritated AF even if she didn't *hate* being tickled. "I don't have them," she said, and jerked away.

He threw up his hands. "Okay. Fine. Whatever. I'll starve."

Samira maintained stern eye contact with Gran so she wouldn't buckle and hand them over. Finally, Kamron retreated to his room.

Samira slipped the keys into the drawer with all the cooking utensils. "Don't let him find these," she said firmly, went back to her room, pulled out her laptop, and googled **Santa Rosa rehabs**. AA clearly wasn't working.

New Horizons looked like a spa with a waterfall and yoga classes and, apparently, a five-star chef. Cash pay or private insurance only, which they didn't have.

She clicked through to the next five sites. Same story. A Reddit on private facilities said they cost anywhere from $20,000 to $75,000. And the public treatment programs had yearslong wait lists.

Her phone buzzed. "Hey, Mom," Samira said wearily.

"Well, hi, baby," Mom said in her slow, honeyed tone. "You sound tired. Everything okay?"

"Yeah, fine," Samira said.

"Samira."

Hundreds of miles away, Erin Murphy could still read her daughter as if she were right there.

"Kamron's drinking again." Samira's throat caught.

Her mother exhaled. "Oh, baby. You'll have to be patient with Kamron while he's on his journey to sobriety."

Journey to sobriety, like he was driving up to Humboldt. Mom had gotten even more "New Agey" after she joined that church in Ashland where everyone wore Birkenstocks and the band played "A Whiter Shade of Pale."

Well, Kamron's "journey" was taking too long; Samira needed him to speed it up.

"I wish he would come up here and stay with me," her mom said.

"You know he won't," Samira said with a tinge of annoyance.

Kamron was still mad at their mother for whatever had happened with their father.

Samira's phone buzzed again with a text from Tara. u okay??? 💔

no, Samira replied. She squeezed her eyes shut. Crying was pointless; *a waste of water,* Grandad called it.

Immediately, Tara called. "Mom, Tara's on the other line."

"All right, baby, I'll call him first thing tomorrow," her mother promised.

Samira clicked through to the other call. "He's drinking again," she said. Her voice broke.

Tara was silent. Finally, she said, "Sami. Can't he go to a treatment center or something?"

"It's hella expensive, T."

"I know." Tara sighed. "My uncle went to one in Malibu. Cost more than his Tesla."

Samira scratched her neck, on which two new welts had appeared. "I can't leave Gran in the fall if he's like this."

"Yes, you can, you're not his mom," Tara asserted.

"I know that," Samira said sharply.

This was one of the differences between her and Tara: Tara would never understand why anyone would take responsibility for someone else because she never had to. Her mom was planning her *gap year* to Dubai and the UK. Total UF.

"I'm sorry," Tara said with a hitch that made it clear there was a caveat. "It's just . . . it's not fair your whole college dream gets blown up because Kamron won't stop drinking."

And that was the other main difference: Tara thought life was fair.

"What are you going to do now?" she asked.

"I don't know. Call his sponsor?"

"His sponsor told you not to call him," Tara reminded her.

"He did," Samira said, the energy draining out of her. "I gotta go, T. I'll text you later."

She slumped against the bed. After an exhausted beat, she picked up her phone again.

Don't do it. It doesn't help. In fact, it usually makes things worse. Don't—

She couldn't help herself. She tapped the app and brought up her mother's abandoned Facebook page, the one on which she had abruptly stopped posting in 2008. It wasn't like she had posted much before—except for that one video. Of her father.

When Samira found it a few years back, she'd watched it over and over. Somehow, it cracked her heart open, stitched it back up, and broke it all over again in the space of three minutes.

Her chest tightened as if she were getting ready to ride the rickety old roller coaster at the county fair. She braced for the precipitous drop, then tapped the video.

Her dad was sitting in a recliner at their old apartment in

Fresno (it felt weird to think of him as *Dad*) cradling a two-year-old Samira in his left arm. She was nestled into his neck, clutching her oatmeal teddy bear.

Right on cue, her eyes rimmed with tears. How many times over the years would Samira have loved to curl up in his lap like that?

His right arm was around Kamron, who sat next to him, happily holding the board book *Guess How Much I Love You*. He must have been about six.

Their father read the book to them, doing the voices for Little Nutbrown Hare and Big Nutbrown Hare. He told them he loved them as wide and as far and as high as he could reach.

That was the part that cracked her heart open. There was her father, sitting in that chair, as real as anything, as if Samira could climb through the screen and right back into his lap.

If only the video had ended there.

Instead, her father looked up at the camera, embarrassed. Maybe from doing the voices? Then he got that same pained expression he was wearing in his military portrait.

"Don't sneak up on me," he said sternly to Samira's mother. "I'm sorry," she murmured. After an agonizingly long beat, he ordered Kamron, "Go to your room." Kamron's face twisted with hurt. As soon as he slid off the recliner, Mohammed stood up and handed Samira over to her mother. The camera jostled, and the video cut off.

That was what did it. The way Kamron's face twisted up in the video when their father sent him away. *That* was what damaged him. And they were all paying the price for it.

In the middle of her Spanish IV homework later that night, it occurred to her that Tara was right. Maybe Samira *should* try to find her father and collect what she and Kamron were owed.

She navigated to Amazon and put the 23andMe genetic testing kit in her cart. Her new Converse high-tops could wait.

In the split second before she checked out, Gran appeared in the doorway, her face ashen white. "Sami," she said, clutching her pocketbook. "We have to go. *Now*. Kamron's been arrested."

CHAPTER FOUR

Henry

Henry lugged his hockey bag through the rink and into the lobby. Mom and Dad stood off to one side while Mama stood on the other talking to Linh.

Mom and Mama looked at him expectantly. Figuring out which one to go to first was a game he could never win.

Before he could make a move, Mama came toward him and draped an arm around his shoulder. "Bet that kid never messes with you again," she said with a wicked grin.

"Good game . . . ?" Linh said with a mock pained look on her face.

Good thing *her* parents weren't there that night. They were already unsure about Henry. They had traveled all the way to Vietnam to adopt Linh and were very protective of her. *I'm the sun; they exist only to orbit me,* she joked.

She had never dated a "jock" before. Henry won her over with his sweatshirt emblazoned with a pack of puppies. In fact, he had a desktop folder filled with baby animals. There was something about their fragility and vulnerability that got to him.

He dropped his hockey bag on the floor. "I'll be right back." Since Mama had gotten to him first, he had to even things up with Mom. They kept a running tally.

"Another game misconduct," Dad said with dead calm.

He never yelled or raised his voice. In fact, the madder he was, the quieter he got, which only made things scarier. Especially since he was six-foot-five and an ex-Marine.

"I don't know why you get like that, Henry," Mom said, her voice ringing with worry. But then, she worried about everything Henry did.

"It's part of the game," he said defensively.

"Did you get suspended?" Dad asked.

Henry shifted from side to side. "Yeah," he admitted.

Mama suddenly materialized beside him. "I gotta go, baby."

"Nancy, your voice carries," Mom said with a finger to her mouth.

"We're not in a library," Mama shot back.

Henry had to get out of the middle before he got caught in the crossfire.

"Me and Linh are going to In-N-Out, okay?" he asked Dad.

Dad looked over at her. "Be home by ten. Not a minute after."

"Yes, sir," Henry said.

He and Linh followed Mama out the door. As soon as they got outside, Mama spun around. "I don't care what they say, you *never* let the other players disrespect you, do you hear me?"

"Yes, Mama," he said.

"Give me a kiss," she said, presenting her cheek to him. "You've got to watch that movie, Linh," she hollered before climbing into her vintage Mustang.

"What movie?" Henry asked, cringing.

"*Good Morning, Vietnam.*" Linh giggled.

"Jesus. Sorry." Henry climbed into her Lexus SUV.

"Old people are always telling me about that movie." She opened the glove box. "Want some weed?"

"Yes," Henry said, rolling down the window as she pulled out of the parking lot. He deflated. "No. It'll get on my clothes. They'll smell it."

She synced her phone to the car's stereo, filling the air with one of those breathy girls. Maybe Billie Eilish. Henry leaned his head out the window.

"Your dad needs to chill." Linh merged onto the freeway. "My parents wouldn't care if I got in a fight. It's *hockey*. Isn't that part of the game?"

"Your parents buy your *weed*." Henry laughed, rolling up the window.

"For my anxiety, yeah. Our therapist says they overcompensate because I'm adopted." She grinned. "Your mom was telling me all about your bio-dad."

Henry groaned. "What'd she say?"

"That he 'could be a millionaire!'"

"She always says that."

Linh pulled into the drive-through. "Aren't you curious about him?"

Before Henry could answer, an In-N-Out associate appeared at the driver's side window. Henry leaned forward. "Two Double-Doubles Animal Style, two orders of fries, a Coke, a vanilla shake—and whatever she wants."

"I'll have a grilled cheese, fries, and a Diet Coke," Linh said, and pulled forward to the pickup window. "There are a lot of issues involved with adoption, you know."

"Well, yeah, but I wasn't *adopted* adopted."

"You're not being raised by your birth parents. It's the same thing."

Henry rolled down the window again and took a moment

to breathe in the cool, night air. Yes, Mom and Dad were technically his aunt and uncle, but Mama had always been around. She took him out to eat on Wednesdays and Saturdays when he was younger and bought him lots of Christmas presents. *Like a divorced Disneyland dad,* Dad always said.

"My therapist says, 'Absent parents are still very present in our lives.'"

Henry handed Linh his debit card and forced a laugh. "I have a bonus mom, that's all."

A deep ridge of concern rose up between her brows. "I don't know, Henry. It's weird. Your moms can't even sit next to each other at your games, and you don't know anything about your bio-dad." She handed him back his debit card. "My parents have taken me to Vietnam twice. They don't try to hide anything about who I am or where I came from."

"I came from *here*," Henry said, growing prickly. Their situations weren't the same.

"You said your bio-dad was Iranian, right?" She handed Henry his red plastic tray and pulled into a parking space under a fluorescent lamp that bathed the car in an iridescent glow.

"Are you making a documentary?" Henry joked. He bit into his first Double-Double.

"No. I think you should know where you came from is all."

Henry reflected on this. "My birth name is Hooman. That's what's on my birth certificate: Hooman Safavi." He rarely told anyone that.

Linh's nose scrunched. "Why do they call you Henry?"

"I guess my parents wanted something more American. My

dad—I mean, my uncle—is an ex-Marine." His face clouded. "Sometimes, he posts anti-Iranian, Islamophobic stuff on Facebook. I pretend I don't see it."

But he couldn't *unsee* it, the pictures of angry Iranian men demonstrating against the US. Dad posted with comments like *they're no better than a pack of dogs*, which inflamed a molten core of anger and embarrassment in Henry.

Linh shook her head. "That is *so* fucked up. And also, why do you even have a Facebook page? It's not 2010. Have you ever asked your aunt and uncle about your real dad?"

Henry blotted his chin with a napkin. "We have this, I don't know, this weird, unspoken understanding I won't ask about my bio-dad because it would hurt their feelings."

Linh nibbled her fries one at a time. "You think about him, though, right?"

The only evidence Henry had of his biological father was the United States Army portrait Mama had given him along with his father's copy of a book by the Persian poet Hafez which Henry kept hidden away in his nightstand.

"Sure. I wonder what he's doing, whether he's happy with his new family—assuming he has a new family. He probably has a new family," Henry said, downcast.

His heart sagged whenever he imagined his bio-dad with a new wife and kids. There wasn't a clear image of him, but there were sounds. Sounds of children's laughter that didn't include him. When he thought about his father's life without him, Henry never felt more alone. So he tried not to.

"I wonder, you know, why he's never tried to contact me," Henry admitted. "But if it's only going to make Mom and Dad uncomfortable, why bring it up?"

"Because he's your *dad*." Linh laughed as if it were obvious. She dipped her fries in ketchup one at a time. "What if you could find him?"

Henry unwrapped his second Double-Double. "I've looked for him before, on the internet. He's not there."

"I mean, through a genetic test."

"Mom and Dad would be so *pissed*," Henry said reflexively. Separating what *he* wanted from what *they* wanted did not come naturally.

"Then don't tell them," Linh said with a sly smile.

"No, I can't do that."

"Yes, you can!"

"No, I really *can't*," Henry said firmly. "My dad would see the charge."

He always got the feeling he was on perpetual probation: one misstep, and they would send him back to Mama. Wash their hands of him. Admit they failed, that *he* had failed.

And, as much as he had enjoyed the occasional sleepover with Mama in middle school, it was like she forgot he was there. She'd stay out with her friends until two or three o'clock in the morning, then apologize all over herself the next day with a batch of blueberry pancakes. *Now don't go telling Jeannie I was a little late,* she'd say with a wink.

Linh picked up her phone. "Hey, Siri. Find 23andMe."

"Linh."

She showed him her home screen. "This is the test I took: Ancestry and Traits."

Henry opened his mouth to stop her, but the possibility of finding his father was opening up again like an elevator door to a previously forbidden floor.

"Should I order it?" she asked, her finger poised above the *checkout* button.

Mom and Dad would be *so* mad. Henry chewed the inside of his cheek. Was it really possible? Could Henry find him?

"Have it shipped to your house," he finally said. "I'll Venmo you the cash so my dad won't see the charge."

"Yesss!" Linh squealed and threw her arms around him.

As soon as she tapped *complete your purchase,* his adrenaline started pumping. And the elevator door slid shut.

CHAPTER FIVE
Samira

Tara hightailed it over to drive them to the county jail as soon as Samira texted her.

Gran sat in the back seat as pale as a ghost. Samira sat in the front seat, staring straight ahead. Tara seemed to know now was not the time for idle chatter and drove in uncharacteristic quiet.

Another DUI. Gran must have given him the keys. She could never say no to him.

Fucking Kamron.

"This is awful nice of you, Tara," Gran said. Her voice shook. "If we don't get there by five o'clock, he might have to stay overnight." She had a death grip on her pocketbook, which was resting on her lap.

"It's okay," Tara said. Her eyes welled up with tears.

Samira would slap her if Tara started sobbing.

The first time he got a DUI, right after he graduated from high school, Grandad had said it might be a good thing. A wake-up call. And it was. For a while. Then he started backsliding. *Because he doesn't work the program,* his sponsor would say.

"He said he was only going to the market for cereal," Gran said, a trembling hand to her forehead.

As if it mattered where he *said* he was going.

Samira stared dead ahead. "What about money for bail?" Her tone was icy.

Her Social Dynamics teacher said overfunctioners often appear unsympathetic during a crisis because they feel they must focus on putting everything back together while it's falling apart. *They* fall apart later.

"I took some cash from the envelope your grandfather left in the safe," Gran said with a hint of apology. The cash in the safe was dwindling. Grandad had left about $1,200 in small bills from his casino winnings. Gran was taking out thirty here and fifty there to give to Kamron. She must have thought Samira would not see the withdrawals.

The sign for the Sonoma County Main Adult Detention Facility came into view: a redbrick, glass, and steel structure that could have been an aging hospital. Tara pulled into a visitor spot. "Should I go in with you or wait here?" she whispered as if they were on a secret mission to bust Kamron out and she was the getaway car.

"We'll need a ride to the lot if his car was impounded. Can you wait?"

"I'm going with you," Tara pronounced.

Samira led the way inside. She would have to take it all in. Be the adult. Bear the responsibility. Gran wouldn't hear anything anyone said about Kamron's court date, fines, impoundment, or the terms of his release. Her only concern would be his comfort.

Tara and Gran followed her, Tara's arm linked through Gran's as Gran clutched her purse like a security blanket.

"Wait here," Samira said firmly. She started for the semicircular bulletproof reception desk dominating the lobby, then turned back. "Gran, your wallet."

Gran glanced around as if a robber were going to burst out of the fake ficus. "Keep an eye on it," she said, her eyes wide with worry.

At the reception desk, a female officer with long black hair pulled into a tight, low bun barely looked up from her computer. "Can I help you?"

"I'm Samira Murphy. We're here to pick up my brother, Kamron. Um, DUI." Her cheeks burned as she said it.

"Deputy Donoghue will be with you in a moment." The officer activated the two-way on her right shoulder. "Murphy's ride is here."

"Are there any fines or fees we need to pay right now? I know bail is all-cash." Samira wanted her to know she knew what she was doing.

The officer shook her head. "He's being released on his own recognizance. Save your cash for the impoundment lot. The releasing officer will give you the court date for his arraignment."

Samira rejoined Gran and Tara at the single row of black plastic-and-metal chairs near the entrance and handed Gran back her wallet. "He's being released on his own recognizance," she said, not bothering to mask her irritation. "But we'll need cash for the impoundment lot."

Tara shuddered. "Do you think they bring murderers through here?"

She was *so* unbelievably sheltered, which was unbelievably annoying. "Of course they do," Samira said. "Where else would they go?"

"He can't be in jail with murderers and thieves," Gran said. Her whole body was shaking. "He's not like that. Kamron is very delicate. And you," she said, gesturing to Samira, "you don't know the whole story. You're too young to remember . . ." She choked up.

Nothing Gran could tell her about their father would justify a second DUI.

Tara draped an arm around Gran's shoulder. "He won't go to prison."

"Yes, he *will*," Samira said.

There was no point in sugarcoating it. This was his second offense. Samira had already googled the mandatory sentence for a repeat offender in California: ten days. Minimum.

Suddenly, a door opened and Deputy Donoghue, who had a kindly face sprinkled with freckles, led Kamron out. He was pale and fragile, holding a clear plastic bag containing his phone, wallet, and a pink slip. Samira strode toward them.

"You his ride?" Deputy Donoghue asked.

"Yes, sir," Samira said, steadying her breath. "I'm his sister, Samira Murphy."

Kamron gazed at Samira through bleary eyes.

"He ran the stop at Brookwood and Sonoma," the deputy said. "Failed the field sobriety test. A breathalyzer revealed a blood alcohol level of one-point-six. Arraignment is in ten days. For the criminal component." He turned to Kamron. "Get a good DUI lawyer. Your car's at Nestor's Towing on Sebastopol Road. Cost ya two hundred bucks to get it out. Cash." He pointed to the plastic bag. "Per se's in the bag. That's your temporary license to drive. DMV hearing will be in thirty days to determine whether you get it back, or whether it's suspended for a year."

Samira made a mental note of everything:

1. Pick up car at Nestor's
2. Google good DUI defense attorney

3. Enter arraignment date into iCal
4. Make sure Kamron calls his sponsor (or call for him—he needs to know Kamron was arrested again)

Deputy Donoghue put a hand on Kamron's shoulder. "You're young, man. You got your whole life ahead of you. Don't let us see you here again."

"Yessir," Kamron said.

Samira restrained herself from punching him just as Gran appeared. "Let's go, honey." She draped her arm around Kamron's shoulder like he was the victim of a terrible injustice instead of the perpetrator.

They got in the car—Samira in the front and Gran and Kamron in the back. "The lot is on Sebastopol Road, just past Dutton," Samira murmured to Tara.

Tara nodded.

"You have to call your sponsor," Samira said to Kamron. "And go back to AA."

"Fuck," Kamron muttered to himself. "I can do it on my own, Sami. I don't need meetings." The hangover was probably hitting.

"Don't swear like that, honey." Gran scolded him like that was the worst of his offenses.

"Um . . . we're here." Tara pulled up in front of the lot with a sign that had a picture of a tow hitch and NESTOR's painted in bright red lettering. "Do you want me to drive you home?" she asked, her face pinched with worry.

Samira opened her mouth to answer.

What she *wanted* was for Tara to drive her straight to *Tara's* house, where Samira would take up residence in the spacious guest room, and Mrs. Asghari would fuss over her and shower her with Larabars and get her a Farsi tutor, and Samira would attend Giants games with Mr. Asghari and eat walnut pomegranate stew with *real* pomegranate syrup and never worry about anything ever again.

"No," she said flatly. "I have to go with Gran and Kamron."

"Call me later," Tara said with a squeeze of her hand.

Samira climbed out of the Mini. "I'm driving," she announced.

She kept her vision focused on the road ahead while her mind raced. Her nonrefundable deposit was due to Lewis & Clark by May 1. Which meant she had exactly three weeks to get Kamron back into AA—whether he wanted to or not.

As soon as she got to her room, Samira tapped the number for Kamron's sponsor, Steve.

He picked up right away. "This is Steve."

She cleared her throat. "Steve, this is Samira Murphy, Kamron's sister. He's been—"

"We've talked about this, Samira." Steve sighed.

"I know, but—"

"No buts," he said. "You can't call me when Kamron's been drinking. That's his job."

Samira switched the phone to her other hand. "I know, but—"

"Samira. *No. Buts,*" he said more firmly.

"But he's been *arrested,*" Samira shouted.

God. Why did no one understand that Samira didn't necessarily *want* to assume all of this responsibility for other people? But if she didn't, who would?

He let out a long, deep exhale with an exasperated motorboat sound. "Goddammit, Kamron. I knew this would happen. He hasn't been working the program."

"He'll go to prison, right?" Samira's throat constricted. It crushed her to think of her big brother behind bars.

"Maybe. Maybe the judge will let him go to a treatment program instead."

Samira's shoulders sagged. "We can't afford rehab."

"First of all, we call it recovery. And he can do it without a twenty-eight-day stay. Kamron needs to get his ass back to AA. In fact, that's the only way a judge might grant him recovery in lieu of jail. But you can't drag him there against his will, Samira. Neither can I."

If it would keep him out of jail, she *might* be able to drag him to AA against his will.

"There is something you *can* do, though," he said.

"What is it?" Whatever it was, she would do it. Anything to help Kamron.

"Get *your* ass to an Al-Anon meeting. You're going to exhaust yourself trying to control his drinking."

"Thanks," Samira said curtly, and ended the call.

Her wheels started spinning. Between attorney's fees and a treatment program (not to mention her student loans), they were going to need money, fast.

She navigated back to her Amazon cart and clicked *complete your purchase.* The genetic test would arrive in three days.

And if Samira could find their father, after she demanded all the back child support they were owed, she would demand an explanation for how he could have loved her and Kamron as wide and as far and as high as he could reach, then abandon them without ever *once* looking back.

CHAPTER SIX

Henry

The minute Henry got home from school, he grabbed a Coke from the fridge, ran upstairs, and locked the bathroom door, even though Dad was at work and Mom wasn't there.

He chugged the Coke and moved aside the decorative tissue box with all the seashells Mom had coordinated with his bath towels, then laid out the collection tube and specimen bag for his genetic test.

Crap. The instructions said not to eat or drink anything thirty minutes prior to collecting his saliva sample. He had just chugged a whole can of Coke. He tapped his phone: 3:27 p.m. He would have to wait till four o'clock. Mom usually got back from tutoring at Kumon by 4:15 p.m. He had to finish the collection before she got home.

The instructional video on YouTube followed by videos of happy family members reuniting gave him chills. What would it be like to hug his father for the first time?

Twenty-five minutes to go.

He went to his room and began digging around the bottom drawer of his nightstand. There it was. Underneath his Westlake High School Athletic Manual and old anime trading cards:

his father's book of Persian poetry. He took it back to the bathroom and locked the door again.

Mama had given it to him after his fifth-grade teacher, Mr. Nassour, asked if he had *any* connection to his Iranian heritage. He told Henry all about Persian New Year and showed him pictures of something called a haft sin: an altar with seven items beginning with the letter *s* in Farsi to symbolize health and wealth and prosperity. He said Persian people put up haft sins for Persian New Year like other people put up Christmas trees.

When Henry asked Mom if he could make his own haft sin, she looked at him like he had asked to join the circus. Dad sat him down and said, above all else, Henry was *American*. There was no need to celebrate "foreign" holidays.

He had stuffed the book in his dresser drawer and hadn't looked at it much since.

He skimmed a few of the poems, which all sounded like they were about love but, according to the introduction, were about God. Several passages had been highlighted, which he had completely forgotten since he was too young to understand the poems when Mama first gave the book to him. These highlighted passages were the only piece of communication, however indirect, Henry had from him.

I wish I could show you when you are lonely or in the darkness,
the astonishing light of your own being.

Henry's chest squeezed. *Lonely or in the darkness*. Exactly the way he felt at times.

He stuffed the book in his backpack. He would read it more thoroughly later. If Mom came home and found him in the bathroom for more than five minutes, she would pound on the door, worried he had a stomachache or the flu or was constipated. When he was little, she routinely gave him a teaspoon of castor oil to keep him "regular."

Henry flipped open the top of the empty collection tube. His saliva needed to reach the fill line—more than halfway up. His mouth was still dry, his nerves were jangled. Yes, Mom could bust in on him, but more important, the man he could only summon as a vibe, his *father,* could be on the other end of a single strand of his DNA.

He tried again to summon the saliva by pressing his tongue against the roof of his mouth and sucking. He spit into the tube. It barely registered.

After what felt like forever, the last bit of spit finally hit the fill line.

Shit. "Henry? Are you in there? Are you okay?"

"Yes, Mom. I'm fine," he said. "I'll be out in a minute."

He snapped the top shut, popped the tube into the specimen bag, placed the bag in the box with the return label, and stuffed the box into his backpack.

When he came out of the bathroom, Mom was waiting for him with a quizzical look on her face. He wouldn't typically bring his backpack into the bathroom.

"I was studying," he said as soon as he saw her. "For the AP Statistics exam. You know, while I was . . ."

"Oh," she said, her mouth forming a little circle of concern. "Do you need some—"

"No, Mom," he said, before she could offer him a teaspoon of castor oil. "I'm going to practice. I'll be home after dinner. Don't wait."

As he ran down the stairs, she went into his bathroom looking for smuggled contraband or evidence of wrongdoing.

She wouldn't find any. He had removed every last trace of the test.

oμo

"That was fire, bro," Daniel said, fist-bumping Henry during their practice scrimmage: red jerseys versus blue. Henry had intercepted the puck, made a breakaway, and scored.

The familiar nothingness had been replaced by a buzzing excitement. In a matter of days or weeks, he could be reunited with his bio-dad.

"Minute to go, then we change everything up," Coach Nielson called from the benches.

Henry saw an opening and skated toward the net. He fielded a pass from Daniel, drew his stick back, and one-timed the puck into the net.

"Whoa, nice job, Henry," Coach called out. "All right. Everyone, come on in."

Henry was getting back on Coach's good side.

They weren't supposed to talk while Coach talked, but Henry couldn't help himself. "I just took that DNA test," he whispered to Daniel.

"Turns out you're a hundred percent that bitch?" Daniel whispered back.

"Owen, Stewart, eyes up here," Coach reprimanded them.

They got quiet.

"Blue team, the red team blew by you. After the break, we're gonna switch it up. Defense, you're moving forward. Wingers to the back."

The players erupted with a mix of shouts and groans at having to play different positions.

"Back in five, let's go." Coach clapped.

Daniel and Henry climbed over the boards and collapsed on the players' bench.

"Whadja have to do, pee in a cup?"

Henry shook his head. "Spit in a tube."

Daniel gulped his Gatorade. "Where do you think he is?"

"No idea," Henry said, guzzling his own.

When he was little, he would ask Mama where his dad was during their outings at Bob's Big Boy for a burger and a chocolate shake on Wednesday evenings. *He could be a millionaire by now for all we know,* she would say with a flourish. But during Thanksgiving one year, he had heard Mom tell one of her brothers that *he could be dead or in prison.* Henry had hoped with all his heart she was exaggerating as much as Mama.

Daniel tightened the laces on his skates. "That'd be lit, man, if you could find him."

Linh said over thirty million people had taken DNA tests, which seemed like good odds.

Coach motioned them back on the ice. "Callahan, Owen, switch jerseys," he said. "Rodriguez, Lewis, do the same."

Henry peeled off his sweaty red jersey and traded it for a blue one.

"Traitor," Daniel said as he jumped over the boards.

"Blue through and through now," Henry said, laughing.

He jumped back on the ice. Now on offense, Henry won the face-off, passed to his right winger, and quickly got into position to shoot when something caught his eye.

Dad was standing at the back of the rink, watching him.

Henry's body flooded with fear. Had Mom called him?

Maybe he had accidentally left the instructions or a piece of packaging from the genetic test in the bathroom.

They would take it personally. As if looking for his biological father meant he didn't care about what they had done for him or appreciate everything Dad had taught him: how to ride a bike, strip down and clean a carburetor, properly mask and paint a wall. Make a budget and stick to it.

Finding his biological father had nothing to do with them.

No. He had cleaned up everything, he was sure of it.

An unlit cigarette hung from Dad's mouth. He loved to tell the story of how he had quit cold turkey after he got out of the Marines. No lozenges or patch for him. But he still needed to suck on that unlit stick of tobacco like a pacifier.

"Hey, wake up," Daniel shouted to him as he skated by.

Henry couldn't afford any more stupid mistakes, but he could not stop worrying he was in trouble. He iced the puck several times and was offsides twice.

After the scrimmage, Henry trudged over to where Dad was standing at the back of the rink. "Hey," he said uneasily.

"Son," Dad said, taking the unlit cigarette out of his mouth. "Not your best play out there."

It was before you got here. Henry tried to laugh it off. "Not used to being a winger."

They stood there for another awkward moment when Dad finally said, "Well, I'm going home. Your mom made mac and cheese."

He never offered to take Henry to Superburger or In-N-Out after practice like Daniel's dad did. He came all this way to stand there and scowl from the sidelines, the story of Henry's life.

"Yeah, see you at home," Henry said, and headed for the locker room when a bitter memory came rushing back.

He was twelve, maybe thirteen. Playing in a hockey tournament up in Fresno, the last place anyone had supposedly seen his father. He had asked Robert if they could look for him while they were there. *Now that would only upset your mother,* he had said.

So Henry had convinced Daniel to go with him to the local Starbucks, where he waited all day for his father to show up—again, like a lost puppy.

It was embarrassing. Truly pathetic.

Well, Henry was almost eighteen now. He didn't need Mom and Dad's approval or permission to find his father. If 23andMe returned a match, he could visit his dad the next day. And there was nothing Robert could do to stop him.

CHAPTER SEVEN
Samira

His sponsor had said Samira couldn't *drag* Kamron to meetings, but here they were at Dierk's for breakfast, after which he was attending an AA meeting at the Veterans Hall right next door. All it took was the threat of a prison sentence.

They sat at a small table for two in the funky little café tucked into a residential corner of Santa Rosa with wooden tables, mismatched chairs, and the best coffee ever.

Kamron wolfed down his breakfast sandwich with bacon, cheddar, and egg and wiped the pesto mayonnaise off his chin. "What time does it start again?"

"Ten o'clock."

No, Samira was not supposed to have googled saturday morning aa meetings santa rosa, but that was the only way she could be sure Kamron would find one.

She sipped her coffee. Kamron was about the same age as their father when that military portrait was taken. She had not yet told him about the genetic test. Maybe she should. "Do you ever think about him? Our dad? Wonder where he is or what he's doing?"

"No," he said sharply. "Why? Do you?"

Samira had *trained* herself not to think about him. Except

on days like Father's Day, when Tara sent texts of her and Mr. Asghari cheering on the Giants from their box seats at Oracle Park. She didn't mean to be cruel. She simply didn't think about how hurtful that might be for Samira.

Anyway, Samira had accepted that her father would never take her to a Giants game or teach her how to change a tire. Or binge-watch *The Walking Dead* with her. Really, she had.

"I, um . . . I ordered one of those genetic tests to see if we could, you know, find him."

"I don't want to find him," Kamron said with an emphatic shake of his head.

"*Why?*" Samira pressed.

Kamron gazed past her at a memory that seemed to appear on an invisible screen. "He was crazy. He would yell. Scream. Mom would cry hysterically. I was scared *shitless*. I'd pee my pants. And Mom didn't do shit about it." His eyes watered. "I remember the cops came once. This officer let me hold his badge."

She touched his hand. "Oh, Kam."

Crap. Maybe this genetic test was a bad idea. "Do you remember anything *good* about him?"

Kamron stared past her again, bringing another image into focus. "He used to kick around a soccer ball with me at a park. In Fresno, I think. I remember he carried you on his shoulders all the time. Ha. I was jealous."

All of a sudden, Samira flashed on the same image: perched high up on her father's shoulders, clutching her oatmeal teddy bear, squealing with delight. She squeezed Kamron's hand.

His face softened. "And he read to us. That book, what was it called . . ."

"*Guess How Much I Love You,*" Samira said, pursing her lips to keep her mouth from trembling.

"That's the one," he said, barely audible.

They sat in mournful silence for a moment while silverware and plates clanked around them.

"If you find him," Kamron said softly, "don't tell me."

A wave of sorrow crested in Samira's chest. Hopefully, if she did find their father, Kamron would change his mind. "We better go," she said, motioning to the server for the check. She fished out the debit card Grandad had given her for emergencies. Getting Kam back to AA seemed pretty urgent.

He stood up and nodded toward the bathroom. "Gotta make a quick detour."

As he made his way to the back of the restaurant, Samira was suddenly gripped with fear that he would somehow sneak a drink.

When he got back to the table, she motioned to his mouth. "You've got something in your . . ."

"I do?" He ran his tongue over his teeth.

"Here, let me see." She leaned over and pretended to inspect them.

His breath was minty, like from a Tic Tac.

He reared back. "Is it gone?"

"Yeah. You got it," Samira said.

That was all it was, a Tic Tac to freshen his breath.

Or to mask the odor of alcohol.

She followed him to the Veterans Hall next door. "I'll be right here when you get out," she said, like a mother dropping her son off at school, which Mom said gave Kamron major anxiety when he was little. Apparently, he tested into the gifted program, but his teachers suggested he delay first grade because he wasn't "emotionally ready." Meanwhile, Samira barreled into kindergarten like she owned the place.

She hated to admit it, but Steve was right. Trying to control his drinking *was* exhausting.

⚬⫿⚬

Samira sat in Gran's Kia at the far end of the parking lot researching the websites of defense attorneys Steve had recommended.

They all looked the same: staged photos of concerned lawyers sitting across from their clients at conference tables. They all said that DUI was a *serious crime with serious penalties.*

Samira tapped the DUI Defense tab for Gregory A. Melnick's site. Immediately, a chat window opened up. **How may we help you today?**

Immediately, she closed the chat window. She wasn't ready to chat with anyone.

Maybe she should call Mom first.

What was the point of calling Mom, who would say something like, *Trust the process, Samira?* Or, *Kamron will be guided to the right attorney.* When Gran told her about the DUI, Mom said it was *an important step in Kamron's journey of recovery.* Everything was a *process* or a *journey* with Mom.

She launched the next website for attorney Beth Woolsey. In her picture, Beth was standing in a super-modern office with a huge art print of an illustration of a car crashing through a wall, which seemed weird for the office of a DUI defense attorney. The car—one of those dinky European models, gray with a tan top—was bursting through a blue wall with chunks of concrete flying everywhere. The license plate said Nov. 9–89.

Before Samira could google what the art print meant, an email notification popped up on her home screen: **Your results are ready.**

The results from her genetic test. Fear shot through her. Her results might be ready, but she wasn't. What if her father was right there, one click away? She had only taken the test three days earlier.

But *holy shit*. What if her father *was* there, one click away? Would he be happy to hear from her? Sorry for all the time they had missed? Willing to pay for Kamron's defense attorney?

Call Tara. Yes, Tara had already gotten her results. She would know how to interpret them.

She held the phone away from her ear while Tara squealed with excitement. "We have to hurry, T," Samira said. "Before Kam gets back from his AA meeting. He says he doesn't want anything to do with our dad."

"That's what he *says*," Tara said. "He doesn't mean it. *Every-one* wants to find their father. Go to DNA Relatives first. See if he's there," she instructed. "I have a *shit ton* of third cousins. My mom said we could be distant cousins of Queen Elizabeth. Am I, like, royalty? What's taking you so long, are you ready? Ooh. What's your username?"

"Michonne05," Samira said, after her favorite character on *The Walking Dead*. She hovered over the DNA Relatives tab. Her palm was sweating.

She closed her eyes, took a deep breath, and . . . nothing. Nothing but a shit ton of third cousins. "He's not there." Her heart unexpectedly tumbled through her chest.

Dammit. She had not wanted to get her hopes up.

"He's not there *yet*," Tara corrected her. "A kabillion people take these tests all the time."

"What if he took the other one?" Samira groaned. She could *not* afford two DNA tests.

"Let's look at the other results. Click on Ancestry," Tara coaxed. "See what you're made of."

Samira navigated to the Ancestry tab. "Forty-nine percent Iranian, forty-two percent Northern and Eastern European, and some other stuff," Samira said flatly.

What a waste of money. Worse, after all those years of *not* thinking about him, she was thinking about her father again, long-dead nerve endings tingling back to life.

While Kamron wanted nothing to do with him.

"Look at the Health results at least," said Tara. "Oh God, please don't let you have that cancer gene."

Samira hesitated. She had largely been spared whatever Kamron and her mother had endured with their father. Of course, *she* would be the one condemned to cancer or Alzheimer's by him.

Just then, the passenger door opened. Samira nearly threw her phone out the window. She didn't want Kamron to see her results, not yet.

"Whoa, what's wrong?" Kamron asked as he climbed in.

"Nothing. Nothing," Samira said. "I'll call you later, T." She quickly tucked her phone in the driver's side panel and plastered a smile on her face. "How was your meeting?"

"Fine," he said, rubbing his eyes. "'I'm Tim and I'm an alcoholic.' 'I'm Kristin and I'm an alcoholic.' It's so depressing."

Samira swallowed nervously and started the car. "You *have* to go, though. Steve said that's the only way the judge might let you go to a treatment program instead of jail."

Kamron slumped in his seat. "I know. I'm such a *fuckup*, Sami. I'm sorry."

Her heart turned inside out to see her big brother so small and scared.

She tried to cheer him up. "Guess what? I found an attorney for you."

At that moment, she had decided on Beth Woolsey. Any DUI attorney who would hang an art print like that in her office had to be badass.

And like Tara said, millions of people took those genetic tests all the time. She could still be one click away from finding her father and making him pay for everything he had done to her and Kamron. He would feel the full force of her fury; she would let him have it.

As long as she could get the image of her squealing with delight atop his shoulders out of her head before she did.

CHAPTER EIGHT

Henry

H*enry*," Linh harshly whispered when she saw what he was doing.

He had discreetly pulled out his phone in the middle of Statistics and was looking at the picture he had taken of his father's military portrait. In it, he's wearing army fatigues against a mottled blue background and a rippling American flag.

He didn't look happy. But then, maybe you weren't supposed to smile in a military portrait.

Henry got the dimple in his chin from him. His deep-set eyes. His left eyebrow was jagged like his. How different Henry's life would have been if his father had stayed in the picture.

The bell snapped him out of his reverie. He looked up to find Linh staring at him. "You're fantasizing about him again, aren't you?"

Henry slung his backpack over his shoulder and frowned. "I'm not 'fantasizing.'" That sounded infantile. Like he imagined his dad was an Avenger or Iron Man.

Linh put her hand on his back as they walked into the hall. "It's okay. It's normal for adoptees to fantasize about their birth parents when reunion becomes a possibility. I did it, too."

Henry stopped and turned toward her. "Linh. Seriously. I'm not *adopted* adopted."

"Okay, *okay*," Linh said as they continued down the hall. "All I'm saying is, it's normal to think about your birth father. Especially now." She held her books tight against her chest.

Crap. He *had* been obsessing. "You're right. I'm sorry." He spun toward her and walked backward. "You still coming over after school?"

Linh's face squinched. "You sure your mom won't care?"

Mom had a way of making his friends—his female friends, especially—feel unwelcome.

He was getting tired of tiptoeing around her, of not inviting Linh over, of Mom hovering around them when he did.

"Honestly, I don't care," he said.

If he could find his bio-dad, he wouldn't be stuck with Robert and Jeannie. And his eighteenth birthday was in two weeks. They would not have absolute power over him anymore. He could move in with Daniel if he wanted and get a job as a bag boy at Sprouts. He could even move in with Mama and go to the community college—the University of Denver be damned.

Linh followed Henry to the two-story mock-Mediterranean on Fair Oaks Circle. He pulled into the driveway and motioned for her to park on the curve of the cul-de-sac, then intercepted her on the porch with a kiss.

She pulled away, giggling, "Your mom could be watching."

"Let her."

He looked directly at the Ring camera but stopped himself from saying, *Hi, Mom.*

Sure enough, when they came through the front door, Mom was standing in the foyer. Clearly, she had been watching them. "Oh, hello, Linh," she said with feigned surprise. She followed Henry and Linh into the family room, where Dad's tan leather La-Z-Boy sectional was positioned in front of his sixty-five-inch flat-screen TV.

Henry deposited his backpack on the barstool at the kitchen counter and immediately went for the fridge. Linh slid onto the other barstool.

"Henry, what time is your practice tonight?" Mom fretted.

"No practice tonight, Mom," he said, balancing two cans of Coke in one hand. "Let's go." He motioned for Linh to follow him up to his room.

Mom watched them for a moment with alarm. "Wait."

Henry threw her a look. He was too old for her to be reminding him to keep his door open.

"Actually, I'm glad you're here," she said to Linh with what Henry knew was a manufactured smile. "We're planning a special dinner for Henry's eighteenth birthday."

This was the first Henry was hearing about it.

"At the Westlake Village Lodge."

The Westlake Village Lodge was one of Henry's favorite special-occasion restaurants. Linh looked to him for guidance. He shrugged. It wasn't like he could boycott the dinner. And their lamb chops were amazing.

"That would be wonderful, Mrs. Owen. Thanks for inviting me," Linh said.

"It'll be nice, just the four of us." Mom tried to sneak that last bit of information by.

Henry's face clouded. "What do you mean, 'the four of us'? What about Mama?"

Mom pursed her lips. "Well, I thought you, Nancy, your dad, and I could all go to Ruby's for lunch the day before."

A *diner*. For lunch. To celebrate his eighteenth birthday. Mama would feel more left out than last Mother's Day when Dad had excluded her from the lavish buffet brunch with the champagne fountain and chocolate-dipped strawberries. Henry had to sneak out later and go on a wild-goose chase for the only dozen red roses left in town. When Mama opened the door, her eyes were red from crying all day. He would talk to Dad about inviting Mama later.

"C'mon," he said, and nodded toward the stairs.

When he and Linh got up to his room, he closed the door. Linh leaned back on his bed with the navy duvet cover and nautical-themed sheets. Henry connected his phone and handed it to her. "Here," he said. "Find one of those playlists you like."

"Getting more adventurous sonically, are we?" She clicked around and launched a playlist with a slow, dreamy quality.

Henry put the phone on his side table and lay down on the bed staring up at the ceiling fan with his hands behind his head. Linh nestled into the crook of his arm. He closed his eyes for a moment and got a little lost in the music.

When he opened them, Linh was looking up at him with her beautiful, crooked smile. He leaned down and kissed her lightly on the lips. "Is this okay?" he murmured.

She nodded. He kissed her more deeply, then rolled onto his side. "What about this?" he asked, sliding his hand gently up her torso. "Mm-hmm," she said.

His hands started roaming all over her body. He whispered, "And this?" every time he ventured into new territory, and she kept saying *yes,* and soon they were enveloped in a make-out fog where he pretty much forgot his own name.

Henry rolled onto his back and pulled Linh on top of him. He wasn't worrying about Mom or thinking about his bio-dad—or thinking about anything, really—just feeling as if his erection was going to burst through his Levi's if Linh kept rubbing up against him.

"Should I get a condom?" he asked, light-headed.

"Yes," Linh said, her eyes half-closed.

He stretched his arm out toward the top drawer of his side table when, suddenly, the playlist was interrupted by the familiar *be-ding* of a Gmail notification.

He nearly flung Linh off the bed lunging for his phone. The Gmail preview contained the subject line **Your results are ready.** "It's the email!" he yelped.

Linh shook off her make-out fog and kneeled behind him. "Oh my God, babe. This is it." She squeezed his shoulders.

He took a deep breath and steadied himself. The home screen was filled with tabs for Ancestry, Health, Traits, and DNA Relatives.

His chest tightened as if he were about to jump out of a plane. He could be one click away from finding his father.

He swallowed. And clicked. At the top of the list were the words **Closest Possible Match.**

Oh, God. Henry's eyes started watering. He had found him. He had found his father. His eyes got all blurry. He wiped them with his sleeve.

"It's okay, babe. It's okay," Linh said reassuringly.

When he looked back at the screen, he did a double-take. The link did not say *Parent*. It said *Closest Possible Match—Sibling.*

A *sibling*?

He scanned the rest of the list: second and third cousins. No father. Of the thirty-five million people who had taken a DNA test, Mohammed Safavi was not one of them.

"It . . . it's not him," Henry said, his chest collapsing.

"What?" Linh grabbed the phone from him. "Babe, you have a sibling!" she squealed.

Suddenly, there was a knock at the door. He and Linh both jumped.

"Henry," Mom called through the door. Somehow, she knew not to open it. "Is Linh staying for dinner?"

"We're going out," Henry said, and held his breath. All he needed was for her to barge in and demand to know what they were doing.

"Okay," she said in a small, wounded voice.

"Henry, you can send a message through the app," Linh whispered. "This is so cool. What do you want to say?"

A thousand thoughts were rushing through Henry's brain, the least of which was what to say to his newly discovered sibling. The only thing he could think of was, *Fuck, Mama lied to me. She never told me she had another kid.* "Mama lied to me," he said, his face wrenched with hurt and confusion.

Linh put the phone aside and took Henry's hand. "Henry, maybe she was young, maybe she had to give the baby up, like my bio-mom. You don't know."

How could Mama let him go through life thinking he was an only child? He felt betrayed. He had begged her *and* Mom for a sibling when he was little so he wouldn't be so desperately alone.

Linh picked the phone back up. "I've got half siblings in Vietnam. I would give anything to connect with them."

"I . . . I don't even know what to say," he said, still in shock.

He wasn't looking for a *sibling*. His brain was all discombobulated. The only two possibilities he had been anticipating were finding his father or not.

His curiosity got the best of him. "What's, uh, its name?"

Linh lay on her stomach with the phone in front of her. "It's a her. I'm assuming. Her username is Michonne05."

"Her name is Michonne?" That sounded fake. Maybe this was a mistake, or a scam even.

"She's a character from *The Walking Dead*. Total badass. I like her already." Linh started typing, narrating as she went. "'Dear Michonne05, Damn, this was a surprise. No one in my family ever mentioned a half sibling, but I'm your brother. How amazing to find each other through a DNA test.'"

"Wait, stop." Henry held up his hand. "Let me talk to Mama first."

Linh sat up, cross-legged. "You don't need her permission, Henry."

It wasn't her permission he was after. He wanted clarity.

Linh rested her hand on his arm. "It's just first contact. Through an email that's not even your *real* email. We won't include your cell number or anything like that. What could it hurt?"

Henry didn't have an answer, just a feeling of unease.

"Henry! Maybe she's your *dad's* kid," Linh said. "Maybe she knows where he is."

That was true. He motioned for Linh to hand back his phone. "Let me see what you wrote." He scanned her message. "Too hype," he said, and started tapping: Hi. I guess we're siblings.

He didn't want to sound overeager.

I'm trying to figure out how we're related. Is your dad Mohammed Safavi or your mom Nancy Vlasek? I'm Henry.

That was simple and straightforward enough.

But . . . Mom and Dad would freak out if they found out, and what if this sibling didn't want anything to do with him?

He wrestled with himself for a full minute and then, with whatever hesitations, misgivings, or second thoughts Henry had, finally clicked *send*.

CHAPTER NINE

Samira

Samira had been up researching the county's DUI programs well past 1 a.m. in anticipation of Kamron's first meeting with Beth Woolsey and had finally found a free outpatient program, like mandatory AA. If he could go, they wouldn't have to pay for treatment.

At moments like these—researching treatment programs for Kamron or planning her grandfather's funeral—she felt a calming sense of completion. Once again, she had averted disaster. Grandad said she was more capable than most adults he knew (*you're the only one with the good sense and fortitude to handle things when I croak, Sami,* is how he put it).

Ordinarily, she would have allowed herself to sleep in the next morning and skip first period, but Mrs. Sandoval had made it clear she couldn't miss any more classes without an excuse. She ducked into the kitchen for her giant travel mug of coffee, and—

WTF?

Uncle Chris, of all people, was standing there, next to the refrigerator with Gran. "Hey," he said tersely, like they were strangers in a supermarket.

He had stepped in to take her to the father/daughter dance in seventh grade; he had brought her a wrist corsage with pink roses to match her dress, took her out for pizza beforehand, and even tumbled onto the dance floor with her for "Shake It Off."

And then he all but disappeared—like her father—because of some blowup with Grandad, without any thought as to how much Kamron and Samira would miss him.

"Uh, hey," Samira replied, uneasy. "What are you doing here?"

He took a sip of coffee and motioned to Gran. "Your grand-mother asked me to come and talk to Kamron. Which I did," he said with a look of distaste, as if he had eaten a sour plum.

Samira bristled. He barely knew Kamron. Why would Gran ask *him*? She set her backpack on the table. "What did you say to him? What did he say?"

"He won't admit he has a problem," Uncle Chris said with a bitter laugh.

"Of *course* he won't admit he has a problem," Samira said. "That's the problem."

Gran waved her hand at him. "You don't know what he went through, Chris, you—"

"I know *exactly* what he went through," Uncle Chris snapped back. "Who picked Erin and the kids up in Fresno, Mom? Who brought them back here? *Dragged* them back. Because Erin didn't want to go."

Uncle Chris was an OF, for sure. The mirror opposite of her mother. He had a nice house in Cloverdale. A good job working for the county. Probably well-prepared for retirement.

And he *could* take charge. Pay for Kamron's treatment if he wanted. But he didn't.

Or wouldn't, which was worse.

"If you keep coddling him, he's going to end up just like his father." He looked Samira directly in the eye when he said this.

She shifted uneasily in the dead silence that followed. "What do you mean?"

Uncle Chris's round face reddened. "Your dad had a lot of issues. A dishonorable discharge from the military, and a—"

"*Chris.*" Gran cut him off sharply.

He dumped the rest of his coffee in the sink. "I'm going to be late for work. Sorry I couldn't be more help." He gave Gran a perfunctory kiss on the cheek and said, "Bye, Sami."

Samira followed him to the door. "I found a DUI attorney," she said with a defensive edge. "We have an appointment today. Kamron might even be eligible for a free treatment program through the county."

"It's not going to work unless he's ready," Uncle Chris said. With that, he was out the door.

Well, she *had* found an attorney who was going to help get Kamron into that free treatment program. Then *she* would be free to be a normal college freshman who worried about dormmates and cafeteria food—and was on her way to selling her million-dollar idea to Barbara or Lori on *Shark Tank*—instead of someone who stayed up until one o'clock in the morning researching DUI programs for her brother when she wasn't supposed to be late the next day.

Samira forged a tardy note from Gran, sleepwalked through school, and nearly fell asleep on the bus ride to the attorney's office. She probably shouldn't have taken a Benadryl at lunch—maybe she was taking too many—but the invisible mosquitoes were relentless that day.

Of course, the day she looked utterly exhausted was the

day a cute, clean-cut receptionist—probably a first-year law student—told her to have a seat in the lobby near the big, weird art print while she waited for Gran and Kamron.

It was even more dramatic in person. She googled it. The print turned out to have been painted right on the Berlin Wall that separated East and West Germany, commemorating the day it came down. Samira found herself falling down a rabbit hole of pictures of tearful families reunited after decades of being torn apart until Gran and Kamron showed up a few minutes before four.

Kamron took a seat in the club chair across from Samira with his eyes closed and his hands folded. Gran sat on the edge of the chair next to him with perfect posture—as if she were being surveilled—clutching her pocketbook.

She and Samira had scraped together $2,500 for the retainer from the rest of the money in the safe and from a small savings account that Gran had kept secret from Grandad (*let's call it my Christmas Club*).

At 4:12 p.m., the clean-cut receptionist called out "Kamron Murphy" with a question mark at the end, even though they were the only people in the reception area.

Samira's cheeks flushed when they passed by. *Smashable,* Tara would have called him. He looked like a Jonas . . . cousin. Samira was desperate to tell him, *Ignore my brother, I've been accepted to Lewis & Clark on a scholarship and am going to make millions one day selling Gran's Tangy Tequila Lime Fudge.*

"I'm Beth Woolsey." A woman about Samira's mom's age with dark brown hair in a pixie cut and wide eyes greeted them. She was all business in her white button-down shirt and pencil skirt. A tattoo of a dove taking flight peeked out from under her sleeve when she extended her right hand.

Samira grasped her hand and shook it firmly. "I'm Kamron's sister, Samira. This is my grandmother, and this is Kamron."

Beth ushered them into her office and gestured for them to sit on a modern, mocha-colored leather couch. She sat opposite them in a similarly modern armchair. A manila file folder lay on the glass coffee table in front of her.

"I know this is a difficult and scary time for all of you." She picked up the file folder and leafed through it. "Why don't you tell me what happened in your own words, Kamron."

He looked away. "I, uh, I met some friends for a beer—"

"Your blood alcohol level was one-point-six, Kamron," Beth said calmly.

This threw him. He fidgeted. "I . . . I know. I left the bar, and I was driving home, and I may have done, like, a rolling stop at the stop sign."

"You *ran* the stop sign." Beth sounded like Siri. "The officer was fully justified in pulling you over. He had every right to give you a field sobriety test, which you failed." She picked up the file folder, pulled out the police report, and handed it to him. "And there were aggravating circumstances. You almost hit a ten-year-old boy on a bicycle."

Samira's mouth opened. Gran gasped.

Kamron's face twisted with genuine shock. "N-no, I didn't."

"You may not remember, but you did. You could be facing up to six months in prison."

Shit, shit, *shit*.

Samira's entire body started itching.

Beth Woolsey didn't know that Kamron used to volunteer at the Boys & Girls Clubs and was the type who gently herded spiders out the sliding glass door because he couldn't stand to see any living creature suffer.

"I don't say this to reprimand you," Beth said in her soothing monotone. "That's not my job. My job is to defend you. But, to do that, we have to be aware of how the judge will look at this."

Samira cleared her throat. "I read about that Sonoma County DUI Program, the court-appointed AA. Do you think the judge would let him do that?"

She wanted Beth Woolsey—an OF, for sure—to know she had done her homework.

Beth stared straight at Kamron with her laser-beam eyes. "No. Not when he never completed the six-month program for first-time offenders two years ago."

Samira felt as if she had been kicked in the gut. She didn't know that. Grandad had handled the whole thing.

She could *not* leave for Lewis & Clark if Kamron went to jail for six months. Forget Kamron, *Gran* wouldn't survive it. She would be sick with worry every day.

"You don't understand what he's been through," Gran pleaded.

"Gran," Kamron said. His face flickered with embarrassment.

She forged ahead. "His father was abusive. He suffered terribly."

"Gran," Kamron said again.

Beth Woolsey sat in her leather armchair, unblinking, for a moment. "If you write a narrative about your traumatic experience, Kamron, in which you sound truly remorseful and indicate your readiness for recovery, the judge may consider residential treatment."

"Residential? Like one of those twenty-eight-day programs?" Gran asked. Her hands were shaking again. "We don't have the money for that."

"What about insurance?" Beth asked.

"I'm on Medicare, the kids are on Medi-Cal." Gran sank back in her seat.

"Medi-Cal covers half the cost," Beth said. "And there are free county resources."

"There's a year-long wait list for those. I checked," Samira said as an air of defeat permeated the room.

And then she was hit with a painful realization. Grandad wasn't there anymore to save the day. If anyone were going to don the red cape and come to Kamron's rescue, it had to be her.

Maybe they *did* have the money if their Medi-Cal insurance covered half the cost. But was she really going to do this? Flush her whole future down the drain for Kamron?

She looked over at him. He was still wringing his hands, his face stark white like the frightened little boy in the Facebook video.

She had no choice. She wanted the brother back who had held her hand while they watched scary movies, the one who shared his Halloween candy with her—and not just the duds like SweeTarts and Laffy Taffy, but the good stuff.

"We . . . we have the money," she said.

Gran's face scrunched with confusion. Beth, who might have been a robot, remained unblinking.

"Between my savings bond and Kamron's, we have over twenty thousand dollars. That should be enough for a Medi-Cal facility."

"You can't do that," Gran said adamantly. "You need that money for university."

Kamron looked at her, searching. "Sami, no," he said softly. "You can't do that."

"We'll do one of those reverse mortgages," Gran insisted.

"The ones where they can take the house if you miss a tax payment? No way," Samira said firmly.

Gran started to cry. "I can't let you do that, honey."

"Yes, you can," Samira said, barely audible, whereupon her body went numb, except for the marauding mosquitoes.

Oblivious to the fact that Samira might *never* be on *Shark Tank,* Beth Woolsey stood up and said crisply, "Make arrangements with a facility and bring your paperwork to court. Be ready to enter the program the day of the arraignment." She arched one perfectly waxed eyebrow at Kamron. "Call your sponsor. Start going to meetings now. And get a list of residential treatment centers from my assistant on the way out."

"Y-yes, ma'am," he said. As soon as they got outside her office, he said, "Samira, I . . . I'll pay you back as soon as I get out, I swear."

Samira's cheeks burned when the clean-cut assistant handed her the list of facilities. There was no point in telling him she had been accepted to Lewis & Clark now. She wasn't going.

⚬|⚬

Everyone went their separate ways as soon as they got home. Samira stopped by the bathroom to pop another little pink tablet.

She collapsed on the bed while her phone buzzed with the tenth or eleventh unanswered text from Tara: hows it going?? 😳 🙏; u ok?? 🥺 💔; stay strong!! 🤎 🖤; and OMG stitch fix came keeping EVERYTHING!!! 💅 🧶 💰.

Samira put her phone down. She wasn't up for texting Tara.

Tara would never have to sacrifice anything for anything. It wasn't fair. But then, life wasn't fair.

Another to-do list was already forming in her head.

1. Research recovery facilities
2. Cash in savings bonds
3. Officially decline admission to Lewis & Clark now that Kamron has detonated it

No matter how hard she tried to escape, she was trapped in a web of his dysfunctionality.

Which reminded her:

4. Find their father and collect the back child support he owed them

A long shot, yes, but if she *could* find him, she might still be able to attend Lewis & Clark and have a shot at *Shark Tank*.

She logged into 23andMe.com and was greeted by several notifications: **You have 19 new DNA relatives. Take the Health Survey. Read your new messages.**

From who, one of her third cousins, twice removed? She tapped the message.

Her head rattled. This couldn't be right.

The subject line of the first message read: **Closest Possible Match—Sibling.**

It *had* to be a mistake.

A second message was from someone named *Zamboni.*

Yes, a prank. Who the hell would call themselves *Zamboni*? And why would they play such a cruel trick on her? She couldn't even bring herself to open the message.

Instead, she FaceTimed Tara, who popped on-screen in the purple polka-dot, ruffle-cuff dress she had just purchased from Stitch Fix. "Oh my God! Why haven't you answered my texts? I've been worried about you."

"Don't talk," Samira said, "just listen. And look." She turned her iPhone toward her laptop. "Did you get this, too? Is it a mistake?"

Tara squinted. "DMs? Yes. I get them all the time, they—"

"Look at the first message!" Samira shouted.

Tara squinted again. "Oh my God, Sami, you have a sibling!"

Samira turned the iPhone back toward her. "No. It's a mistake, right? Or, like, spam."

Tara futzed with the tag on her dress while trying to hold her phone. "Sami, no. It's not a mistake, there are no 'mistakes' in DNA. Either you're a match or you're not. If it says you have another sibling, you *have* another sibling."

For a moment, Samira couldn't breathe. She'd been knocked off her feet without warning. Her mind went uncharacteristically blank. She uttered a sentence she hadn't uttered in ages. "Wh-what am I supposed to do?"

"Open the message," Tara commanded.

Samira sat there staring at the screen, immobile. She could be opening Pandora's box. "I should call my mom first."

"Click first, call later," Tara said, taking remarkable control of the situation.

Samira clicked and stared intently at the screen, reading and rereading the message, unable to speak.

"What does it say, what does it say?" Tara asked, pulling the tag off her dress with her teeth.

"It's . . . a boy. I mean, he's a boy. I mean, he's my brother, my brother is a boy. You know what I mean." Her brain was scrambled.

"*Whoa.* Another brother. What does his message say?"

"It says, *Hi. I guess we're siblings. I'm trying to figure out how we're related. Is your dad Mohammed Safavi or your mom Nancy Vlasek? I'm Henry.*"

"Mohammed Safavi! Sami, he's your dad's son. You *have* to write him back," Tara said, making a to-do list for Samira. "Then you can call your mom."

Samira's head was spinning. "Am I supposed to have a *relationship* with this person?"

"Don't you *want* a relationship with him?"

"I don't know!" Samira flopped back on her bed. "One brother is trouble enough for now."

"Oh no. Is Kamron going to jail?" Tara's face twisted up.

"Hopefully not." Samira sighed. "Not if the judge lets him do a treatment program instead."

Tara had finally stopped fiddling with her dress. "I thought you couldn't afford it."

"We couldn't." Samira closed her eyes, overcome with exhaustion. "Unless we combine the savings bonds my grandad left us."

Tara's forehead scrunched. "Then how will you pay for college?"

"I'm not," Samira said, and felt like throwing up. She had worked so hard to get accepted and to save her share of tuition.

"Oh, Sami, no!"

She tried to smile but couldn't swing it. "I'll enroll at the community college. Or, who knows? Maybe take a gap year with you."

Tara looked like she might cry. "You were super excited. You got the Lewis & Clark hoodie and everything."

"It's just a sweatshirt," Samira said, but the minute she said it, her eyes welled up.

"Want me to come over?" Tara offered.

"No," Samira said. She blinked several times. Suddenly, her body felt as if it were under a weighted blanket; like she could fall asleep and not wake up for a hundred years. "I need a nap. Then I'll call my mom."

The Benadryl she had taken caught up to her.

The minute she closed her eyes, she didn't drift off so much as fall off a sleep cliff through dinner and into breakfast the next morning.

CHAPTER TEN

Henry

It had been three days since Henry had messaged Michonne05. She (he? they?) still hadn't responded. What were they waiting for?

His one-game suspension was up. He should have been happy he was allowed to play in that week's game. Instead, he was preoccupied with how to ask Mama if she knew anything about a half sibling—without mentioning anything about a half sibling—when they went out for pizza afterward.

He let a goal slip by and failed to stop several two-on-ones. When Henry glanced up at the stands on a line change, Dad had that perpetually dissatisfied look on his face. Mom was wincing, as usual.

Mama sat behind them. He could not directly ask her, *Did you have another kid?* He had to be more subtle than that.

Finally, he found his groove in the last two minutes of the game. Daniel went on the attack from the defensive zone and quickly passed Henry the puck, which he crisscrossed right back. Daniel took a slap shot and scored.

They still lost.

After the final buzzer, Henry trekked over to where Mom and Dad were standing by the double doors. "What happened out there?" Dad said. His questions always felt like accusations. A vertical frown line intersected his brow.

Henry was too nervous about his conversation with Mama to care. "Off day. Don't forget, I'm going out with Mama tonight."

"No. We didn't. Forget," Mom said with an awkward smile. Smiling was not her native language.

As soon as they left, he made his way over to Mama.

"If Coach had played you more, we would have won," Mama declared.

Dad didn't seem to think Henry could do anything right. Mama didn't seem to think he could do anything wrong, which, weirdly, was just as annoying.

"Let me get changed," he said.

"Okay, baby. I'll be right here waiting for you."

⚬✕⚬

"You didn't have to pay." Mama bit into her cheese and pepperoni at the pizza place next to the rink. She ate with a lot more gusto than Mom.

"It's okay," Henry said, separating a slice of his pepperoni and meatballs, which he could enjoy since Linh was not there bugging him to be a vegetarian. "I get an allowance from Mom and Dad."

She wiped her face with her napkin and grimaced. "Well. They can afford it."

He shouldn't have said that. He tried not to praise Mom and Dad too much around Mama. And that night, Henry needed her loose and chatty.

"Oh, man, I forgot," he said with a tap of his forehead. "They have Fanta here." He stood up. "You want a glass of wine or something?" Wine would loosen her up.

"Sure. You got a fake ID?" she teased.

He stepped up to the cashier. "Fanta and a glass of red wine for my mom," he said, gesturing to her.

"It's for me. I'm his mother." Mama waved, calling out across the room. She would wear a sandwich board emblazoned with I'M HIS MOTHER if she could.

Henry returned to the table with their drinks and set her glass down on a napkin, then slid into the red booth opposite her.

She took a sip. "It's good. And I know wine, remember. I used to wait on some of the most important people in Hollywood."

She loved reminiscing about her time waitressing at a restaurant in Burbank, near all the movie studios, before Henry was born.

This was his opening. "Is that where you met my dad?"

She took another sip of her wine. "Yep. Used to come in there after his shifts as a security guard and sit at the bar. Have a beer. Just to see me."

Mama looked older than her fifty years. But Henry had seen pictures of her when she was young: petite, with strawberry-blond hair. She looked flirty, always making faces at the camera.

He took a big bite of his pizza. "How come you didn't marry him?"

Her lips pursed. "He was married at the time."

This was news. Henry played it cool. If he made too big a deal out of it, she would clam up.

"He told me he was separated. We got involved. Next thing I know, you're coming along."

As nonchalantly as possible, Henry said, "Do you know where he is?"

She shook her head. "Nope."

He shoveled another bite into his mouth. "Did he have any other kids?"

Mama paused, mid-sip. "Didn't mention any."

Henry swallowed nervously. "Did you?"

Her face got all contorted. "What?"

He hesitated a half second. "Have other kids?"

She dabbed her lips with her napkin. "Why would you ask that?"

Henry played it off. "Just, you know, wondering if I have any siblings out there."

"You might," she said, and took another sip of wine. "But if you do, they're not mine."

Not hers. Which meant Michonne05 *was* Mohammed Safavi's daughter.

"Where do you *think* he is?" Henry pushed.

"Who knows? Could be a millionaire for all we know," Mama said, as she always did, raising her glass in a mock toast.

Henry kept the questions coming before she shut down. "Why didn't he try to see me?"

She downed the rest of her wine and looked him directly in the eye. "Robert and Jeannie were supposed to help out, you know, on evenings and weekends when I was working. Your dad was still in the picture then. All of a sudden, they were your legal guardians, and they wouldn't let him come around." Her face hardened. "Jeannie couldn't have her own children, you know."

Henry shifted uneasily. This was clearly not something Mama was supposed to tell him.

He had a million more questions about how he had come to live with Robert and Jeannie, but as soon as he popped the last bit of pizza into his mouth, Mama grabbed her purse, stood up, and said, "You ready?" For her, this conversation was over.

"Yeah, yeah," Henry said, scrambling to his feet.

When he walked Mama out to her car, she hugged him tight and said, "I never 'gave you up.' Don't you ever forget that."

"I won't," he promised.

A surge of anger swelled in Henry's chest. All these years, he had been led to believe his bio-dad had abandoned him. That, in some way, Mama hadn't wanted him, either.

His mind raced on the drive home. He was going to confront Mom and Dad and demand to know why they had taken him from Mama and worse, wouldn't let him see his bio-dad.

"Don't do it," Linh warned when he called to tell her about his conversation with Mama. "Don't say anything you can't take back. Make contact with Michonne first."

Since she knew more about this whole adoption thing—even though he wasn't *adopted* adopted—than he did, he would wait.

He laid out his sweaty gear in the laundry room, raced upstairs, and pulled out his laptop. No wonder Michonne hadn't responded: his note sounded rushed, like he wasn't taking the whole thing seriously. He would message her again and tell her—

"Henry."

Dad was standing right there in the doorway.

"Jesus," Henry said under his breath and snapped his laptop shut. Dad never knocked.

He leaned in the doorframe with his arms crossed. "Did you accept admission to U of D yet? We have to send in that deposit."

"I will," Henry said quickly. He wanted to get back to messaging Michonne.

But his dad remained in the doorway. U of D wasn't what he really wanted to talk about. Henry braced himself.

"Your mother said you want Nancy to come to the Westlake Village Lodge with us for your birthday dinner."

"I do," Henry said coolly.

Robert flashed one of his patronizing smiles. "All they do is bicker, you know."

"I know," Henry said. They weren't going to exclude people from Henry's life anymore.

"Well." Dad chuckled. "It's not going to be a very enjoyable evening."

"I want her to come," Henry said firmly. He wasn't backing down.

"Henry," his dad said, growing impatient. "We'll have a perfectly fine lunch the day before at Ruby's."

"Mama will feel left out if she's not included," Henry argued.

Robert's jaw set. "Nancy will feel aggrieved no matter the situation."

"Then let's not go," Henry said, irritated. He put his laptop aside. "Let's order pizza from Domino's. That'd be fine by me."

Robert's head cocked. "You know we're not ordering Domino's," he said in a low voice. "You know your mother has her heart set on the lodge."

She had her heart set on excluding Mama and was using a birthday dinner at Henry's favorite restaurant to do it. Well, Henry was done playing Who's Your Favorite Mother?

After a long, difficult silence, in a quiet voice filled with maximum fury, Robert said, "I'll tell your mother to make the reservation for five, then," and shut the door.

Whoa. Henry had won! He had battled his dad and *won*, which never happened.

With a burst of adrenaline, he flipped back open his laptop, logged into 23andMe, navigated to Messages, and started typing.

> Hi there. Sorry my last email was so short. I thought I'd tell you a little more about me, so you know I'm for real. My name is Henry Owen. I live in Westlake Village, in Southern California. My mom—my biological mom, I have two moms, it's a long story—anyway, my mom said she didn't have any other kids, so we must have the same dad: Mohammed Safavi. Is that your dad? I'd like to talk to you about him if you know where he is. Please write back, if you can. You can call or text me at 555–437–2406.

This time, without a moment's hesitation, Henry clicked *send*.

CHAPTER ELEVEN
Samira

The pillow over her eyes couldn't block out the sun that streamed into Samira's bedroom. Her mouth was dry. She fumbled around for her phone.

Ten o'clock, as in 10 *a.m.* She had slept for more than fifteen hours. Her brain was foggier than the mist rolling down from Mount Tamalpais and onto the Golden Gate.

All at once, everything came rushing back.

1. They had to get Kamron into recovery
2. She had to decline admission to Lewis & Clark to help pay for it
3. They had another brother

They had another brother.

It didn't seem real. Where was he? What was he like? Was he younger or older? Did he look like her or Kamron? She was curious. But also cautious. She didn't know anything about him and did not need the entanglement right now.

Plus, as much as she might have wanted to tell Kamron about him, she couldn't. Not now. Not when all he should be worrying about was his arraignment.

She sat up and tried to focus her vision. Mom. She needed to talk to Mom about this other brother, even before she told Gran.

Samira tapped her mother's contact. As usual, she took forever to answer. Samira's index finger was poised above the big red X when she finally picked up.

Without even saying hello, Samira blurted, "Did our dad have another kid?"

Which caught her mother off guard. An instant eternity elapsed. Samira held the phone out in front of her to make sure they were still connected.

"Why?" Mom said carefully. "Did someone contact you?"

"Yes. Through one of those genetic tests."

"You took one of those tests, baby? What were you looking for?" She sounded hurt.

Samira stood up. "The test is not the point, Mom. The point is, we have another brother."

There was a difficult, awkward silence during which Samira urgently scratched her ribs.

"No. I didn't know that," Mom said, her voice heavy with regret. "We . . . we separated around the time I was pregnant with you. I don't know what happened afterward."

Samira picked up the military portrait and held her father's melancholy gaze. "So, you didn't know he had another kid? You don't know anything about him?"

Another long, difficult silence.

". . . no."

Samira put the portrait back, facedown. She hadn't thought about how it might feel for her mother to learn that their dad had a child with another woman. She softened. "His name's Henry," she said.

"Does he want to meet you? Do you want to meet him?"

One good thing about Mom was that she probably wouldn't care if Samira did want to meet him; she'd say Samira was on a *journey of reconnection.*

"Not till after Kamron's arraignment." Samira scratched her ankle. "Mom, do you have *any* idea where our dad is? We could sure use that back child support right now."

"No, honey. I don't."

Samira's voice rose. "Why did he go? What *happened?*"

Mom hesitated. "Samira. I don't want to say anything that could turn you against him. He's still your father. If you could shift your focus away from anger toward forgiveness, then—"

"Forgiveness for *what*? I don't even know what he did! Uncle Chris makes him sound like a monster."

"He wasn't a monster, he was *suffering,*" her mother said sharply. "Your uncle doesn't know what he's talking about. It broke my heart that I couldn't reach him."

Samira wasn't getting anywhere asking questions about her father. "Are you coming down for Kamron's arraignment?" she asked with growing exasperation.

"I'm going to try and get the time off work."

"*Try* and get off work? He's your son, Mom," Samira snapped.

"I know, Samira," Mom said more firmly. "But he's not talking to me right now. And I don't know whether I would be more of a help or a hindrance."

"It would help *me,*" Samira said grudgingly. If only everyone knew how hard it was for her to ask for help.

"I'll do my best to be there, baby," her mother promised. "And your grandmother told me about the brave and beautiful thing you did for your brother. I wish I were in a position to pay for it. But your sacrifice won't go unnoticed."

It probably would. Samira's sacrifices mostly went unnoticed.

After they hung up, Samira went back to searching for affordable treatment programs. An ad appeared at the top of the results for Sunrise Acres—*Where Each New Day Dawns with Hope.* Samira wasn't getting hers up. Of the places she had called that accepted Medi-Cal at reduced rates, few had availability.

"Sunrise Acres, where each new day dawns with hope," a receptionist chirped.

"Hi, my name is Samira Murphy, and I'm calling to see if there's availability for my brother, Kamron. He's an, um, an alcoholic."

It was embarrassing to admit it, and "alcoholic" was not the sum total of him.

"Just one moment." The receptionist put Samira on hold, who suffered through a smooth jazz version of "Here Comes the Sun." She was not in the mood to be uplifted.

Finally, the receptionist returned. "Yes. We have a bed opening up next week."

"And you accept Medi-Cal?" Samira asked with zero energy because they probably didn't.

"We do," the receptionist said.

"Y-you do?" Samira said, now jolted awake. "You . . . you take Medi-Cal? Like, we would pay the Medi-Cal rate?"

"Yes, we have three beds dedicated to Medi-Cal patients, and one is opening up next week," she repeated more slowly and clearly.

Samira was ready to cry tears of joy, which would *not* be a waste of water. "Can I sign him up? My brother. He has to get in recovery because he got a DUI, and . . ." She was babbling.

"Let me get your email, and I'll send you the paperwork."

Oh my *God*. Maybe there was something to Mom's hippie church after all! Kamron *had* been guided to the right place. Samira was elated.

Plus, she got the satisfaction of crossing yet another task off of her to-do list.

◦⦉◦

It wasn't a bad omen, necessarily, but Samira did find it odd that on the day of Kamron's arraignment, she, Gran, and Kamron were wearing the exact same clothes that they had worn to Grandad's funeral: Kamron in his navy jacket and tie, Gran in her black pantsuit, and Samira in a long black skirt and emerald-green silk tee—a cast-off from Tara, who was barraging her with texts: good luck!! ✳✳ can meet you there if you want 🤲 🖤 🖤 🖤 lmk 🗞

There were also several texts from Mom asking how Kamron was doing and if Samira could please keep her updated. She was not able to get off work, which was okay. Kamron claimed he didn't want her there anyway.

Samira answered both with a quick call u later.

Kamron rolled Grandad's old Samsonite suitcase—stuffed with clothes and toiletries for a possible twenty-eight-day stay—out to the car and heaved it into the trunk. Gran paused outside the passenger door as if she might sit in the back seat with Kamron but slipped into the passenger seat instead.

Samira climbed into the driver's seat and locked eyes with Kamron in the rearview. "It'll be okay," she said, because what else could she say?

He didn't respond.

In fact, no one said much during the twenty-minute drive to the Sonoma County Superior Court. "There's your uncle,"

Gran said when Samira pulled into the parking lot. Uncle Chris made it unanimous: he was wearing the same charcoal-gray wool sports coat he had worn to Grandad's service.

As they walked toward the concrete-and-steel courthouse, he strode toward them. "Hey, Mom, Samira." He shook Kamron's hand and draped an arm around his shoulder. "You're gonna be a new man in twenty-eight days, buddy."

Great. He had probably jinxed it.

The corners of Kamron's mouth wobbled into a smile.

Samira telepathically pleaded with him not to cry.

They all entered the courthouse, where Kamron's sponsor, Steve, was waiting for them in front of Courtroom 15. He threw his big grizzly arms around Kamron and gave him a bear hug. "You got this, brother."

A minute later, Beth Woolsey came out of the ladies' room toting her leather messenger bag, wearing a black pencil skirt and a leopard-print blouse—another bold choice. "Is everyone here? Are you the admissions director for Sunrise Acres?" she asked Steve.

He gestured to the courtroom. "He's in there."

"Good. Are you ready?" she asked Kamron. Before he could answer, she said, "Let's go," and led the way inside.

◑◐

Samira kept scratching her left calf with her right shoe while Kamron was read his rights during the arraignment: his right to an attorney, right not to incriminate himself, etc.

He sat at the defendant's table with Beth Woolsey and the admissions director for Sunrise Acres opposite a younger woman, the assistant district attorney, who sat at the plaintiff's table. Samira, Gran, Uncle Chris, and Steve sat in the public benches, pretty much like the *Law & Order* episodes on a permanent loop after Grandad got home from work.

"And how do you plead?" the judge asked Kamron without glancing up from her docket.

"Um, guilty, Your Honor," Kamron said, barely audible.

"Speak up, please," the judge said with a South Asian accent.

Beth Woolsey motioned him to stand up. "Guilty, Your Honor," he said again, more clearly.

The catch in his voice pierced Samira's heart.

"Plaintiffs agree to alternative sentencing?" the judge asked, making notes on the docket.

"Yes, Your Honor," said the assistant DA.

Finally, the judge looked up at Kamron. "What do you have to say for yourself?"

Her tone sounded skeptical. Samira's mouth went dry. If she denied the alternative sentence, Kamron would go to prison.

Kamron's hands shook as he read the statement that Beth Woolsey had helped him prepare. "I am sincerely sorry for my actions and the pain I have caused my loved ones." He glanced over at Samira and Gran, who wiped away a tear. "My . . . my drinking and driving . . ." He choked up. ". . . my drinking and driving endangered the lives of others, including a little boy. I know I need help. I know I need to enter recovery. I'm asking you to allow me to get treatment at Sunrise Acres so I can go back to being a productive member of society."

That part sounded like Beth wrote it.

"More than anything," he said sincerely, "I don't want to be a burden to my sister and my grandmother any longer." Again, he looked over at Samira and Gran.

Kamron stirred such a confusing mix of emotions: anger,

sympathy, sadness. And yes, guilt that he had been traumatized by their father, whom Samira could barely remember.

The judge lasered in on him. "You understand you must complete this program in order to fulfill your sentence and that the charges against you will not be dismissed until you have?"

Kamron nodded dutifully. He looked so pale and scared.

"Then answer in the affirmative," the judge said sharply.

"Yes, ma'am, I mean, Your Honor," he said, voice cracking.

There was an agonizingly long pause. Samira's heart was at the top of a roller coaster, suspended in midair.

Finally, the judge said, "Then I accept the county's recommendation for alternative sentencing and remand you to the custody of Sunrise Acres."

Samira closed her eyes. Gran clutched her hand. The judge pounded her gavel. "This court is adjourned."

Samira, Gran, and Uncle Chris walked a shaky Kamron to the Kia to retrieve his suitcase while the Sunrise Acres van idled nearby. Samira hugged him tight. "You'll be okay. And we'll see you in two weeks," the earliest possible date she and Gran would be allowed to visit.

Uncle Chris teared up when he shook Kamron's hand. "I'm proud of you, son." Steve gave him another bear hug. "First couple of days are rough. It gets easier."

The Sunrise Acres admissions director stood by patiently until Gran finally let him go. "You'll be okay, honey," she said with one last hug. He climbed into the van looking like he was being abducted. Samira couldn't watch.

On the drive home, Gran sniffled and said, "Your grandad did this. I asked him to watch over Kamron and he did." If Grandad had *really* been watching over them, Kamron wouldn't have gotten a second DUI in the first place. But Samira felt a weight lift. It was now on Sunrise Acres to worry about Kamron.

∞

Samira had barely gotten home when Tara burst into her room with an armful of snacks: Tate's Chocolate Chip Cookies, sea salt and vinegar Kettle chips, and spicy pistachios from the Persian market. She hopped on the bed and sat cross-legged. "Oh my God! Are you okay? Was it like *Intervention*? My mom watches that show all the time because of my uncle."

Samira sat across from her and tore open the Kettle chips. She hadn't eaten since breakfast. "Kind of, I guess." She let out a morbid laugh. "Only the intervention was court-ordered."

Tara's eyes welled. "How was he?" Her emotions were always so close to the surface.

Samira winced at the image of Kamron climbing into the van. "Scared. We can't see him or talk to him for two weeks. There's a family thing at the end."

Tara cracked a pistachio and motioned Samira for her empty travel mug to deposit the shell. "My mom was supposed to do that, too. My uncle never made it to the end."

Samira's eyes widened. "Kamron *has* to. It's court-ordered."

"I know, I *know*," Tara said excitedly. "I wasn't implying he wouldn't. I was just saying . . ."

Shit. Samira googled, **what happens if you fail court-ordered drug alcohol treatment?** when a Gmail notification popped up: a message from 23andMe. "Oh God," Samira said with a weary sigh. "Another DM from Zamboni."

"What does it say?" Tara said, breathless.

Samira scanned the message quickly. "His full name is

Henry Owen. He's from Westlake Village. He just wants to find our dad. He left his phone number," she said, and immediately regretted it.

"Let's call him." Tara wrested Samira's phone from her.

Samira tried to snatch it back. "Tara, I'm serious. I want to take this slow. I'm not up for a big reunion right now. We don't know anything about him."

Tara surrendered Samira's but grabbed her own phone and started tapping.

"What are you *doing*?"

A big smile spread across her face. "Found him. Henry Owen. Yep, Westlake Village, California." She giggled. "He has an Instagram with, like, fifteen followers. He goes to Westlake High School." She kept tapping. "He hasn't posted anything—not even a profile pic—but he's tagged in some pictures with a girl named Linh." Tara expanded the image with her thumb and forefinger. "He doesn't look like a serial killer, Sami. All he wants to do is find your dad."

Samira crumpled up her Kettle chip bag. "Well, I don't know where he is."

"Can't you call him and tell him that?"

Leave it to Tara, a textbook UF, to underestimate the fallout of connecting with a newly discovered half sibling. He could: 1. Be a serial killer (he *could*). 2. Be a jerk. 3. Want more of a relationship than she was ready for.

Tara's eyes were glued to the screen. "He plays hockey. Someone named dannyboi tagged him in a team photo. Ooh. I wonder which one *he* is."

"Lemme see," Samira said with mild irritation. She scrolled through the Instagram images, then wished she hadn't. Henry Owen did *not* look like a serial killer. He had brown skin and green eyes and a kind face with some sadness lurking underneath. Like Kamron.

And their father.

"Oh, Sami. Just call him," Tara said, her voice oozing with sympathy.

Samira's heart sank. She wanted to help. But it wasn't the right time to reach out. Was it?

She exhaled. "If I call him and tell him I don't know where our dad is, do you think he'll quit DMing me?"

Tara threw her arms around Samira. "I can't believe I'm here for this with you."

Samira had to laugh. "All I'm going to say is that I don't know where he is." She took a deep breath. "Here goes." In the second it took before the call connected, she reconsidered. Honestly, she wasn't ready to—

Too late. It was ringing. Even if she hung up, he would see her number and call back.

"Hello?" a male voice said.

She could still hang up. Pretend she didn't know it was him if he called back.

Better to get it over with. "Is this Henry Owen?"

"Yes! Yes, it is."

He might have known it was her, but she said it anyway. "This is Samira Murphy. I'm, um, I'm your sister."

CHAPTER TWELVE

Henry

Henry glanced around frantically. Michonne05 had finally called him back!

At the worst possible moment.

The Devils were minutes from taking the ice. Henry was all suited up—Daniel was already out there warming up.

He couldn't *not* take the call. This was his sister. His heart was *galloping* through his chest.

"Hey, hi, hello, Samira! Thanks, thank you for calling. Can you give me one second?"

He muted the phone and raced to the rink as fast as he could, balancing on the edge of his skates. "Hey, Coach. I need a couple of minutes in the bathroom."

"Hurry it up," Coach said before marching off to the bench. "Henderson. Use the wall."

"Sorry about that," Henry said, racing back to the bathroom where he could get some privacy. The announcer was already introducing the players.

"Where *are* you?" she asked.

"I'm at a hockey game. I play hockey." His voice was shaking.

"Oh. Right. 'Zamboni.'"

His cheeks flushed. Linh had given him that username. Now it sounded silly.

Henry made a beeline for the last stall, closed the door, and locked it. He glanced around. There was nowhere to sit except on the toilet. "Wow. I can't believe you finally called."

"Yeah, sorry it took so long. So, your dad is Mohammed Safavi?" she asked.

"Yeah. He is. I mean, he's my bio-dad. I have another dad. And two moms." He was not coming off as cool and collected as he might have wanted to impress his new sister, who might have information about their father.

"Are we sure they're the same guy?" she said with an embarrassed laugh.

How could they not be? They were a DNA match.

"I mean, could it be a mistake?" she asked.

Jesus. What if it was a mistake, and they *weren't* the same person?

"I have a picture of him," Henry said, too eager. Dammit. He was going to overwhelm her.

"So do I," said Samira. "Let's text each other."

Henry quickly launched his photo roll and tapped the image of his father.

"Hold on, I'm taking a picture of my picture," Samira said.

"Here it comes," Henry said, sending her his father's portrait. He held his breath until her text came through.

"Holy shit." She gasped.

"What? Wh— Oh my God." Henry gasped, too.

Hers was the exact same photo as his: their father's US military portrait!

"It's him." Henry's voice cracked again. He cleared his throat and said in a stronger, deeper voice, "It's him, that's our dad."

Just then, the announcer's voice boomed over the PA. "Ladies and gentlemen, welcome to the final home game of the regular season for your Westlake Ice Devils."

Henry jumped up. "Listen, I'm so sorry, but can I . . . can I call you back? Right after the game, I swear. In, like, ninety minutes. At six-thirty."

". . . uh, sure," Samira said.

But she didn't sound sure.

"Okay. Okay! I'll call you back at this number. Thank you."

Henry almost slipped running back to his locker. He threw the phone in his hockey bag and ran back to the ice, trying not to trip on the edge of his skates. He was vibrating with excitement.

He glanced up at the stands. Mom, Dad, and Mama were there right at the exact moment his sister had called him.

His sister!

This was going to be the longest game of his life.

⚬│⚬

The game wasn't the longest of his life. In fact, it flew by. Coach commended him for staying in his zone, and he executed the backhand and drop passes he had been practicing perfectly. He was full of adrenaline, but it was different. Without the driving anger or dread.

He told Daniel about Samira on their first line change as soon as they hit the benches. "She called. My sister, Michonne05. She's a she. Her name's Samira. Right before the game," he bubbled. "I'm going to call her back after."

"All this time, you thought you were an 'only.'" Daniel

drenched himself with his water bottles when Coach Nielson motioned them back onto the ice.

By the third period, Henry had gotten three assists. Plus, he didn't drop his gloves once. The minute the final buzzer sounded, he hurried over to where Mom, Dad, and Mama were waiting for him in the stands. "Good game," Dad said, which was about as high as the praise ever got.

"You're the fastest one out there," Mama bragged.

"There's a pot roast with carrots and potatoes waiting for you in the slow cooker at home," Mom chimed in.

"I'm, uh, I'm going to In-N-Out," Henry said. He needed an excuse to call Samira without anyone eavesdropping.

Mom's face dropped. "Pot roast is your favorite."

"Baby back ribs are his *favorite*," Mama asserted.

Mom rolled her eyes.

They *constantly* argued over the most trivial things.

"It's Daniel's birthday," Henry lied.

Mom looked puzzled for a moment, as if she remembered Daniel's birthday was actually in February. "Well. It'll keep till tomorrow."

"I'll see you when I get home. Bye, Mama," he said with a quick wave and took off in the direction of Daniel and his dad.

"Bye, baby. See you at your birthday dinner," Mama called after him.

"Don't yell, Nancy," Mom reprimanded her. They squabbled all the way out the door.

"Hey," Daniel said as Henry teetered over to them. "I was just telling my dad about your—"

"Shh." Henry nodded in the direction of his parents. "They don't know anything about her yet. I told them we were going to In-N-Out for your birthday."

Daniel's face scrunched. "Why?"

"So I can talk to her in private," Henry said.

Daniel laughed. "Right on. If it's my birthday, you're paying."

"All right, son, I'll see you this weekend," Mr. Stewart said with a squeeze of Daniel's shoulder. "Good news about your sister, Henry. I hope she can help find your dad."

"Thanks, Mr. Stewart." Henry motioned to Daniel. "I'm supposed to call her in ten minutes."

He dashed in and out of the shower in record time, threw on his sweatpants and hoodie, tossed his hockey bag in the back seat, and waited for Daniel in his truck. He kept tapping his phone to check the time. He texted Daniel, **you coming?** just as Linh texted him, **hey babe, how was the game? get in any fights?** 🏒 **call me** 🌸

Linh! There was no time to tell her; it was already 6:27 p.m. **good game, call u later.**

The minute Daniel came through the double doors, Henry pulled the truck up and hopped out. "What are you doing?" Daniel asked. Henry tossed him the keys. "You drive. I need to concentrate." Daniel hopped into the driver's seat.

Henry jumped into the passenger side and exhaled forcefully to steady himself. "Okay. Here goes," he said, and tapped Samira's number.

CHAPTER THIRTEEN
Samira

Samira had expected to tell Henry she didn't know their father's whereabouts, apologize for not being more helpful, and gracefully end the call. The day her brother had been sentenced to a treatment program for a DUI was *not* the day to begin a relationship with a new one.

And now she had to wait for him to call back.

There was something about his voice, though. He sounded nervous. And vulnerable.

Probably a UF. She did *not* need another underfunctioner in her life. But that photograph. *That photograph.* The brother she never knew had the *exact* same photo of their father on his nightstand—or his phone, or wherever. Maybe it was a sign.

"Oh God," Tara whispered. "I got goosies from the portrait thing. When is he calling back?"

Samira was stress-eating the pistachios. "After his game. At about six-thirty."

Tara broke her chocolate-chip cookies into bite-size pieces, which she sandwiched between two Kettle chips. "How could you *not* want to meet him?"

"I do. Maybe. Eventually. After Kamron gets out of recovery. Or I don't know. Maybe not."

Tara carefully constructed another chip/cookie sandwich. "Sami, the genie is already out of the bottle. You can't stuff it back in. He's your *brother*. Why not get to know him?"

Samira licked the spice off her finger. "We know his name is Henry Owen. I wonder if his mom is American—I mean, you know, not Iranian. Like mine."

"*Thank* you," Tara said with mock indignation. "Iranians *are* American."

"You know what I mean." Samira's brow furrowed. "Wait, he said he has two moms."

"*Two* moms?"

Samira pressed on. "He lives in Westlake Village. It's a nice area. He's probably rich." She looked around and frowned. "Richer than we are."

"What does being 'richer' matter?" Tara said.

Of course it mattered. If they were rich, she could have gotten Kamron into a treatment program with Pilates and private chefs. If they were rich, Samira would still be going to Lewis & Clark. Rich people were frustratingly oblivious to the benefits of being rich.

"He goes to Westlake High," Samira continued, "and you said the girlfriend who tagged him in all the Instagram photos is Linh. See? We know a lot about him." She closed her eyes. When she opened them, she was staring right at the portrait of her father. "He thinks I know where our dad is, T. He's going to be so disappointed."

"He's not going to be disappointed," Tara assured her. "He's your brother."

After they had finished all the snacks, she squeaked, "It's almost six-thirty! C'mon. Get ready. He could call any minute."

"He said he would *around* six-thirty. And I've got to pee." She rolled out of bed.

"Hurry up," Tara called after her. "You've got a bunch of texts from your mom, you know."

"Put my phone down," Samira hollered back. She made her way down the hall, closed the door, and perched on the toilet.

A strange sadness swept over her. How many times had she cleaned up in here after Kamron had gotten sick at two or three o'clock in the morning? Trudging to the laundry room for Lysol cleaner and rubber gloves, armed with Glade Sheer Vanilla to overpower the stench of tequila and lime. His first night in recovery. He must be terrified.

She tore off a couple of pieces of Charmin Ultra to dab her eyes before finishing up. His sponsor said if he could just make it through the first ten days—

Oh, Lord. Tara was talking in that fast, high-pitched tone she got when she was nervous.

Apparently, that was another thing about Henry Owen: he called exactly when he said he would. Samira made a beeline back to her bedroom.

". . . season tickets to the San Jose Sharks, but we hardly ever go, even though I want to, I was just telling my mom, we should go more often because hockey looks really fun and . . ." Tara noticed Samira standing there with her arms folded. "Uh, anyway, Samira's back with her tea. She went to make some tea, that's all she was doing." She muted the phone and whispered, "I didn't tell him you had to pee."

"I guess you met my friend, Tara," Samira said with an apologetic laugh.

Tara motioned for her to keep the phone on speaker.

"Yeah. She sounds like a real hockey fan," Henry said appreciatively.

"Yeah, she sure is," Samira said with an anxious laugh. "So, how was your game?" She had better ease into her bad news.

"We won. Made the playoffs, I think."

This was weird. Especially with Tara staring at her like a wide-eyed emoji.

"Your friend said you live in Santa Rosa," Henry said.

"Yes. We do."

There was an awkward pause. If he would just ask about their father, she could end the call. She let out another anxious laugh. "This is so weird."

"*Totally* weird," Henry acknowledged.

Tara threw Samira an exasperated look and texted: ask him what grade he's in

Samira read the text. "Um, you said you go to Westlake High. What grade?"

"A senior."

Samira nodded knowingly. "So am I. My mom said she and our dad were going through a rough patch when she got pregnant with me."

"My mom said he was separated when she got pregnant with me," Henry said.

"Wow. They must have been pregnant around the same time. When's your birthday?" Samira asked.

"April twenty-eighth," Henry replied.

"Mine's October seventeenth," Samira said.

"Another big brother," Tara whispered with tears in her eyes.

Samira shushed her. "Is your mom Iranian or, um, white? I thought, you know, with your name."

"Oh. Yeah. My bio-mom is Nancy Vlasek. She's, like, Russian and British, I think. The name on my birth certificate is Hooman Safavi. My aunt and uncle are the Owens. They started calling me Henry and changed my last name when they became my legal guardians."

"The last name on our birth certificates is Safavi, too," Samira said. "Me and my brother. My mom changed it back to her maiden name when they got divorced."

"You . . . you have a brother?" Henry asked with anticipation.

Crap. Samira had not meant to mention Kamron.

"Uh, yes. Kamron. With a *k*."

Henry cleared his throat. "Does he have the same dad as us?"

She couldn't lie to him . . . could she?

She couldn't. ". . . yes. Same dad. He's two years older than we are."

Still, it felt like a betrayal to talk about Kamron when he wasn't there, when he had just started recovery. When he didn't even know about Henry.

"I have an older brother," Henry said excitedly to someone else in the car.

Samira was determined to wrap up the call before Henry could ask any more questions about Kamron. "Henry, there's something I have to tell you."

Tara reached over and muted her phone. "Why are you in such a hurry?" she harshly whispered.

Samira swatted away her hand. Time to take charge. "Henry, I know you're trying to find our dad, and I'm really sorry, but I don't know where he is."

"Oh . . . oh. Oh," Henry said. His voice rang with disappointment. "Uh . . . when, when was the last time you saw him, if you don't mind me asking?"

Samira exhaled. "I don't remember. He was gone by the time I was two, maybe three."

"Same," Henry said, downcast.

"Have you asked your moms about him?" Samira grimaced. Silly question. Of course he had.

"Mom, I mean my aunt, said he could be dead or in prison. Mama, my bio-mom, said he could be 'a millionaire.'"

Samira shook her head. "My mom has no idea where he is, either."

A grim silence fell over them.

"No one will talk about him," Henry said, the frustration in his voice mounting. "Not my mom or my dad. I mean, my aunt and uncle, you know, the ones who are raising me."

"Is that why you have two moms: your bio-mom and her sister?" Samira asked.

"Yeah," he said. He sounded completely crestfallen.

"I live with my grandparents, my mom's parents. Well, my gran. My grandad just passed."

"Oh, I'm sorry," Henry said. Another awkward silence followed.

Samira felt compelled to offer some useful piece of information before she hung up. "When me and my brother were little, we lived in Fresno with him. I don't really remember it."

"Fresno! Yes. That's what my dad said, I mean, my uncle. He said my dad lived in Fresno." Henry sighed. "I just want to know what happened, where he is. I really thought I'd find him with this DNA test."

Even though Samira had planned to get off the call as quickly as possible, the OF in her was taking over. They could:

1. Visit all the websites that track missing relatives
2. Ask their moms for his Social Security number
3. Contact their relevant matches on 23andMe.com
4. Push relatives like Uncle Chris to tell them what they knew

"Everyone's left a digital trail," she declared. "I bet we could find him if we tried."

"Yesss!" Tara mouthed.

Samira couldn't help herself. "There are websites we can search, all those cousins we can reach out to on 23andMe. If we had his Social Security number, we could trace him that way. And maybe he'll take the test one day and we'll get a DM from him like I got from you."

"I'm totally down to find him," Henry said with overwhelming enthusiasm.

Tara clapped like a baby seal.

As the significance of what Samira was getting herself into began to dawn on her, she was again overcome by the urge to hang up. "Okay, I'll text you a list of things we can do, and then we can . . . do them."

"O-okay." His voice dropped. He seemed disappointed she was ending the call so soon.

"I'll text you," Samira said. "Um, okay, then . . . bye."

As soon as she hung up, her body went limp with relief. It was too much to deal with Henry on a day that had already been too much.

Samira put her phone on her nightstand, crawled into bed, and pulled the afghan around her. "I'm not ready for this, T." She yawned. Only 7 p.m., but she was wiped out.

Tara gathered up their empty wrappers. "This is going to be a good thing, you'll see."

She also said something about Instagram, but Samira didn't hear her clearly since she was already half asleep.

CHAPTER FOURTEEN
Henry

Henry stared at the screen for a moment after Samira hung up. "Why do you think she wanted to hang up so fast?" he said, his face twisting with hurt.

"Dude, it is *weird*," Daniel said, funneling a handful of fries into his mouth. "She's your sister, but you've never met. Don't get all emo on her first thing."

"I'm not," Henry said. But he was. She didn't seem to want to talk to him as much as he wanted to talk to her. It stung.

Daniel polished off the last bite of his burger. "She's gonna help you find your dad. That's what you wanted, right?"

"Yes, but . . . that's before I knew I had a sister. And a brother, too."

"Yeah, that shit's bananas." Daniel laughed.

Henry unwrapped his Double-Double. He kept going over their conversation, convinced he had said something wrong. "She didn't seem to want to talk about Kamron."

Daniel crumpled his wrappers and stuffed them into the paper bag. "You're too thirsty. Don't worry. You'll meet her in due time. Where is Santa Rosa, anyway?"

Henry googled it. "About eight hours north of here, past San Francisco."

Daniel whistled. "We had a tournament up there once, re-member? At that Snoopy ice rink."

If Mama had moved up north to Santa Rosa, closer to his dad, instead of staying in Southern California after they split up, he might have grown up with a sister and a brother. He hadn't even met them, and Henry already felt a sense of loss around Samira and Kamron.

He stuffed the rest of his burger and fries into the paper bag and hopped out of the passenger side. "Let's go. I want to get home and call Linh."

Daniel climbed over the shifter and deposited himself in the passenger seat. "Home, Jeeves." As Henry pulled out of the parking lot, Daniel pulled out his phone. "Ha. Look at that. I got a new follower on Insta: Tara Asghari."

"Yeah? Is Samira on there?" He had no idea what his sister looked like.

Daniel tapped his phone. "What's her last name?"

"Murphy."

"Yep." He laughed. "Dude, she has fewer followers than you. Barely posts anything." He kept tapping. "Tara's tagged her in a bunch of posts, though. Here's a good one." He held up his phone. "Lot better-looking than your ugly mug," he teased.

Henry glanced over and was met by the widest smile he had ever seen. Only yesterday, the girl in the picture—the girl with thick black hair, brown skin, and a great smile—was a total stranger. Today, that girl was his sister.

And together, they were going to find their father.

◁▷

When Henry got home, all he wanted was to get upstairs and call Linh without having to talk to Mom and Dad while he kept replaying his conversation with Samira.

The kitchen and family room were dark. Good. That meant everyone was asleep.

Henry deposited his jersey, socks, and athletic cup on top of the washer in the laundry room and headed for the kitchen. He tossed his backpack on the counter, grabbed a Coke from the refrigerator, and started for the stairs.

"You're home."

"Jesus, Mom," Henry jumped. "Why are you sitting here in the dark?"

She was at the dinette table with only the under-cabinet kitchen lights on. "Waiting for you, like I always do," she said with affected good cheer.

Her overprotectiveness felt more and more like surveillance. "I'm almost eighteen. You don't have to wait up for me anymore," he said in a tone Dad would have found disrespectful, but he was worrying less and less about what Dad thought.

"I can't sleep until you're home safe. You know that. Did Daniel have a nice birthday celebration?"

"Uh, yeah."

I found my sister, he wanted to shout. Mom would simply pretend he was speaking another language, which she did when confronted with unwelcome information.

She stood up and started for the stairs, then turned back. "Oh, I forgot to tell you," she said of something she almost certainly did not forget. "I booked a photographer for your birthday. You know, the one who always takes our Christmas portrait? I thought he could take some nice pictures of us before your birthday dinner."

Henry's chest tightened. Family photographs were a nightmare. Mom and Mama jockeying to get prime position next to him, Mom always reprimanding Mama for not coordinating her outfit with everyone else's.

"Mom, we don't need a whole photo shoot," Henry argued. "Linh could take some pictures with her iPhone."

Mom's smile flagged. "He does such a good job organizing everything."

He didn't have the energy to fight her. There was too much else on his mind.

"Okay, yeah, whatever," he said, and went upstairs.

⬦

"I can't believe I missed it, babe," Linh said sleepily. "I'm so happy for you."

Henry sat on the edge of his bed, scanning the list of his second and third cousins on 23andMe. "Why do you think she wanted to hang up so fast?"

Linh yawned. "You have no idea what was happening in her life before you contacted her. She probably had no idea she was going to find a half sibling by taking a DNA test. You didn't. You didn't even want to message her at first."

"True," Henry admitted. None of his second cousins seemed to have Iranian surnames. "She didn't want to talk about our brother."

"This was your first conversation. You may have to take things slow, but you'll get there. And I've got to get to sleep," she murmured. "We'll talk about it all tomorrow."

Henry was nowhere near sleepy. More wired than tired. Instead of showering, he googled find missing relatives.

A site he hadn't seen before called Truthseeker popped up. He quickly entered his father's first and last name plus California as his last known place of residence. A pop-up notice appeared: **Did Mohammed Safavi live in Fresno, California?**

Whoa. Henry clicked *Yes.*

The taskbar resumed running. Another notice popped up: **Is Mohammed Safavi between the ages of 35 and 49?** Henry did the math. His dad was born the year of the Iranian Revolution in 1978. His pulse raced. *Yes.*

A countdown clock appeared under the taskbar. He would be able to access his report in five minutes . . . three minutes and thirty seconds . . . With each update, his heart started pounding faster and faster. Could it really have been this easy to find his father all along?

Two minutes and twenty seconds. *Jesus.* It was taking forever.

Maybe the website was a scam. His heart sagged.

Right when he was about to bail, a final notification popped up: **Your report is ready.** All he had to do was enter his name and email address. Done.

And then his phone number. Henry hesitated. *Was* this a scam to get his personal contact information? But then how did they know his father had once lived in Fresno?

It might be a scam, but it might be legit. And imagine what Samira would say if he were able to tell her that, before their search had even begun, he had found their father.

He entered his phone number. And then, just as the cover page of the report appeared, another dialogue box popped up: **Payment information.**

Dammit. There's no way he could use his debit card. Dad tracked his purchases to the penny. Henry would have to wait until he could use Linh's credit card and Venmo her the cash.

He barely slept that night. He was on the cusp of something, he could feel it. When they found him, maybe he, Samira, and their brother . . . what was his name?

Right. Kamron with a *k*.

Anyway, they could all visit him. Together.

CHAPTER FIFTEEN
Samira

The air was cold and sharp, the sun rising against a cornflower-blue sky as Samira walked to the bus stop. Poppies in a neighboring garden had burst into a blaze of orange glory. Nature had a way of rubbing it in. The sky could fall, but the poppies would still bloom in April, as they did on the day Grandad was laid to rest.

The yappy Chihuahua followed Samira along the fence line, squeaking and squawking while she tapped her mother's contact. Hopefully, Mom had their father's Social Security number.

She picked up quicker than usual. "Hey, Mom," Samira said with a yawn. Benadryl hangovers were brutal.

"Samira, I texted you all day yesterday and left several voice mails," she said, pissed. She never got pissed. "Why didn't you respond?"

"I was busy with the arraignment, and I . . . I fell asleep," Samira said. When this was all over, she needed to quit Benadryl cold turkey.

"Your gran said he looked very shaken," her mother said, her voice full of concern.

If she was *that* concerned, she should have been there. "Of *course* he was shaken," Samira said with exasperation. "They put him in a *court-ordered* treatment program."

Dammit. The conversation was veering off-track, and Samira had not asked about the Social Security number. "I'm sorry, Mom. I'm tired, and I, um, I was talking to Henry last night."

"Is that one of Kamron's friends?"

"No, he's my . . . my other brother."

Still weird.

"Oh. Right," her mother said wistfully, as if she had been left out of something. "The one you met through the test. How was it?"

Samira was still processing their interaction. "Okay, I guess. I haven't told Gran yet."

"Is he older than you? Younger?"

Samira hesitated a beat. "Same age."

"Oh. Oh," Mom said, her voice tinged with hurt as she put the pieces together.

Samira passed the Great Powerhouse Church Gran had once tried to make Grandad attend. He said he already prayed on Sundays: *for three kings to go with my aces in the hole.*

"He wants to find him, our dad," she said. Dead silence. The nose of the bus came into view. Her mother still hadn't replied. "Mom?"

"Yes, I'm still here," Mom said. "How will you do that? Find him, I mean?"

The bus pulled up. Samira hopped on, taking her usual seat in the back. "I'm sure he left a digital trail."

"Possibly," Mom said. For some reason, she sounded doubtful.

Samira gazed out the window at the elementary school and the sea of ladybug and Spider-Man backpacks, the parade of doting parents sending their kids off to kindergarten. She had been cheated out of so many moments like these.

"Have you ever *tried*? To find him, I mean?"

"Well, no. Not since we . . . we split up."

"Do you have his Social Security number?" Samira pressed.

"I would have to look for it."

The bus turned on Santa Rosa Avenue, minutes away from Samira's stop. "You didn't write it down somewhere?" Samira still knew Grandad's by heart. She'd needed it to contact Social Security and the bank after he died.

"It could be in one of the boxes I have in storage. I'd have to go through them," she said.

As usual, whatever Samira needed from her mother, she wasn't going to get. She exhaled with frustration. "I've got to go, Mom. I'm here at school. Oh, and there's a Family Week," she added, "at the end of Kamron's treatment. We're supposed to go. You, me, and Gran."

"I'll be there. If I can't get off work, I'll bring him here for our own week of reconciliation."

"It would probably be better if you did the one with me and Gran," Samira said, irritation creeping in.

"I'll try my best, baby."

Always *trying*.

"But Samira, you must trust that everything is unfolding for Kamron's best good no matter how it might look to you now."

"Right," Samira said, even though the only thing she could ever truly trust was herself.

◑◐

"Maybe we could drive down for Henry's playoff game," Tara said while walking Samira to Spanish class before peeling off to AP French. "They start tomorrow according to Daniel's Insta story."

Samira stopped suddenly. "You're *friends* with Daniel on Instagram?"

Tara turned back. "Yes, I told you that last night." She frowned. "You look super tired. Are you using the Glossier concealer I got you for your birthday?"

"I *am* tired and we're *not* going to their playoff game," Samira said crossly. "I don't even want to *think* about meeting Henry until after Kamron is out and we're sure he's going to be okay. I mean, look at your uncle."

"Oh, I forgot to tell you! He went to Peru, did ayahuasca, and totally quit drinking."

Great. If Kamron's treatment program failed, Samira would only have to raise another twenty grand to send him off to Peru.

"Samira," Mrs. Sandoval called out from down the hall.

The day just kept getting better. "Yes, Mrs. Sandoval." Samira attempted a chomper, but the muscles around her mouth were too tired to cooperate.

Mrs. Sandoval caught up to them. "You haven't accepted admission to Lewis & Clark yet. Why is that?"

Why did Mrs. Sandoval have to be the *one* adult in Samira's life who kept track of her to-do list? "I'm waiting for Decision Day to make it official," Samira said, trying not to look at Tara.

"And you skipped fourth and fifth periods yesterday. Did you forget our agreement about attendance?"

Crap. Samira had forgotten to turn in her excused absence form before the arraignment. "I had a family . . . thing."

Mrs. Sandoval adopted her wide, sad-eyed look. "You're so close to the finish line, Samira. Don't stumble before you get across." She touched Samira's arm and continued down the hall.

Tara's face twisted. "Why didn't you tell her you're not going to Lewis & Clark?"

Samira had no answer. It wasn't like she was expecting to collect that back support from her father or win the lottery before May 1. They shuffled on toward Spanish class.

"And why didn't you tell her you had to skip school for Kamron's arraignment?" Tara demanded.

"Why? What's she going to do about it?"

"She could help. You *never* let anyone help," Tara said with her own wide, sad eyes.

True, Samira didn't ask for help often. But it wasn't like there was some knight in shining armor standing around waiting to come to her rescue.

They stopped in front of Samira's Spanish class. "Listen. After Kamron gets out, we'll *think* about planning a trip down south, okay?" Tara would hound her for the foreseeable future if Samira didn't throw her a bone.

"Yay!" Tara jumped up and down. "I'll tell my mom to start looking for an Airbnb. Oh! And I saw Olivia this morning—remember, the barista from Aroma's with the pierced eyebrow?—anyway, they asked if I wanted to grab a bite sometime! And they said they have a cute, straight friend if you want to double."

The last thing Samira wanted was to go on a double date.

She had more immediate worries including her phone call with Henry that afternoon. She hadn't made much progress on her action plan to find their father.

If she were being honest with herself, it was because, deep down, she feared that was futile.

CHAPTER SIXTEEN

Henry

Henry hurried home after school and ran upstairs. The report on his dad from Truthseeker.com was supposed to come as soon as Linh paid for it, and Samira was calling at 3:30 p.m., in about twenty minutes.

While he waited, Henry checked for new matches on 23andMe .com. Like Linh said, their dad could take the test at any time.

Nothing. Not even a new third cousin.

He searched **mohammed safavi facebook** and got twenty pages of results, including a chiropractor in Vancouver and an Iranian high school student. None of them were his dad. Finally, the report from Truthseeker.com came through.

Henry steadied his breath and clicked on the document. Right off the bat, the name and birthdate were correct: October 31, 1978, on Halloween during the year of the Iranian Revolution Mr. Nassour had told him about.

Immediately, he scrolled down to the section titled Possible Associates. There were several people with Persian surnames and an Erin Murphy. Wasn't that Samira's last name?

She could be Samira's mother. And the report confirmed that his last known address was in Fresno. Henry's heart exploded. It was him! It had to be.

He called the first phone number in the Contact Information section. His foot tapped a mile a minute while he waited for an answer. Wait till he told Samira!

We're sorry, the number you have reached has been disconnected. If you feel you have reached this number in error . . .

He dialed the second number and held his breath.

Welcome to Verizon Wireless. The number you dialed has been changed, disconnected, or is no longer in service . . .

He called the three other numbers listed and got the same response. His heart sank.

In the section marked Location History, there was a bunch of pin drops on a map: one in Los Angeles, one in Fresno, one in San Francisco, and one in Georgia. The most recent occupancy date was 2017. There didn't appear to be *any* current phone numbers or addresses.

He rushed through the rest of the report. There were no social media or business profiles, no licenses of any kind, or any financial information. His last known employment was as a security guard for an insurance company in Fresno—in 2017. It was like his father had disappeared.

Oh, God.

Was he *dead*?

Jesus. His phone buzzed and snapped him out of this morbid contemplation. "Hey, Samira," he said, feeling discouraged.

"Hey," she said. "So, I have a plan. I pulled together a bunch of websites: Instant Check, Public Records Finder, Truthseeker—"

"I tried that one," Henry interrupted. "It's a total rip-off. I got the report. It's him: his name, the right birthdate, from Fresno and everything. But that's about it. All the phone numbers were disconnected; his last known address was in 2017." He didn't mention his worst fear.

"Oh. Okay," Samira said. She seemed taken aback by his tone.

Henry wanted to hang up. "Maybe he doesn't want to be found."

"We don't know that," Samira said. "That's what we're trying to find out."

"Right," Henry said. "Sorry." He wasn't being much help.

"The second thing on my list is to contact our relatives with Persian-sounding surnames on 23andMe to see if they have any information."

Henry navigated to the DNA Relatives tab on the 23andMe .com website. "I don't see any." He kept scrolling. "Wait, here's a third cousin: Shirin Mansouri."

"DM her," Samira said. "We should check our matches a couple of times a week."

She seemed on top of everything, which made Henry feel more hopeful.

"Step number three: we've got to find his Social Security number. My mom didn't have it. Can you ask yours? Or your moms? How did you end up with two moms again?" She laughed.

Her laughter put him at ease.

"Mama is my bio-mom. Mom is her sister. Mom and Dad—I mean, my aunt and uncle—they're a lot older. More stable. They started babysitting me when I was little, when my bio-mom was a waitress at this restaurant where a bunch of celebrities came in."

Henry's cheeks got hot. Why did he say that?

"Anyway, when I was two, they became my legal guardians. I guess our dad wasn't around much then." Somehow, Samira cushioned the sting since she was in the same boat.

"Was that weird?" Samira asked. "Did they try and pretend they were your real parents? I mean, not your 'real' parents, but . . . you know what I mean."

His brow scrunched. He had to think about it. "Mama was always around. But I did call them 'Mom' and 'Dad.' It *was* kinda weird," he admitted. "Mom and Mama can be competitive about me, but it's not really about me, you know?" Oddly, he felt as if he could confide in Samira, this stranger who was also his sister.

She laughed again. "No, I don't know. No one here is competing over me."

Why did he say that? It did sound like bragging. "What about you? You said you live with your grandparents?"

"Just my gran," Samira said.

Henry cringed. "Right. Your grandad died. I'm sorry. Is your mom close by?"

Samira didn't answer.

Right when he was about to tell her *forget I asked,* she said, "She moved up to Ashland, in Oregon, two years ago. She teaches art there, her dream job; it took forever for her to find it."

Maybe she was like Mama, always going from one job to the next. "Do you visit her much?"

"Sometimes," Samira said. "And she comes down for holidays."

She sounded sad about it; Henry didn't push for more details. "Is, uh, is Kamron there?" His voice wobbled. He didn't want to sound *thirsty* as Daniel had warned.

"Um, no. He's out."

Henry's unease crept back in. For some reason, Samira did *not* want to talk about him.

And now everything felt awkward.

Samira cleared her throat. "Okay, the last thing is, do you

have any other relatives who might know where he is or what happened to him? I can talk to my Uncle Chris. He said . . ."

She stopped herself from saying whatever it was her uncle had said about their dad.

". . . he might know something, who knows?"

At that moment, the front door opened. "Henry?" his mom called out from the foyer.

"My moms have a bunch of brothers and sisters," he said, dropping his voice. "They all live in Ohio. I wouldn't know how to reach them."

He didn't want Mom to catch him talking to Samira. But he didn't want to be rude. Their relationship was as delicate as a bubble that could burst at any minute.

"Let's start with the 23andMe thing and go from there," Samira said.

"Okay, yeah," Henry said. The staircase was creaking, which meant Mom was coming upstairs. "Hang on a minute," he murmured just as she opened the door.

"There you are," she said. "Did you not hear me calling you?"

"Uh, no." He pointed to his earbuds. "Listening to music while I study."

Mom surveilled the room as if he were hiding someone under the bed. "Dinner will be ready at six."

"I'll be down then," Henry said, her cue to leave.

She hesitated, then finally closed the door.

And opened it again. "The photographer is coming at four-thirty on your birthday."

"*Okay.*" Henry nodded impatiently. The minute his mother closed the door, he went back to Samira. "Sorry about that," he said, his voice hushed. "That was my mom. I haven't told anyone about you yet." God. That sounded awful, like he was embarrassed about her. "Except for my friend Daniel and my girlfriend," he hurriedly added.

"I haven't told everyone about you, either." She half laughed. "Only my mom and Tara."

Meaning, not Kamron. Henry couldn't help but take it personally. Why was she so determined to keep them apart?

"Speaking of Gran, I . . . I have to go pick her up at the library," Samira said.

"Oh. Yeah, of course," Henry said, hoping it wasn't simply an excuse for Samira to hang up. "I'll DM that third cousin and check my DNA relatives twice a week."

"Okay, then. We'll, um, we'll talk soon," she said.

"Sounds good," Henry said.

But it wasn't. What if they couldn't find their father? And what if their search was the only thing keeping them connected? He could lose Samira and Kamron before he had even met them.

He sat for a moment, then grabbed his backpack, pulled out his father's book of Persian poetry, and opened to a random page on which his father had highlighted: *Your heart and my heart are very, very old friends.*

If Henry had grown up with Samira and Kamron and their father, he would have had an entirely different family. Their hearts would be "old friends." The alternate reality of what could have been unfolded in his mind like a movie.

A movie for which he was determined to create a happy ending.

CHAPTER SEVENTEEN

Samira

Samira didn't need to pick up Gran from the library. She needed an excuse to hang up. The sense of control that usually gave her comfort was beginning to overwhelm her. Why had she volunteered to spearhead the search for their father?

Her phone buzzed again. God. If it was Henry calling back . . .

Unknown caller. It might be the community college returning her call about registration. She answered before the call disconnected.

"Sami, it's me."

"Kamron!" Samira broke into a chomper that was 100 percent genuine. "I didn't know you'd be allowed to make phone calls until—"

"You've gotta get me out of here." His voice was full of fear. "They've got me in here with a bunch of addicts: heroin and meth. Cocaine."

"Kamron, you're not supposed to be calling," Samira said, the panic in her voice rising.

"I know, I know." He talked in a hushed tone over the sound of a television in the background. "But Sami, I'm in here with *hard-core* addicts."

"We're not supposed to have contact with you for two

weeks. If you get kicked out, you'll go to prison." Her insides were in free fall.

"That's in-person visits. After the first twenty-four hours, I'm allowed one phone call every other day if I do all my chores." His voice got muffled like he had cupped the phone with his hand. "I swear, I don't feel safe in here."

He sounded scared. Really scared. The invisible mosquitoes attacked. Samira grabbed her comb and fought back, frantically scratching her head. "Have you talked to your counselor?"

"They don't want to hear it. They say it's all the same. But I've never done *heroin*."

"Well . . . avoid them." *Why* did he have to make everything so difficult?

"This place is not that big. I'm really scared, Sami."

He sounded desperate. God*dammit*. What was she supposed to do?

"Can you call someone? Like my attorney? Maybe they'll let me do outpatient. I'll go to meetings five days a week, call my sponsor every day, I swear."

"Okay, okay," Samira relented because she had no choice. She could *not* let Kamron get kicked out of the program. "I'll call the admissions director."

What the *hell* were they doing at this treatment program for which she had blown up her acceptance to Lewis & Clark and possibly her million-dollar idea? Weren't *they* supposed to be responsible for him now?

She foraged for the Sunrise Acres brochure in her desk drawer and flipped through it; Hartford Blakey was the admissions director. Hopefully, he could help.

"Sunrise Acres, where each new day dawns with hope," the receptionist chirped.

"I need to speak to Mr. Blakey, please. This is Samira Murphy, Kamron Murphy's sister."

"One moment."

Samira's skin was stinging so badly, she would need to take an oatmeal bath and slather herself with calamine lotion the *minute* she got off the phone.

"Hartford Blakey."

"Mr. Blakey, this is Samira Murphy. I'm Kamron Murphy's sister and—"

"Right, we met at his arraignment."

"Yes, so . . ." She stood up and started pacing. "I just got a phone call from him, and he says he's surrounded by hard-core addicts, like heroin and meth addicts."

"Using is using, Miss Murphy."

"Yes, but he has a *drinking* problem, he's not a drug addict."

"I'm aware of that." Hartford chuckled. "Addiction and alcoholism are two sides of the same coin. We treat 'em the same way."

"Oh. Right," Samira said. She had to admit, it made sense, even if it did rebut Kamron's entire argument. "But still. He says he doesn't feel safe," she pleaded.

"That's normal. First two weeks, ten days of treatment, they think of any excuse to leave."

She panicked. "But he can't, right? He can't leave?"

"Well, it's not like there are inside locks on the doors. Listen, alcohol has been Kamron's coping mechanism for years. But, like I tell all our residents, the demons are not without, they're within. He's having to face some hard truths without his crutch right now."

Samira cautiously lowered herself onto the bed. "So this is normal?"

"Completely. This is the reason we keep family away for the first two weeks. If you're co, your first instinct will be to rescue him."

Samira's nose scrunched. "*Co?*"

"Dependent."

"Oh, no. I'm not co-dependent. I've just had a lot of responsibility handed to me since my grandfather died, and . . ." Suddenly, her throat constricted. Her eyes stung. She swallowed hard. ". . . and anyway, I understand. I'll call Kamron back and tell him."

"Kamron is only allowed one five-minute call every forty-eight hours. He can call you again on Sunday if he has earned that privilege."

"I, uh, all right then. Thank you, I guess."

"Thank you for calling," he said cheerily. "I look forward to seeing you during Family Week. When we learn about boundary-setting."

As soon as they hung up, the tears spilled. Kamron hadn't completed his first treatment program. What made her think he would finish this one?

She needed to talk to someone about the call and, for a split second, contemplated calling Henry. He seemed like a good guy who would be a good listener. Plus, he didn't come with the baggage of Tara, who would be too emotional; Gran, who would be in denial; or Mom, who would insist it was all part of Kamron's "journey." And he *was* her brother.

But he didn't know Kamron. And she really didn't know Henry.

Samira trudged into the kitchen. Maybe she could convince Gran to whip up a batch of Tangy Tequila Lime Fudge to cheer her up. It *was* still a million-dollar idea.

Gran was staring out the kitchen window at the old oak tree in the backyard.

Samira squinted at her. Perhaps she wasn't giving Gran enough credit. Perhaps Samira *could* talk to her about Kamron. "Gran," she said softly.

Gran didn't hear her. "Kamron used to sit up in that tree like a little monkey. We couldn't get him to come down," she said with a faraway look in her eyes. "He's such a fragile spirit."

Samira deflated. Gran was consumed with worry about Kamron; this was not the time to tell her about the call. Besides, as Grandad used to say, Samira was the one with fortitude. She gave Gran a kiss on the cheek, took her big travel mug of coffee into the bathroom, and climbed into her oatmeal bath before the invisible mosquitos ate her alive.

Samira tried to keep herself occupied with the housecleaning that Sunday, but she was on edge all day dreading Kamron's call. It had been forty-eight hours.

The day before, she broke down and told Mom about how Kamron wanted to leave. Mom responded exactly as Samira had expected: with a string of words punctuated by *process, journey,* and *trust,* which was frustrating when all Samira wanted was a way to make him stay.

After all, her future depended on it. She could *never* leave Gran and go off to college if Kamron didn't get his shit together.

She had vacuumed, mopped the kitchen floor, and was now practically scrubbing the porcelain off of the tub when her phone buzzed. Her heart jumped. Samira scrambled to remove her rubber gloves, ready to give the big speech she had prepared that would convince Kamron to stay (he would go to prison, he was letting Gran down, etc.).

"Hey, Henry," Samira said with a mixture of relief and uneasiness. She wasn't accustomed to getting calls from him.

"Hey, Samira," Henry said. "Do you have a minute to talk?"

"Sure." It would keep her mind off of Kamron. She sat down on the toilet.

"I heard back from that third cousin, Shirin Mansouri. She said she thinks her great-aunt might be related to our great-grandfather. She's going to look into it."

Not exactly a major breakthrough. "That's great, Henry. Who knows where it will lead?"

"I also asked my bio-mom if she knew his Social Security number. She didn't."

"Neither did mine," Samira said with a deep sigh. "I guess it's not on a marriage license."

After a discouraging beat, Henry said, "I wish I had *some* memory of him. He left when I was a baby." He cleared his throat. "Do you? Have any memories of him? You know, that you'd feel comfortable sharing."

"Uh . . ." Samira bought herself a moment to think. She didn't have any *direct* memories.

Maybe she could text him the video. But that might make him feel even more excluded from their father's life.

"He . . . he used to take us to the park in Fresno and kick a soccer ball around with Kamron. Kam said he carried me on his shoulders a lot." She got that flash of herself on her father's shoulders, clutching her oatmeal teddy bear. Her chest seized; she stifled the tears like a hiccup. "Kam said he read to us."

"Oh," Henry said.

Samira could hear the longing in that single syllable. It hurt her heart. She had better tell him the truth, though, the whole truth, about Mohammed Safavi.

"Henry, Kam also said he had these episodes where he was full of rage, screaming in Farsi. Making my mom cry. He even said the police showed up once."

"Oh." Henry got very quiet.

"I didn't want you to think he was, like, perfect," Samira apologized. Not when Kamron's situation was proof that he wasn't.

"Yeah, of course, no. I didn't think that at all," Henry insisted.

After another awkward moment, Samira changed the subject. "Um, how are your playoff games going?" Might as well try to end the call on a more upbeat note.

"Our first game is Wednesday," he said, brightening a little.

"What position do you play? I know *nothing* about hockey."

"Defense. I'm the one who stops the puck from going in the net."

"It's exciting to watch." Samira had been to a San Jose Sharks game once with Tara.

"It is. What about you? Do you 'sport'?"

Samira smiled. "No. But I went to all of Kam's practices for soccer and Little League."

"Well, sports need spectators," Henry said.

He had a good vibe about him.

"What are your extracurriculars?" He groaned. "'Extracurriculars.' Can you tell I've been ass-deep in college admissions lately?"

"Yeah," Samira said, rueful. She still hadn't officially declined Lewis & Clark.

"What do you like to do outside of school, I mean?"

Plan my grandfather's funeral. Find a treatment program for my brother. She didn't have the time or money to play a sport or take cello lessons like Tara.

"Um, I watch *Shark Tank*." She winced. "Okay, that sounded ridiculous. What I mean is, I used to watch it with my grandfather all the time. I want to go on the show one day."

"Really? Doing what?" He sounded genuinely interested.

Samira hesitated. Oh, why not? "My gran has all these . . . *interesting* recipes, but there's one that everybody loves: her Tangy Tequila Lime Fudge. It's amazing, Kamron's favorite."

She was about to reassure Henry that the alcohol burned off the tequila, but it didn't matter because Henry didn't know that Kamron was an alcoholic.

"Anyway, I want to be the next Wicked Good Cupcakes," she bubbled. "They just sold their company for millions of dollars." It felt surprisingly good to share her dream with him.

"That sounds amazing. I'd like to try it one day." He paused for a moment, then said, "Is, um, is he there? Kamron . . . ?"

Dammit. This was all her fault. She had opened the line of questioning. "No, he's out." She simply wasn't ready to talk about him.

Clearly, he was disappointed. After an awkward beat, he stammered, "Okay, well . . . it . . . it was great to talk to you, I'll keep checking our DNA relatives and searching online, and . . . it's only a matter of time."

"Yeah. Call me if you find anything, and I'll do the same," Samira said with a tinge of regret.

She really did want to talk to him. Just not about Kamron.

Not on a day when he might call and beg her to bust him out, for which she had stayed up till midnight the night before worrying, waiting.

He never did call, which should have been reassuring but left Samira with an oddly uncomfortable sense of uncertainty.

CHAPTER EIGHTEEN

Henry

Be patient, babe," Linh said, rubbing Henry's arm. "Give it time." Henry, Linh, and Daniel had arranged themselves in a semicircle on the quad during lunch. Linh sat next to him. Daniel sat across from them, devouring his sub sandwich.

It had been two weeks since Henry had gotten his DNA results. He had DM'd five second and third cousins. Not one had any real information about his father. Plus, Samira was acting weird about Kamron, and it unnerved him. Why was she so determined to keep them apart?

"What if we never find him?" Henry worried.

Linh and Daniel exchanged sympathetic glances. Linh speared a piece of grilled salmon from her salad. "What do you *know* about your father, like, what are the facts? Have you written them all down? Maybe there's a clue in there somewhere."

Henry pushed his PB&J aside and fixed his brow in concentration. "I know he was born in Iran right after the revolution in 1978. He came to the United States when he was, like, two or three. I think his family lived in San Francisco. He was in the army. He worked as a security guard and lived in Fresno from . . . I'm not sure through 2017." He looked up. "That's all I know."

"That's a *lot*, babe," Linh said.

"Wait." Daniel snapped his fingers. "The military. Can't you ask the army to search for him? Tell them you're his kid?"

Henry had never thought of it. "Yeah. Good idea. I will."

And then, something Samira said popped into his head: *The police came once.* And Mom had said, *He could be dead or in prison.*

Daniel's dad was a Ventura County sheriff.

"Hey, do you think your dad could do a search for him?" Henry asked. "To see if he's ever been, you know, arrested?"

Daniel's brows shot up. "You think he's been arrested?"

Linh cast Henry a sympathetic glance.

"I heard my mom say something like that," Henry said.

"I'll ask," Daniel said as the bell rang. Henry extended a hand to Linh while Daniel took off across the quad.

Linh looped her arm through Henry's. "So, Mama's coming to your big birthday dinner on Friday. That'll be interesting."

"Yep," Henry said, his lips flattening into a straight line.

During his eighth-grade graduation celebration, Mama locked herself in the bathroom after Mom went on and on about Henry's first day of kindergarten, which Mama had missed. Still, including her still seemed better than excluding her.

"If they fight, I'll have my phone ready," Linh teased. "We'll get an epic TikTok out of it."

"They're not gonna fight," Henry said. But he knew full well they might.

⚭

Henry had forty-five minutes before he had to leave for the game to research whether the army could help find his father. It *was* a good idea. He should have thought of it sooner.

He closed the door to his room, popped open his laptop, and googled **find an army veteran**. A website with a link to **Search Military Records** appeared. His heart sped up as it always did when he was checking his DNA relatives or talking to Samira or doing anything that could result in finding his father.

The pop-up box asked for dates and locations of service. Henry didn't know anything about his father's time in the military except that he had been in Afghanistan before Henry was born.

Another search result promised that Henry could **Find Military Service Records**. But the website said that the records were only available to veterans or next of kin.

Next of kin. Dread settled in the pit of his stomach. Someone would have notified Mama or Samira's mom if he had died, wouldn't they?

He clicked on another government site but, again, he had to know his father's dates of service and where he was stationed. Plus, the site said it *cannot release personal information about a veteran such as a home address*, so what was the point?

Nothingness was overtaking him again, a feeling of disconnection. Of rejection. Obviously, his dad wanted nothing to do with him—otherwise, why would he make himself so hard to find?

And now he only had twenty minutes to get ready and psych himself up for the first playoff game against the Falcons. Linh was coming—with her parents. He launched his workout playlist on the drive to the rink and blasted Kendrick Lamar. Lamar, who promised Henry everything would be all right.

He lugged his hockey bag to the locker room as Daniel hustled past. "Dude, you gotta be on the ice in, like, five minutes."

"I *know*," Henry said. He slipped out of his sweats and into his hockey pants and pads. His jersey felt like a weighted vest.

He couldn't afford an off-game. He had to maintain his stats and not look like a loser in front of Linh's parents. This was only the second game they had ever attended.

When he hit the ice, Linh shouted, "Woo! Go, Henry!" He held his stick up and managed a feeble wave. Mr. and Mrs. Brennan sat under their UCLA alum blanket.

His parents sat an entire section away from them; they weren't very good at socializing. Thankfully, Mama was at work. She would have talked their ears off, which would have embarrassed Mom.

He skated around the rink and fell into a familiar rhythm. Good. His head wasn't in the game, but maybe his body was.

The first and second periods whizzed by. He got a penalty late in the second period for hooking—the blade of his stick "accidentally" wrapped around number sixty-four, a Falcon winger's waist—but he busted out of the penalty box right at the buzzer to block Sixty-four's shot on goal. The second period ended with Henry's team up 2 to 1.

Dad had what would pass for a proud smile on his face. Linh's parents got so caught up in the game that they were on their feet, cheering. Mr. Brennan almost spilled his latte. "Looking good, Henry," he called out.

"Fuck yes, flexin' for the in-laws," Daniel said as they skated toward the locker room.

They tumbled onto the benches in the locker room with all the other players. A box of Gatorade protein bars was passed around. Despite how well he was playing, Henry wasn't hungry. He couldn't stop thinking about his father. He shouldn't have set this whole process in motion when it was destined to end in disappointment.

When he got back on the ice, Henry was clumsy. Sixty-four

breezed by him, headed for a breakaway. Henry chased after him, tripped on a pit, and slid right into Sixty-four, whose skates came out from under him.

The whistles sounded immediately. Henry was banished to the penalty box again. Sixty-four took a penalty shot and tied the game. The Falcons' game-winning goal came minutes later.

Henry wasn't even on the ice, but he couldn't help feeling he had personally lost the first game of the playoff series for his team. And he looked like a loser in front of Linh's parents.

He trekked over to where they were waiting for him by the boards, plastered on the fakest smile he could, and said, "Hey, Mr. and Mrs. Brennan. Thanks for coming."

"Good game, Henry," Mr. Brennan said. "Especially that second period."

"Yes, good game," Mrs. Brennan said with an awkward smile. "And, uh, happy birthday. Linh said your birthday is Friday."

"Yeah. Thank you," Henry said, downcast.

"I'll call you later," Linh said with a squeeze of his hand.

After they left, Henry spotted Daniel's dad heading for the exit, which reminded him. "Mr. Stewart." Henry caught up to him before he could make it out the back double doors.

"Henry." Mr. Stewart patted his arm. "Good game, let's keep that temper in check."

"Yeah, I will," Henry said. He dropped his voice and kept an eye out for Mom and Dad. "Uh, did Daniel ask if you could maybe do a search for my bio-dad?"

"He did," he said, his face full of apology. "I'm sorry, Henry, I'm not allowed to do unauthorized searches. But listen, you can do a search of public records yourself: the DA's office, the sheriff. Maybe the county courthouse where you think he might have been—" He clammed up.

Henry felt a presence behind him.

"Robert, how are you?" Mr. Stewart boomed to let Henry know Dad was standing right there.

Had he heard anything Henry had said?

"Good game, Henry," Mr. Stewart said, and backed away toward the double doors.

Henry turned and forced a smile. "I'll see you and Mom at home," he said. He was going to In-N-Out first to conduct a search of the Fresno Sheriff's Office and DA in private.

Before Dad could answer, Henry made a beeline for the locker room and showered as quickly as possible. He beat Daniel out the door and parked in a remote corner of the In-N-Out lot, where he wolfed down a Double-Double before digging out his laptop.

Once again, his heart sped up, only this time through a combination of fear and apprehension. What if his dad *was* in prison? Ultimately, it seemed better to know than not know.

He navigated to the Fresno County Sheriff's website, clicked on **Inmate Search**, and entered **Mohammed Safavi**. Henry held his breath.

No result. A tiny wave of relief washed over him.

Next, he searched **fresno district attorney**. There were several links on the Criminal Division page, but none of them were to search arrest records.

Was this going to be another dead end like his search for military records?

He pushed forward. On the Fresno.Courts.Ca.gov website, there was a Case Information page with a Smart Search box where Henry entered his father's name—last name first and first name last—and hit *Enter*.

The results were taking forever to load. It was probably—

Fuck! Oh *fuck*. There it was: a single result for Safavi, Mohammed with a link to case number W050796: a felony arrest on August 31, 2017, the year he seemed to disappear.

Holy *fuck*. Henry felt sick, like he might throw up.

He forced himself to click on the case file. At the top was a summary of information for the People of the State of California v. Mohammed Safavi including a note that read: **Remanded to the custody of Salinas Valley State Prison.**

Jesus Christ. *Prison.*

What was Henry supposed to do now? How was he supposed to have a relationship with a dad who was in prison?

He exited the site as quickly as he could; he did not bother scrolling down for detailed information about his father's offense. It was a felony conviction. That was all he needed to know for now.

He would call Linh. She could look for him.

Or Samira. This was her father, too. Yes, he would call Samira, and together they would find out exactly what terrible crime their father had committed.

CHAPTER NINETEEN

Samira

I t's Captain Marvel. Brie Larson. Not even close," Olivia the barista with the pierced eyebrow said with a triumphant sip of their watermelon margarita.

"If you don't count Spider-Man," Victor—their "cute, straight friend," who was actually Olivia's twin brother—said as he chugged the rest of his margarita.

Apparently, they had just celebrated their twenty-first birthday.

They both had brown skin, wavy black hair, and close-set brown eyes. Olivia had the pierced eyebrow and Victor had gauges. Somehow, Tara had convinced Samira that going on a double date would "take her mind off things."

"Who's your favorite?" Olivia nodded to Samira.

"Uh, Black Panther?" She didn't know—or care—enough about the Marvel Cinematic Universe to have a favorite character.

At least she was getting a free chile relleno with a side of rice out of it. Unless Victor Venmo'd her for her share of the tab.

And the giggly, girlie afternoon she'd had with Tara, during which she let Tara "contour" her face, *did* take Samira's mind off things—even if she did look like a nighttime news anchor.

Thankfully, by the time the conversation turned to the Star Wars Expanded Universe, the server came out balancing his big tray. Samira moved her phone aside to make room for her plate. "Can I get you anything else?" the server asked.

Olivia pointed to their glass and Victor's. "Another round."

"You're not driving, are you?" Samira asked with alarm.

"No, Mom," Olivia said with a dismissive laugh.

"Ow," Samira squeaked after Tara nudged her under the table, but she had to speak up if they were in danger of driving drunk.

While Tara and Olivia flirted their way through shared fajitas, Victor squinted at Samira. "You're going to the CC next year, yeah?"

"Um, yeah," Samira said. She felt nauseous admitting it, especially when she hadn't officially declined admission to Lewis & Clark.

"I'm there, majoring in automotive technology," Victor said. His words were slurring.

Tara would surely nudge Samira under the table again if she said automotive technology was not a "major" but a vocational field of study.

Her phone buzzed with a call from an unknown number. She ignored it. It had been five days since Kamron called, and she had created a contact for Sunrise Acres. If it were him, the number wouldn't show up as an unknown. Besides, there was nothing she could do for him anyway; she may as well enjoy her chile relleno.

"I'm specializing in engine repair." Victor flashed a bleary-eyed thumbs-up.

"My, uh, my grandad taught me how to change the oil and clean the fuel filter on my gran's car," Samira said. Finally, *something* in common.

"Bae knows about fuel filters," Victor gushed to no one in particular. He had to be about one margarita away from throwing up in the parking lot.

Samira's phone buzzed again. Again, she ignored it.

Seconds later, a text came through: sami it's kam call me back at this #

Shit. Whose phone was he calling from? She was not calling him back.

"When do you, um, when do you get your degree?" she asked Victor, distracted.

He gulped his drink and burped. "It's a two-year thing. I'm on the four-year plan."

Samira's phone buzzed with another text: sami call me please

She turned her phone over. She was not calling Kamron back.

Victor pushed his margarita toward her. "Want a sip?"

"I'm . . . no, I'm not twenty-one."

Her phone buzzed again. Reluctantly, she turned it over. The text said simply, 911.

Samira stood up. "I'll be right back."

Tara flashed her a look of concern. "Where are you going? Want me to go with you?"

"No, no. No," Samira said, rattled. "Stay here. I . . . I'll be right back."

"Where's she going, is she going to pee, man, I gotta pee," Victor rambled as Samira hurried toward the exit.

She stepped outside and tapped the number Kamron had texted her, then stopped herself. They weren't supposed to have contact. He *wasn't* supposed to be calling her.

She was about to head back inside when another text came through: 911!

Against her better judgment, she tapped the number.

"Oh, Sami, thank God," Kamron said in a hushed tone.

"You're not supposed to call. Whose phone are you calling from?" she reprimanded him.

"This dude, Aaron. The heroin addict. He smuggled it in."

Samira threw her hands up. "The one you said you were scared of?"

"Yeah, he's cool. Everyone in here is cool. Except for the counselors. They're *harsh*. They treat us like inmates."

"But you're not an inmate, you're an in-patient," Samira snapped.

"No, but Sami . . ." He started to break down. "I'll go to another place, I swear."

"You'll go to *jail*," Samira said sharply. "You begged the judge for this. Goddammit, Kamron. I blew up my college admission for you!"

"I know, I know. I'm so sorry. I want to come home." He started to cry. "I can do it from home, I swear. I'll wear one of those ankle bracelets. You gotta help me, *please*."

Dammit. She could not shake the image of the sad little boy in the Facebook video. But why did *she* always have to be the grown-up?

"Sami, what's going on?" Tara suddenly materialized beside her.

Samira quickly muted her phone. "It's Kamron. He's having a rough night. It'll be okay, go back inside."

Tara eyed her suspiciously. "Are you sure?"

"Yes. Go."

She took a deep breath. As hard as it was, she *had* to stay strong. Grandad was counting on her. "I can't help you, Kamron," Samira declared. "The director *said* the first ten days are the hardest. You're already more than halfway through that."

"He doesn't know what he's talking about," Kamron cried.

"Yes, he does!" Samira said. "Everyone who works there is a recovering addict or alcoholic. It's in the brochure."

"Sami, please," he pleaded. "I'm begging you. Get me out of here. *Please*."

The corners of Samira's mouth quivered, but she fought it, even as a little boy sporting a giant birthday sombrero passed by holding his dad's hand.

"I can't."

She hung up. Her phone rang again almost immediately. She was ready to block Kamron's number when she saw the caller ID: Henry. She had better answer; she had missed several calls from him already. "Hey," she said, completely drained.

"Hey, sorry to bother you." He let out a little nervous laugh. "Uh, how . . . how are you?"

Maybe it was because he asked about *her*, someone had finally inquired about *her* well-being, that within a split second, she lost the fight. She could not sandbag the flow of tears.

"Samira? Samira, I'm sorry. Is this a bad time? I can call back."

"No, no," Samira said, wiping her eyes. "It's . . ."

She may as well tell him. "Kamron just called. He . . . he's in treatment for alcohol, and it's not going well." She managed to laugh through the tears at her gross understatement. "That's why I never wanted to talk about him."

"Oh, Samira. I'm sorry. That must be so hard on you."

The crying turned to sobbing. Finally! Someone who understood the toll it took on her to worry constantly about Kamron.

"It *is*. He had to go because he got a DUI, his second," she said between sobs. "And he has to *stay*, or he'll go to prison. But he wants to leave."

"Oh shit. Must be hard on him, too."

"It is," Samira said between sniffles.

Henry was quiet for a moment. "This is probably a bad analogy, but at the start of every hockey camp, *everyone* wants to go home. They work us *so* hard. We're exhausted from all the drills. After a couple of weeks, though, we get in the flow. By the end, everybody's glad they came. Maybe he just needs to get in the flow."

Samira's tears began to subside.

"Bad analogy, I know."

"No. No, it's not," Samira assured him. "It was helpful. Really."

"And I can't imagine how hard it must have been for your brother to get a DUI right after your grandfather died. *Our* brother, I mean," Henry said delicately. "Is it okay if I call him that?"

Our brother aroused an odd feeling in Samira: partly protective—would Henry judge him?—and partly proprietary. Kamron was *her* big brother.

But she couldn't deny the truth of their DNA.

"Yeah. He is," she acknowledged. "He's your brother, too."

"I hope I get to meet him one day. I bet, underneath everything, he's a good guy."

"He is." Samira squeezed her eyes shut.

Just then, Tara and Olivia came out with Victor stumbling behind them. Tara handed Samira her purse. "We're not going to coffee, we have to drive him home," she said, nodding to Victor with major annoyance.

"Hold on," Samira murmured to Henry. "I'm finishing up my blind date from hell."

Tara leaned in and frowned. "Your mascara is totally running," she said as if that were the evening's major issue.

"I *know*," said Samira. "It's fine."

Victor peeled away from the group just in time to throw up in the bushes.

"Oh, gross," Tara squealed.

"I'll take an Uber," he shouted and sat down with his head in his hands.

Tara looked to Olivia, who shrugged. "He'll take an Uber."

"Call me tomorrow," Tara said to Samira, who nodded.

"I'm back," Samira said to Henry with a deep exhale.

"So, how'd it go? The blind date."

"Terribly." She snorted. "My date just barfed in the bushes."

"Well, that's not very romantic," Henry deadpanned.

Samira's face relaxed into a faint smile. Suddenly, she smacked her forehead with her palm. "Oh, God, you've called several times and I never called you back. Is everything okay?"

"Uh, yeah. I just . . . I found a . . . a third cousin who said her mother might know our dad's whereabouts."

He wasn't a good liar. There was something he wasn't telling her. But she didn't have the energy to probe any further. "Oh. Well. That's good news."

"Yeah, she said she'd look into it."

"Great."

There was a moment of strained silence.

"Hey, do you have a ride home?" Henry said suddenly, his voice full of concern. "I can stay on the phone with you till you get there."

Samira's heart melted. This person she barely knew wanted to look out for *her* like Kamron used to before their roles reversed.

"I drove separately. In anticipation of a disaster like this."

"All right, well, drive safely, and I'm always here if you need to talk."

"Okay," Samira said. "And Henry, thank you," she said with deep conviction. She *was* thankful for him.

She riffled through her purse for her keys, passing Victor on the way to her car. She couldn't leave him in the parking lot like that.

She circled back and rooted around his jacket pockets till she found his cell phone, which she held up to his face and . . . yes! Was into his home screen. She tapped the Uber app, booked him a ride, and slid the phone back into his pocket.

"Hey," she said loudly, right into his face. "Hey, Victor."

"Huh?" He came to.

"Your Uber's on the way."

"Yeah, okay, thanks." He put his head in his hands again.

Right before she got into her car, he called out, "Hey, can I get your number?"

Hopefully, no one would run him over before the Uber got there.

CHAPTER TWENTY

Henry

Maybe Henry should text Samira to make sure she got home safely.

Maybe that was too much.

He couldn't tell her the real reason for his call. Not when she was so worried about Kamron. No wonder she never wanted to talk about him. A pit of worry was already forming in *his* stomach, and he had never met Kamron.

Linh said it was normal to be confused when the connection doesn't go as anticipated, but how could he have anticipated *this*? Of course it wasn't the right time to tell Samira. Henry was still in disbelief himself.

But the truth was staring him right in the face, even if Henry could not bring himself to click on the case number again to find out exactly what his father had done. His insides were a roiling mix of fear and shame and anger. Why the hell did his father have to prove Mom and Dad *right*?

He called Linh. She would help him sort it out.

"Hey, babe. What time should I be over on Fri—"

"He's in prison," Henry spat out.

"*What?* Who?"

Everything came tumbling out. "My *dad*. He's in prison. I

found him on this website, a website for Fresno County—the DA, the courthouse, I can't remember—anyway, there was a case file for Mohammed Safavi, and he's in state prison, Salinas Valley State Prison, and—"

"Babe, *babe*. Slow down," Linh commanded. "Take a breath. Okay. You found your father. He's in prison. Are you sure it's him?"

"*Yes*," he said, channeling his frustration toward her. "The arrest date was in 2017, the year he disappeared on that Truthseeker report."

Linh was silent for a moment. Then, very gently, she said, "Babe. You're upset now, but—"

"—but what? I won't care that my dad's in prison tomorrow?" Henry snapped.

"Henry," Linh said in a soothing voice. "Sleep on it. You might change your mind and decide you want to, I don't know, write him or something."

"No, I won't. I wish I'd never tried to find him," he said pointedly, as if it were Linh's fault that he had.

"Okay, Henry," she said as if she were speaking to a five-year-old. "It's late. I know this is hard for you. We'll talk about it in the morning." She hung up.

Crap. He hadn't meant to be mean to her, but he wanted the father in the military portrait: the hero. The patriot. A man who read poetry. Not a *prisoner*.

Poetry. Impulsively, he reached for his backpack, pulled out the book of poems by Hafez, and opened it to a random page. His father had highlighted: *You yourself are your own obstacle, rise above yourself.*

What a joke. *He* wasn't the obstacle.

◦┃◦

The next morning, as he pulled on his sweatpants and a T-shirt, the memory of what an asshat he had been to Linh came rushing back. He grabbed his phone and texted: sorry i was so sassy last night 🙁 will be better today, promise 🖤

She and Daniel tried to cheer him up at lunch with a sprinkled cupcake to celebrate his "birthday eve." But nothing either of them said or did was going to change the fact that his eighteenth birthday—the day by which he had hoped he might have connected with his bio-dad—was going to suck.

◦�‖◦

Henry was all tangled up in his sheets that night tossing and turning. After what seemed like hours, he reached over and tapped his phone: 12:35 a.m.

As expected, his eighteenth birthday was off to a crappy start.

He managed to drift off around three o'clock and didn't wake up until Mom knocked on his door announcing, "Henry, I made your favorite French toast for your birthday breakfast."

She and Mama would try to one-up each other all day. He used to get a kick out of it.

"I'm coming," he said flatly. The nothingness was overpowering.

Goddammit. This was his one and only eighteenth birthday. Somehow, he had to shake off the nothingness and make the day a happy one. Samira had texted, happy birthday, enjoy your party with a gif of a cat in a birthday party hat, which was nice. Thanks, he texted back. No party, fancy dinner w/ gf & parents.

When he came into the kitchen, Mom gestured grandly to the dining room table. "It's the kind you like, with toasted almonds and raspberries." A side of applewood bacon and warmed syrup were on either side of the French toast.

He sat. She poured herself a cup of coffee and sat down at the table, gazing at him.

He froze mid-bite. "What?"

"I can't believe you're eighteen." She got that dreamy look she always got when reminiscing about Henry's childhood. "You were the cutest thing I'd ever seen when you first came to us."

Henry drizzled more syrup on his French toast. "How old was I then?"

Her nose wrinkled as she calculated. "Let's see. You had just started walking. And you knew how to say 'juice' and 'peas.' Which meant 'please.'" She loved these memories. "Probably around fifteen or eighteen months."

"Why did I come to live with you and Dad?" Henry asked as if he were cross-examining a hostile witness.

He had never gotten a straight answer. *Nancy was young, she needed our help.* They always made it sound like they were the heroes of the story but never explained exactly why.

Mom's face tensed. She grasped Henry's hand. "Now. We've talked about this. Nancy was young. She needed our help. We watched you on evenings and weekends and then, eventually, you stayed." She squeezed his hand. "We're so happy you did."

Henry pulled his hand away. "Where was my dad?"

Mom pursed her lips and took a careful sip of her coffee. "Well, I don't know. He wasn't much in the picture by then."

A whole chunk of Henry's childhood was missing, time he would never recover, and no one would tell him the truth about what had happened.

"Thanks for breakfast," he said, and stood up abruptly.

"You're welcome," Mom said, her face screwing up with

disappointment. She seemed to know the conversation didn't go the way Henry had wanted.

He went back to his room and pulled up the Fresno County courthouse website again. All he had to do was click on the case number to find out what his father had done and to see how long he'd be in for.

Henry shut his laptop.

Not on his birthday.

There would be plenty of time to investigate what had happened to Mohammed Safavi later. He wasn't going to spoil this day.

Henry held Linh tight, breathing in her orange-scented hair, feeling her heartbeat against his.

He had gone outside to wait for her. He couldn't take any more of Mom and Mama bickering in the backyard while the photographer set up for the birthday photo shoot that was unnecessary anyway when Linh could have taken a few pics with her iPhone.

He had only seen Linh briefly that morning. Henry had signed himself out of school after third period—since he was now eighteen—and gone to the rink for an open skate with all the moms and kids. He was free to skate as aimlessly as he wanted, bobbing in and out of traffic, rescuing an errant four-year-old here and there.

It was great. It definitely got his mind off of . . . things he would rather not think about.

Linh squeezed him back. "How *are* you?"

"Better now that you're here." He held on tight. If only they could celebrate by themselves.

"Oh! Your present. Hang on." Linh leaned into the driver's

side of her SUV and retrieved a small gift bag billowing with clouds of tissue. "Happy birthday, Henry."

Henry parted the clouds. Inside was a black braided leather bracelet. The clasp was inscribed *Linh ♥ Henry*. Henry beamed. "Help me put it on."

Linh fastened the bracelet around his wrist. "I do, you know," she said with a flirtatious grin.

"Me, too," he said, and pulled her in for a deep kiss.

Mom and Dad did not routinely say it—*I love you*—to him or each other. The words didn't come naturally. He wasn't exactly sure what it felt like to be in love, but it must be how he felt about Linh.

Before Mom or Mama could come looking for them, Henry led her into the backyard where the photographer had arranged everything as if it were a magazine cover shoot.

"There's the birthday boy." Mama sounded like she had already had at least one glass of wine. She was wearing a neon-pink pullover.

Mom hated neon pink.

"Hello, Mrs. Owen, Mr. Owen, Ms. Vlasek," Linh said with a nervous smile.

Mama draped an arm around Linh's shoulder. "Now, I told you, call me Nancy."

Mom frowned at Mama. "Hello, Linh," she said.

"Linh, how are you?" Dad nodded, loosening the collar on his dress shirt.

"We ready to get started?" the photographer asked, impatient. Tufts of gray hair sprouted out from under his baseball cap.

"Yes," Mom said. "Let's start with Henry."

The photographer positioned Henry in front of the bamboo backdrop strung up with lights and clicked away.

"Now father and son," Mom commanded.

Dad stepped into the frame and draped an awkward arm around Henry. No one would ever mistake *them* for father and son. He was more like a coach than a dad, always ordering Henry to *do this* or *do that*. If he failed to do it, there was hell to pay.

Worst of all, he made Henry feel ashamed to be part Iranian (*we're American*). To be Mohammed Safavi's son. And maybe he should be.

"Now the three of us." Mom inserted herself on the other side of Henry.

Henry caught a glimpse of Mama, whose mouth had hardened into a straight line.

After the photographer snapped a couple of shots, Mom motioned to Linh. "C'mon, Linh. Let's get one of the four of us."

"We'll do you next, Mama," Henry hollered before she felt too left out. Jesus, it was exhausting trying to keep the peace between them.

Mom got in the middle of Dad and Henry. Linh stood on the other side of him.

The minute the photographer said, "Got it," Henry motioned Mama over. "C'mon, it's your turn, Mama."

"Yeah, c'mon, Nancy, in your *hawt* pink," Linh said. She put her arm around Mama's waist.

They made goofy faces at the camera while Mom stood off to the side and *her* mouth hardened into a straight line.

The story of his life.

◦|◦

Henry pulled up to the valet. Mom led the way into the restaurant; the walls were paneled in knotty pine and dotted with mounted deer heads. They all followed the maître d'—a man about Dad's age, with the air of a royal butler—to a big round table for five. Henry was determined to keep the peace between Mom and Mama. Especially with Linh there.

"Henry, you and Linh sit there. I'll sit here," Mom said, and took the seat next to him. Dad sat next to her. Mama harrumphed and sat next to Linh. The restaurant was lit with the glow of votive candles at each of the tables covered in white linens.

"Here are your menus," the maître d' said. "Are we celebrating a special occasion tonight?"

"Oh yes. Our son's eighteenth birthday," Mom said, and squeezed Dad's hand.

Our son. Mama's eyes flashed with anger.

The server appeared at their table. "Can I get you anything to start? Something to drink?"

"I'll have a glass of cab, whatever you have open," Mama said with a tense smile.

Mom pursed her lips and gestured to Dad. "We don't drink."

"I'll have a Diet Coke," Dad said.

"Me, too," said Henry.

"Make it three," Linh chimed in.

The server tapped his iPad. "Very good. Anything to start?"

Mom brushed Henry's hand. "Now, you order anything you like. You can get an appetizer, both of you." She scanned the menu. "The ribs or the sliders. Linh, you might like the pork belly or the—"

"They can read, Jeannie," Mama said. "Linh is a vegetarian. She wouldn't want the pork."

Mom glowered at Mama. "Are you, Linh? I didn't know."

"Yes, but . . ." Linh quickly opened her menu. ". . . I could start with the roasted beets or shishito peppers. The peppers, I'll have the peppers," she said like her life depended on it.

"Johnnycake for me," Henry said, and sat back in his chair, annoyed. Couldn't Mom and Mama get along for *one* night, especially with his girlfriend there?

"No starter for me," Dad said.

"Me, either. Except for that wine," Mama said.

"Yes, ma'am, coming right up." The server hightailed it to the bar.

Mom looked around and pasted on a smile. "Isn't this nice? All of us here together."

"Yeah, great," Henry said flatly.

"It is," Linh echoed.

The air was thick with tension.

A busboy appeared with warm dinner rolls and herbed butter. Dad tossed his roll to Henry. "Think fast. And enjoy the carbs while you can."

The server reappeared with Mama's wine. "This is our Caymus Special Selection." After he had left the table, she swirled and sipped. "It's good." She winked at Henry. "Want a sip?"

"Nancy," Mom whispered harshly. "He's not twenty-one. The server could get in trouble. We could get kicked out."

"Oh, calm down," Mama said dismissively. "It was just a joke."

"Happy birthday, Henry," Dad boomed, to defuse the tension.

"Yes, happy birthday." Mom cast Henry one of her adoring gazes. "You were such a good little boy. He was such a good little boy, Linh."

"Was he?" Linh grinned.

"Oh, yes. We would take him to the doctor for his shots. He

would turn his little head and have this stoic look on his face. But he never cried. Remember, Bob? He never cried."

"I remember. He was one tough kid."

Mama took a big, purposeful gulp of her wine. She *hated* these memories.

"Here we are," the server said, setting down Henry's johnny-cake and Linh's shishito peppers. "Careful, the plates are hot."

Mama took another big gulp of her wine. "You didn't cry the day you were born, either."

Oh shit. Henry froze.

Dad cleared his throat.

This was a clear violation of their unspoken cardinal rule: *never* acknowledge Mama had given birth to Henry, which would remind Mom that, technically, Henry wasn't her son.

Linh bit into one of her shishito peppers. "This is delicious," she gushed. "If anyone would like to try one."

No one did.

Mama continued. "The doctor got you out, cleaned you up, and handed you to me. You fell asleep right on my chest. Not a peep out of you," she said with a raised glass.

"Nancy, that's not appropriate dinner conversation," Mom hissed.

"It's his *birthday,* for God's sake," Mama said, raising her voice. "How is it not appropriate to talk about the day he was born?"

Mom folded her arms. "Well, you don't have to get so *graphic*."

Mama let out a bitter laugh. "I didn't mention the emergency C-section or how I had to have twenty-five stitches, now, did I?"

Henry shifted uncomfortably; he could feel everything spinning out of control.

"No one needs to know about that." Mom nearly spit.

Mama pounded the table with her fist and pointed to Henry. "*He* does. You pretend he popped out of thin air. Well, Henry wouldn't be here if it weren't for me. I'm his *mother*."

Linh clutched Henry's thigh right above his knee.

Henry was having one of those out-of-body experiences—like when he dropped his gloves—floating above the action. Numb to it. Watching as a detached observer.

"You're his mother? *You're* his mother?" Mom said, still harshly whispering so as not to draw any more attention. "Who potty-trained him? Taught him to read? Took him to Boy Scouts and . . . and hockey practice for the last *twelve* years?"

Mama's face twisted with anger. "*I* would have done those things, too, but I never got the chance because you *stole* him from me."

Henry's mouth opened. *Stole?*

"You were out *carousing* in bars." Mom was no longer whispering. "And if we hadn't taken him from you, protective services would have."

Mama was now halfway out of her seat. "I was not 'carousing,' I was *waitressing*—"

"You stayed after hours, you and his 'father,' who's never done a damn thing for Henry his whole life." Mom pointed an accusatory finger at Mama. "You were unfit, the both of you."

In an instant, a flash of deep crimson streaked across the table like a comet.

Mom shrieked.

"Holy shit," Linh gasped.

Dad jumped out of his seat.

Mama had thrown her glass of wine at Mom, whose blouse was now dripping with red. Everyone in the restaurant was staring at them.

Dad turned to Henry. "Goddammit. I *knew* this would happen."

Henry snapped back into his body and stood up. "Let's go," he said firmly to Linh.

Mom tried desperately to blot her blouse with a white linen napkin. "No, Henry, please. It's your eighteenth birthday. We're here to celebrate," she said, as usual, in complete denial.

Mama stood up. "If you're going, I'm going with you."

"No, you're not," Henry said unequivocally.

"Are we ready to order here?" the server asked before fully taking in the carnage.

Dad sat back down and said, steely-eyed, "I'll have the cowboy rib eye." He gestured to Mom. "She'll have the rainbow trout. Everyone else is leaving."

"Very well, sir," the server said, and quickly collected the menus.

"Henry, please," Mom said, her eyes rimmed with tears.

Linh gathered her purse. "Um, thank you, Mr. and Mrs. Owen."

"Henry," Mama called after him. "*Henry.*"

Linh scurried to keep up. But Henry didn't stop until he got out the double doors.

ᴏᴊᴏ

"Is there a twenty-four-hour dispensary around here? I think I'm having a panic attack." Linh fanned herself in the passenger seat of Henry's truck as they wended their way down the path that led back to the freeway.

Henry took her hand. "I'm sorry you had to see that." He couldn't shake the image of his mother's blouse covered in red. For a split second, it looked like blood.

She held his hand to her chest. "It's okay. Where are we going now?"

Henry let the road whiz by as he considered his next move. "I gotta get away, at least for a day or two."

"You can stay with me," Linh said brightly.

Henry shook his head. "I can't do that to your parents, draw them into this whole thing. There's a campground in Pismo Beach, about two and a half hours from here. We've done team retreats there. I can car camp."

"I'll go with you."

He and Linh, alone, in a sleeping bag, under the stars. Now *that* would be a birthday present.

As tempting as it was, Henry said, "No way."

Linh deflated.

"You're a *minor*. I could get in a lot of trouble. I just need a night to think."

"Okay," she said mock grudgingly.

As soon as they got home, Henry snagged his sleeping bag, toiletries, and a change of clothes and walked Linh to her car. "I love you," he said. He needed to say it, clearly this time.

She threw her arms around him. "I love you, too." He pulled away before things got too heavy. He had to get to the campground and check in before 10 p.m. It was already a quarter past seven. "I'll text you when I get there."

"Henry, be careful," she called after him.

He jumped into his truck and texted Mom and Dad: need some space, back tomorrow, then turned on Do Not Disturb, turned off Find My Friends, and sped out of the cul-de-sac listening to Linh's Chill playlist.

He didn't want to think about anything as he drove, not even lyrics.

∞

The playlist must have put Henry in a trance. Before he knew it, he was entering the North Beach Campground. He paid the overnight fee and pulled into his campsite by 9:22 p.m.

He desperately needed to pee. He checked his phone on the way to the bathroom. Mom had texted: Henry please call us and tell us where you are. Please come home. 💔

Her emoji did not move him. He responded: I'm fine, with a friend, will call tomorrow. And he texted Linh: I'm here, moon is full, beautiful, have to come back w/u.

He went straight from the bathroom to the beach. The moon was peeking through a veil of fog and reflecting on the water. He got as close to the water as possible and sat down. The sand was damp and the air salty. A text came through from Mama: sorry about your birthday, sorry Jeannie can't face the truth. He didn't respond.

How could Mom and Mama have such drastically different versions of how he came to be with Mom and Dad? All he wanted was the truth. Was he surrendered or "stolen"? Did Mama abandon him or not? Did his bio-dad want anything to do with him or not?

He stayed out by the water's edge for over an hour. The sound of the waves was hypnotic.

Finally, he trudged back to his truck at around eleven. Before he reclined the front seat and bundled up in his sleeping bag, he pulled out the book of poems, fanned the pages twice, and stopped the third time in the middle. His father had highlighted: *This place where you are right now, God circled on a map for you.*

What did that even mean?

But as he was drifting off to sleep, it hit him: what he would do next. A way he could get clarity around whatever had happened in the past.

Henry was going to visit his father in prison.

CHAPTER TWENTY-ONE

Samira

This was the first Saturday morning Samira had woken up before ten o'clock. Mainly because Friday was the first night for which she didn't need a double dose of Benadryl to fall asleep.

Kamron hadn't tried to call or text since Wednesday night, which was a good sign. The director must have confiscated that cell phone. Monday would be his eleventh day in recovery. Maybe he was finally accepting that he needed help.

A rare feeling of hope was crawling out of the wreckage of the past few weeks. Samira sat up in bed and pulled open her laptop. Maybe she was finally ready, too. She logged into the Lewis & Clark portal and tapped the Accept or Decline Admission button. In the half second she wavered before clicking *decline,* her phone buzzed.

Why was Henry calling her at 8 a.m.? Had he heard back from that third cousin?

"Hey, how are you?" Samira said. "How was your fancy birthday dinner?"

He let out a bitter laugh. "You ever seen the fight scene between King Kong and Godzilla?"

"That bad?" She could not imagine having *two* mothers

fighting over her and showering her with gifts but, apparently, it sucked. "Are you okay?"

"Yeah. Listen, I have to tell you something."

He sounded serious. Samira put her laptop aside and scrambled to insert her AirPods.

"What is it? Are you okay?"

"I, uh, I found him. I found our dad."

A rush of air filled Samira's lungs. "You *found* him? How? Where?"

"I did a search."

"Wh-where is he?" Something about Henry's tone made it clear he wasn't behind a white picket fence waiting to hear from them all these years.

Henry hesitated.

Oh, God. He was dead. Samira had not made enough of an effort to meet him and now—

"He's in prison. Salinas Valley State Prison, the one in Soledad."

Samira's mouth remained open. "In *prison*? What for?"

"I don't know," Henry said. "But I'm going to find out. I'm on my way to see him now."

Samira squeezed her eyes shut, trying to make sense of everything Henry was saying, but not everything was making sense. "You're going to see him *now*?"

Henry let out a deep sigh. "I went to this campsite in Pismo Beach last night. I had to get away. Soledad is only about a two-hour drive from here."

Samira did not know how to respond. The brother she had never met was on his way to meet the father she never knew. "Why?" was all she could think of to say.

"To get some answers, I guess. Ask why he disappeared, if

he ever tried to find me. I think it's the same distance for you," he said tentatively. "If you want to meet me there . . . ?"

Everything was coming at her so fast. She threw off the covers but couldn't seem to get up.

"I mean, I can ask about you, too," Henry hurriedly added. "If you want. So you don't have to make the drive. Or I can, you know, wait until we can go together."

What *would* Samira say to him? A list started forming. First, what the *hell* did he do to her mother and Kamron? Second, why did Uncle Chris have to come and get them? And, yes, did he ever think about her or try to get in touch with her?

She swung her legs over the side of the bed, then paused.

A prison waiting room was *not* where she wanted to meet her new brother, even if they were there to see their father.

"You go," she said with a pang of regret. "I can visit him another time." She managed a weak laugh. "I'm sorry, Henry. It's a lot to take in, and a prison waiting room is not where I pictured our first meeting."

"Yeah, I understand," Henry said, but he sounded disappointed. "I should be there by eleven. I'll call you after."

"O-okay," Samira said, not entirely certain this wasn't a dream. After they hung up, she sat in bed, perfectly still, trying to absorb the shock.

She was at a loss for what to do next. She couldn't tell Gran. She hadn't even told her about Henry. And Tara would ask a million questions for which Samira had no answers.

She snagged the comb off her nightstand, scratched the welt on her calf, and launched the Facebook video, then paused on a thumbnail of her father smiling, his right arm outstretched, Kamron grinning in his lap.

If only they could have freeze-framed this moment, before her father—God, what did he do? Why was he in prison? He wouldn't be paying that back child support now.

She tapped her mother's contact. Mom would know. The minute she answered Samira blurted, "Henry found our dad. He's in prison."

Her mother was speechless. "I . . . *How?* How did he find him?"

"I . . . I don't know." Samira had forgotten to ask specifics. "But did you know about this?" Was it another secret that had been kept from her?

"No. I didn't." Her mother's voice was shaky.

Samira's whole body tensed. "Was he, like, a terrible person?" she said, her voice rising.

"*No*. He wasn't a terrible person."

She was *sick* of the lies. "Uncle Chris said he was a traitor. He said—"

"*No*. That's not true," her mother said emphatically.

"—he said he had to 'come and get us,'" Samira shouted over her. "Why, Mom? *Why?*"

"What are you yelling about?"

Gran suddenly appeared in the doorway.

Samira swallowed hard. "I'm, uh, telling Mom about Kamron."

Gran took a few steps toward Samira and hollered into her AirPods, "He's doing great, Erin. It'll be eleven days on Monday. We get to see him next Saturday."

"Tell Gran I said that's great," her mother said with forced cheer.

"Mom says that's great," Samira said flatly.

"I'll call you later," Gran shouted again into Samira's Air-

Pods. "I made some French toast," she said at regular volume. "The spicy kind with ginger and nutmeg and a dash of cayenne."

Samira wanted to scream, *who the hell puts cayenne pepper in French toast?* But instead, she said, "Thanks, Gran. I'm not hungry."

After Gran closed the door and went back to the kitchen, her mother asked, "Is Kamron really okay?"

"I don't know," Samira said, and collapsed back on the bed.

In *prison.* It hit her again: her father was in prison.

"Samira, I know this is hard," her mother said gently. "I'm not trying to make everything a mystery. Maybe you could write your father if you have questions."

"Okay, yeah," Samira said curtly. "I will. I gotta go. I have a bunch of homework." She was not writing her father in prison.

Just then a text from Tara came through: come for shahs of sunset dinner tonight 👋🍽 with mader & uncle Hooman 🇮🇷🇮🇷 for kabob and cherry rice from Daryoush???!!! 👏👏👏

Even though kabob with cherry rice was her absolute favorite, Samira would not be sitting through a Saturday dinner with Tara's family, including her doting grandmother and uncle, harboring this shameful secret about her father. No thanks, T, she texted back. homework.

Her mouth began to tremble. Her father was in prison, her brother in treatment, and Grandad was gone, along with Lewis & Clark.

She allowed herself to cry until her tear ducts were dry, then slipped on a sweatshirt, pulled on her jeans, and made a mad dash to CVS to replenish her stash of Benadryl. Something told her she was going to need it.

CHAPTER TWENTY-TWO

Henry

As the 101 freeway veered inland away from the coast, the landscape got browner and drier—and hotter. Henry's University of Denver sweatshirt was not the best choice for the heat, but he needed it to stay warm at night and hadn't anticipated this side trip.

His brain was buzzing with various scenarios for the moment he would come face-to-face with his father. They would probably meet in one of those prison visiting areas he had seen in the movies with the stainless-steel tables and stools. His dad would be shocked to see him as a grown man. And he would be an *old* man. Well, older than his military portrait.

Henry had so many questions: Why did he leave? Why was he here? Did Mom and Dad "steal" him from Mama? Did he think about Henry or ever try to contact him?

A need to pee interrupted his fantasies. The familiar green-and-white logo appeared up ahead for the King City Starbucks.

His phone was blowing up with voice messages and texts from Mom. Henry please call us we're so worried; please let us know you're okay; Dad says he wants you home tonight.

Henry texted back: don't worry I'm fine, will be home tonight.

Mama sent another text that said simply: Don't let them bully you.

He popped in and out of the Starbucks and climbed back into the truck with a PB&J Protein Box and bottled water. All he had eaten since morning was a stale bran muffin from 7-Eleven since that was all that was left.

The closer he got to Soledad, the flatter and more desolate the landscape became. As he neared the exit, CORRECTIONAL FACILITY signs began to appear. His heart was thumping.

He pulled into the dusty, gravel-covered visitor lot plastered with warning signs: WARNING—VEHICLES UNDER SURVEILLANCE, WARNING—VEHICLES SUBJECT TO INSPECTION, WARNING—THE FOLLOWING ITEMS ARE PROHIBITED. The list included tobacco, firearms, and drugs.

Henry grabbed his water bottle and phone, made sure he had his wallet with photo ID, and headed for the visitor center—a good three-block walk—which was plastered with the same warning signs.

The industrial gray-and-black waiting area overflowed with families: what looked like parents and spouses and siblings and kids. Some laughed and joked while they waited; others—maybe first-timers, like Henry—looked as confused and scared as he was. Lockers and vending machines lined the far wall. Several windows were marked CHECK-IN HERE.

Henry's stomach curdled as if he had drunk sour milk. He had no idea what to do first but was too embarrassed to ask.

Check-in had to be first. He got in one of three lines and became obsessed with a sign outlining what visitors could bring into the visiting area: fifty dollars in dollar bills and coins; a comb without a pointed end; two keys on a ring with no other attachments (there were five on Henry's); up to ten "appropriate" photographs; and a deck of cards, all in a clear plastic bag.

Not only had he never been in a prison before, Henry had never even met anyone who had been *arrested*. He was as out of place as a goalie at a figure-skating competition.

"Ow!" He jumped. Something had struck him in the ankle. He looked around with wild eyes.

It was only a runaway Matchbox car. A sheepish little boy with a mop of black hair and a missing front tooth scrambled over, clutched his car, and scurried away.

For the next ten minutes, Henry debated whether to turn around and run, to forget about his father and pretend he had never come, when the clerk called out, "Next."

He stepped up to the window; his hands were shaking. "I . . . I'm here to see Mohammed Safavi. Case number . . ." He grabbed his phone out of his back pocket and tapped on the note he had made. ". . . W, zero, five, zero, seven, nine, six."

"Did you fill out an application?" asked the clerk, an older woman whose hair looked anchored in place by a gallon of hair spray.

"Application?"

She gestured to a sign posted on her window: ALL VISITORS MUST COMPLETE AN APPLICATION. "The visitor's application. It's on the website."

Henry swallowed nervously. "No, I didn't."

A little sigh escaped her mouth. "You have to fill out an application first. And then make an appointment." She glanced beyond him as if she were about to say, "Next."

Henry shifted slightly to maintain eye contact. "How long does that take?"

"Depends. Once you're approved, the inmate will contact you." She shifted to the left.

The *inmate*, the father he had never met, had to *approve* him as a visitor? He should have clicked on the case number sooner.

"We . . . we've never had contact," Henry said, desperation creeping in. "It's my dad, I've never met him. I only just found out he was here."

"You'll need to fill out the visitor application. He still needs to approve you. You can do it online, with your phone. What did you say his name and inmate number were?"

"Mohammed Safavi, inmate number, uh . . . uh . . ." Henry entered the wrong passcode twice before accessing his notes. His face turned beet red. "I only have a case number."

"Spell his name, please," the clerk said with another impatient sigh.

Henry did.

She frowned at her computer. "He's not here."

Just then, a baby began to wail. Henry must have misheard her. He leaned in. "What?"

"Mohammed Safe . . . Safeway, right?"

"Safavi."

"He was transferred to Oregon State Penitentiary. Didn't you do the inmate search on our website before you came?"

Henry's cheeks were on fire. "Yes, but . . . I didn't read through the case file."

The clerk looked back at the screen. "His date of transfer was August 13, 2019."

"*What?*" Henry nearly shouted. He steadied himself. "Why . . . why was he transferred?"

The clerk shrugged. "Prisons do swaps for various reasons."

Henry shifted back to the right. "Well . . . could I—"

"Honey," she cut him off gently but firmly. "Your dad is not here. If you want to see him, you'll have to contact the Oregon State Penitentiary."

Henry stood there for a moment, immobile.

The clerk offered him a sympathetic smile. This time, she did not try to look around him.

"Okay, thank you," he said, voice cracking, and strode toward the exit. As soon as he got outside, his face was wet with tears. He leaned over with his hands on his knees to catch his breath. His stomach lurched as if he might throw up the PB&J.

Suddenly, there was a hand on his back. "It's okay, man, it's okay." Henry stood up and found himself face-to-face with a heavyset biker dude covered in tattoos. "This place is rough, I know. I did a dime in Corcoran. But you're bringing hope to whoever's in there."

Henry's face grew hot again. "Yeah, man. Thanks." As he loped off, the heavyset man called after him, "It'll be okay, son. Keep your head up."

Henry barely made it into the truck before he broke down. What a stupid wild-goose chase. The whole thing. Why did he even want to find his father in the first place? And what was he supposed to tell his parents? He dreaded calling Samira.

"Hey," she answered excitedly. "How did it go?"

Henry cleared his throat. "It didn't."

Samira was quiet.

"He's . . . he's been transferred to Oregon State Penitentiary. Which I would have known if I had checked the website." His face twisted. "I'm sorry, really sorry."

"Henry, it's okay," she said. "I wouldn't have known to check the website, either."

Her understanding only made him feel worse.

"I mean, at least we know where he is now."

"Yeah," Henry said, his voice getting lower and slower.

"What are you going to do now?"

"Go home, I guess." He laid his head back on the headrest and closed his eyes. "Jesus. The last thing I want to do is face my parents."

"Well . . . you could come here," Samira said.

Henry opened his eyes. "Come here? What do you mean?"

"I mean, if it wouldn't get you grounded for life, you're only about two hours away. And you probably won't be this close for a while. *Especially* if you're grounded for life."

Henry's mouth opened. "I . . . I . . ."

"You can stay in Kamron's room for the night."

Dad would be furious.

Mom would be worried sick.

But she was right. This might be Henry's last opportunity to meet Samira in person for a long while. And anyway, what could Dad do, have him arrested?

"Send me a pin drop," he said, instantly overcome with excitement.

As soon as Samira texted him the pin, he texted his mother: Staying with a friend tonight, all good. Will call soon, I promise.

Immediately, his phone rang before he could put it back on Do Not Disturb. He debated not answering but tapped the green button. "Hi, Mom."

"Oh, Henry." She was crying hysterically. "Where are you, why haven't you called, we've been so worried we—"

"*Mom*. I'm safe, don't worry," Henry interrupted. "I'll be home tomorrow, I promise."

The phone rustled. "Where are you?" Robert asked with deliberate calm.

"I'm safe, don't worry," Henry repeated. "I'm staying with a friend tonight. I just needed some space."

"Where. *Are*. You?"

"With a hockey buddy, up north. Near that Snoopy ice rink. I'm *fine*. Can you . . . can you just trust me on this?"

"Trust is earned," Robert snapped.

"I've earned it," Henry snapped back. "I do my chores, I do my homework, I don't party. All I'm asking for is a night or two to myself."

Robert was quiet for what felt like the next twenty minutes. At long last, he said, "I want you home tomorrow night. Do you understand?" His teeth must have been grinding down to nubs.

"Yes," said Henry, who was doing cartwheels inside.

"And reply promptly when your mother or I text you," he said sternly.

"Yes, sir," Henry answered.

"We *will* see you tomorrow night," Robert said. That was an order.

Henry hung up and punched the air. He had won. Again.

He called Linh with an update and texted Daniel, then got back on the freeway.

Holy. Shit. Henry couldn't contain the goofy grin that was now plastered on his face. He was about to meet his *sister*!

CHAPTER TWENTY-THREE

Samira

Oh no. What had she done? Samira had told Henry he could "come here" without thinking.

It wasn't that she didn't want to meet him. But the house was a mess. And she hadn't told Gran, who would be back from her weekly Target run any time. And it was weird enough *talking* to this brother she had never known. Now she was going to *meet* him IRL.

She had to clean! Quickly. Samira sprinted to the laundry room for Gran's cleaning caddy with the N95 mask and rubber gloves left over from the pandemic. The fumes from the Lysol Power bathroom cleaner were overwhelming. But the toilet, sink, and tub had to be spotless for Henry. She would share Gran's bathroom while he was there.

The faint ring around the tub and mildew in the corners wouldn't disappear no matter how hard Samira scrubbed. She finally gave up and laid fresh towels on the vanity.

He would arrive in less than ninety minutes. She still had to vacuum and clean the kitchen. And Kamron's room. Oh God, Kamron's room must be a disaster.

It was. She picked up the dirty clothes strewn across the

floor and had just begun to strip the bed when Tara called. "So, I'm bingeing *Queen Charlotte*—"

"Can't talk, T," Samira interrupted her.

"Don't talk, then," Tara said. "Just listen to *me* talk about Queen Charlotte and King George, who are both so *ridiculously* hot, I—"

"Tara, I *can't* talk," Samira said more firmly while removing the cases from Kamron's pillows. "I have to clean . . . Henry is coming over."

Tara emitted a high-pitched sound to rival a dog whistle. "He's coming *here*? Now? I . . . I know 'here' means 'there,'" Tara stammered. "But why?"

Samira threw the sheets in the laundry basket and sat on the bed. "He found him, T." She exhaled. "Our dad. Henry found him." She hesitated. "He's in prison. Henry went to visit him in Soledad and found out he had been transferred to Oregon."

Tara got all discombobulated. "Wait. *Back up*. How did you find out he was in prison?"

"Henry did a search or something."

Tara's voice dropped. "Sami, could he be, like, a *murderer*?"

"No! No. I don't think so. God, I don't know," Samira said. She glanced down at her phone. A half hour had elapsed. Henry was now only an hour away. "Tara." Samira stood up. "Honestly, I can't talk. Henry is on his way here *now*. The house is a disaster."

"I'm coming over," Tara announced. "I'll help you clean."

As much as Samira loved her, Tara had a full-time house-keeper. She didn't know how to clean. And Samira wanted her first meeting with Henry to be just the two of them.

She picked up the laundry basket. "Thanks, T. I've got this. Maybe you can come over after your dinner."

Tara squealed again. "You should come to our dinner tonight. Both of you. There'll be tons of food. I'll be on my best behavior, I promise."

"Let him get here first. I'll text you later."

As soon as they hung up, Tara started texting Samira icebreaker questions like: *Are you a dog or cat person? What's your favorite holiday? What's your favorite food?*

Samira was not worried about conversation starters. She and Henry had plenty to talk about. She needed to clean Kamron's room and vacuum before he got there.

Just then, Gran hollered, "Sami, I'm back. I got you your tampons."

Samira quickly slipped off the rubber gloves and found Gran in the kitchen. "I got some canned pumpkin," she reported, "to make my famous pumpkin parmesan casserole."

"Gran, I have to tell you something," Samira said. The urgency in her voice matched the look on her face.

"What is it? Is it Kamron?" Gran asked, her voice ringing with alarm.

"No," Samira said. "Come here, sit down." She led Gran to the dinette and grasped her hand. "I've been in touch with someone." She struggled to find the right words.

Just say it.

"My brother. We have another brother, me and Kamron."

Gran gasped. "A *brother?*"

"A half brother, Henry. He found me through a DNA test on 23andMe." Samira closed her eyes. "I'm sorry. I wanted to tell you sooner."

Gran sat for a moment, stunned. Her face flickered with hurt. "Wh-why did you take a DNA test?"

"I wanted to find our dad," Samira said, her voice evenly split between apologetic and defensive. "To see if he could help pay for Kamron's treatment." She didn't mention her student loans, which would make Gran feel guiltier.

Gran's whole face fell. "It doesn't surprise me. Your mother and father separated right around the time she got pregnant with you."

"She told me," Samira said.

"She knows about this?" Again, Gran looked hurt. Clearly, Samira should have told her sooner. "Well." She put a shaky hand to her cheek. "Where does he live? Are you going to meet him?"

"We've talked on the phone, but, um, that's the thing." She squeezed Gran's hand. "He's on his way here now."

Gran looked like she was going to faint.

"It's a long story," Samira said with a pleading look. "I'll explain it all soon. He was in the area, I told him he could stay in Kamron's room. Just for the night."

Gran stood up and glanced around in a daze. "I . . . I'll make dinner for you. Fried chicken and mashed potatoes. Maybe those green beans you love with the capers."

No way would Samira allow Gran to serve Henry fried chicken coated in crushed Fritos or those green beans with the capers Samira hated. Plus, Gran would not be able to stop herself from bad-mouthing their father. And Henry might not be able to stop himself from mentioning that their father was in prison.

"Uh, Tara invited us for dinner," she said. If Henry wasn't down for it, they could get pizza at Rosso. "You can make us your special cheddar pancakes for breakfast." By then, she would have forewarned Henry about her cooking. "But Gran, we've got to get the house clean. Henry will be here in"—she checked her phone again—"less than forty minutes."

They sprang into action.

After Gran had cleaned up the kitchen—stuffing half-opened cereal and cracker boxes back into the pantry—and Samira had tidied up her room, she changed into her nicer jeans, dabbed on a little Glossier concealer, brushed her hair, and waited for Henry on the edge of the couch opposite Grandad's recliner. Gran waited in her room to give them some time together.

Samira couldn't help but wonder what Grandad might have thought about the whole thing. He would like Henry, she was sure of it. He was starting to seem like an OF, which would be a relief, although Samira did not have enough information to render an official decision.

Her phone buzzed with a new text notification. Her stomach backflipped. He was here.

It was only Tara: don't forget 2 truths & 1 lie 🤨 for ice breakers ⛄

Which reminded Samira: dinner invitation still open? for both of us?

OMG, YES!!!!!! 👏👏👏🙌🙌🙌 ARE YOU COMING??

Samira replied, Let me see what Henry wants to do when a car pulled up outside.

This was it.

Her stomach did an entire floor routine with a roundoff. It seemed like a dream, but he was real. Henry Owen was real, and she was about to meet him.

CHAPTER TWENTY-FOUR

Henry

Henry's truck idled in front of Samira's house. He craned his neck toward the passenger side to make sure the street number was correct. Yep, 61761 Victoria Lane.

An uncontrollable urge to laugh came over him. He was about to meet his *sister*. He debated whether to bring in his overnight bag, which seemed presumptuous. Though Samira did say he could stay in Kamron's room.

He would bring it. He opened the driver's side door.

He should have brought a gift: cupcakes or flowers, or whatever was appropriate for meeting a half sibling for the first time. After a couple of quick rabbit breaths to steady himself, he hopped out. "Samira," he called out to her.

She was waiting on the porch for him with a big, broad smile.

"I found it, no problem," he said, and immediately cringed. Of course he had found her house; he had Google Maps and a pin drop.

They came face-to-face for the first time. A lightning bolt zinged through him. His sister was standing *right* in front of him.

"I can't believe it's you," she said with a shake of her head.

"We don't look that much alike," he blurted.

God. He was saying all the wrong things.

"I know." She laughed. "But *you* look exactly like Kamron."

She had the best laugh. Was it okay to hug her?

"Come in, come in," she said, motioning him in.

He would follow her lead on the hug.

"You want something to drink? You must be thirsty." She led him through the living room—past a sofa, an old recliner, and an upright piano—and into the kitchen.

"Water would be great. This is nice." Their house was smaller and more dated than Henry's, but it felt cozy.

"My grandad built it back in the sixties. Can't you tell?"

"The whole house? That's amazing."

The kitchen wallpaper was covered in cheery flowerpots and bows. This was a place where he could relax or make a mess without anyone panicking.

"Have a seat." Samira gestured to the dinette table and pulled a pitcher of water out of the fridge. "So, no major traffic coming across 580, the Richmond Bridge?"

"No, no," he said. "No traffic."

Their conversation was mundane—yet monumental. She filled up two mason jars and sat opposite him at the dinette, this sister he hadn't known until a month ago. A big oak tree dominated the backyard out the kitchen window; the lawn was turning brown.

He raised his glass to her. "Thanks for asking me to come," he said.

"Thanks for coming."

He took a sip of water, then gulped the whole thing. "I told my parents I was staying with a hockey buddy. We've played tournaments up here at the Snoopy ice rink. Do you know it?"

She grinned. "Every birthday party from third grade onward

was at Snoopy's Home Ice. You'll never see me in a pair of skates again."

He grinned, too. "You probably had bad rentals. And the ice wasn't properly Zambonied."

"Zamboni. Right. That's what that means. How'd you get into hockey anyway?"

It was weird to talk to her like this. She could be any girl he had just met, but she wasn't. They shared a history, a common purpose. DNA.

"My mom and dad, I mean, my aunt and uncle." His words got all jumbled. "Someone posted sign-ups for youth hockey at my dad's work, and he signed me up. I might be a freshman starter for the University of Denver."

Jesus. Why did he say that? He wasn't one to brag; he didn't even want to go to U of D. He wanted to take a gap year.

"You're going off to Denver. Cool," she said, resting her chin on her hand.

"What about you?"

Samira stood up to retrieve the pitcher and refill their glasses. "Me? Oh, I, uh, I got accepted to Lewis & Clark."

"That's cool. And how . . . how's Kamron?" Maybe he shouldn't have asked. It was not clear what was appropriate small talk.

Samira tapped her home screen. "Hasn't called or texted since Wednesday."

"Have you told him about our dad?" he said, hushed, as if someone were eavesdropping.

"I haven't even told him about *you*."

Henry winced.

"It's not you," she assured him. "It's him. He's not in a great place." She sat back down and tapped her phone again. Her face crinkled. "Do you want to see a video of him? Our dad?" For some reason, she sounded uncertain.

"You have a *video* of him?" Henry asked, awed. "*Yeah*. I want to see it."

She turned her phone toward him and tapped *play*. Henry took in a little gasp of air when their father appeared on-screen, at least a decade older than his military portrait. He was reading to Samira and Kamron *Guess How Much I Love You*, doing the voices for Little Nutbrown Hare and Big Nutbrown Hare.

A pressure built up in Henry's throat. He could *not* cry in front of Samira, not when they had only just met.

"The next part is sad," Samira said, and pulled her phone back. "He realizes he's being filmed and gets embarrassed."

Henry would have liked to see it, but he didn't push. "Oh! I have a book from him, a book of poetry." He fished it out of his backpack. "By this Persian poet, Hafez. I open it all the time to a random page and, whatever he's highlighted, it's like he's talking to me."

His cheeks ignited. That sounded weird.

He handed the book to Samira, who leafed through it. "Can I try it?" She beamed like a little kid holding a Magic 8 Ball, closed her eyes and opened to a random page. "Oh my God." Her eyes watered. "Look at the highlighted passage."

She pushed the book back to Henry. The highlighted passage read: *And love says, "I will, I will take care of you," to everything that is near.*

They held a look, Henry and his sister. His *sister*.

"Well, hello, Henry."

An older woman who must be Gran came into the kitchen. He jumped up and extended his hand. "Hello, Mrs., uh, Mrs. Murphy?"

She grasped his hand with both of hers. "Oh, honey, call me Gran." She turned to Samira. "He looks just like Kamron, doesn't he?"

"He does," Samira agreed.

Gran's expression grew pained. "I don't think Samira's mother knew about you."

A twinge of guilt pinged Henry's heart.

"But I'm happy you've found each other." Gran gestured to the refrigerator. "Now, I offered to make you a fried chicken dinner, but Samira said you were going to Tara's and—"

"Yes. We are." Samira stood up and cast him an apologetic look. "Tara invited us to dinner. A family thing with her aunties and uncle. There'll be mountains of Persian food: kabobs, rice, tahdig, ghormeh sabzi. Do you like Persian food?"

"I've never tried it," he was embarrassed to admit. There was a Persian restaurant in Westlake Village, but it was "too ethnic" for Dad.

"You'll love it. C'mon, I'll show you Kamron's room."

Henry grabbed his duffel bag. "Nice to meet you," he said to Gran.

"We'll have more time to visit tomorrow morning during breakfast. I'm making my famous cheddar pancakes."

"Don't ask," Samira murmured as he followed her down the hall to an old-fashioned bathroom with pink and mint-green tile. "Here's your bathroom. Everything's clean. I'll use Gran's for tonight. You have to, uh, hold down the handle for a count of ten. You know, to flush." She continued on to Kamron's room.

"I don't want to know what happens if I don't, right?" Henry said.

"Things get . . . stuck." She giggled.

"What 'things'?" He snorted.

They were like two fifth graders. She opened the door to Kamron's room. "The sheets are fresh. I vacuumed and dusted."

"You didn't have to do all that," Henry said. He laid his duffel bag on the bed. His room was twice the size of Kamron's. The floors were scratched, and the walls needed paint, but it seemed like Kamron's space. "You sure he won't mind if I stay here?"

"I mean, he probably would," Samira conceded, "but he's not here."

Henry became transfixed by the anime posters on the opposite wall: several pixie-ish characters whose mouths were open, gaping in horror. They were kind of disturbing. "I guess he likes anime?"

Samira studied the posters. "Loves it." After a beat, she said, "Hey, I'm sorry Gran sprang dinner at Tara's on you. Her cooking is kind of an . . . acquired taste. If you're not down for a big group thing, there's a great pizza place called Rosso."

"No, no, I am," he insisted. He sat on the edge of the bed. "Does Tara know about Dad?"

Samira leaned against Kamron's desk. "Yeah. I told her. I hope that's okay."

"Yeah, yeah." He was quiet for a moment. "Should we do that inmate search on him?"

"We will," Samira said. "But maybe not tonight, okay? You only just got here."

He allowed a smile. "Okay."

She pushed herself away from the desk. "The thing about dinner at Tara's is, it's early. At, like, four o'clock." She tapped her phone. "Which means we have to leave in a half hour. I'm going to get glamorous. I'll see you in thirty minutes."

She left for her room and closed the door. Henry called Linh and told her his first meeting with Samira went better than expected and that they were having a real Persian dinner with Tara's family that night.

No matter what was in store for him with Mom and Dad when he got home, he was determined to savor the next twenty-four hours.

CHAPTER TWENTY-FIVE
Samira

Your mom threw her drink in your mom's *face*?" Samira couldn't help but laugh at the absurdity, sitting in the passenger seat of Henry's truck. Gran needed the Kia for her book club meeting, and he didn't seem to mind driving. He gawked at all the passing scenery: the vineyards and orchards, the old-growth oaks.

"Yep," he said. "And my mom was wearing a white blouse."

He felt familiar. Not like a brother, not yet. But maybe, over time. No need to rush.

Samira's nose wrinkled. "Wait, which mom is which again?"

"Mama, my bio-mom, threw her drink at Mom, the one who raised me."

"Got it," Samira said. She let out a deep sigh. "God. I would have thought having two moms would be totally amazing, but . . ."

"Yeah, totally *not* amazing," Henry said. "Like I said, it's not about me. It's more like they're in competition with each other."

"Healdsburg Avenue is your exit," said Samira, an admitted back-seat driver.

"Right, two-point-six miles." Henry nodded to the map app

on his phone. "My girlfriend says Dad blew a big hole in the center of our lives. That's why my moms fight."

Samira puzzled over this. "But he's not even around."

"I know. She says, 'Absent parents are still very present.' Her *therapist* does. She's adopted."

Samira considered this. "He's definitely the ghost haunting Kamron."

The longer she went without getting a text or desperate phone call from him, the more she allowed herself to believe he might make it through.

As they exited the freeway and started down Alexander Valley Road, Samira said, "Tara's uncle's name is Hooman. Did you ever want to go by that name?"

He thought about it for a moment. "No. My mom and dad couldn't have handled it."

"When I was little, I wanted to change my name to Samantha. Samira was so . . . *weird*. I had never met another Iranian until I met Tara. I'm glad I didn't. Change my name."

"There are a couple Iranian kids at our school. I don't really know them." Henry made the turnoff and started climbing up the dirt road that led to Tara's house. "Things would be different. You know, if we had grown up with him. And each other."

As soon as they pulled into the circular driveway—whose muscular old oak Tara had nicknamed Kumeil after Kumeil Nanjiani bulked up for that superhero movie—she came running out to meet them and threw her arms around Henry. "Oh my gosh, Henry, it's so nice to meet you. I'm so glad I talked Samira into calling you."

Samira threw Tara a look.

Henry smiled warmly. He got it.

He couldn't help but gape. Samira was used to the Asgharis' six-bedroom, five-bathroom villa by now. She wasn't as gobsmacked by the great room with its soaring twelve-foot ceilings and custom-built stone fireplace. Or the kitchen that looked like something out of *Top Chef*. She *did* still get a thrill out of the private screening room with its own popcorn maker.

"Come in, come in," said Tara. "Everyone is here."

Samira probably should have forewarned Henry he would be accosted by all of Tara's relatives: her aunties and grandmother and Uncle Hooman.

Mrs. Asghari grasped Henry's hand and kissed him on each cheek. "Henry-jon, welcome." She still pronounced her *w*'s as soft *v*'s. "Samira-joon," she said with the same kiss.

"'Jon' and 'joon' are terms of endearment in Farsi," Tara boomed.

Samira also should have forewarned him about Tara. She had not inherited her mother's quiet elegance. Mrs. Asghari's hair was pulled back in a sleek, ballet bun; she wore simple, tailored trousers under a cashmere sweater. She gestured to the great room where Tara's aunties—technically, her greataunts—and Uncle Hooman were sitting. "Come in. We are so happy you can join us."

"Henry-jon, welcome." Uncle Hooman rose and extended his hand. He was older than Mrs. Asghari, but he seemed younger, more mischievous, and always a bit disheveled.

"Nice to meet you, sir," Henry said with a shake.

"Listen to this guy," Uncle Hooman teased. "Calls me 'sir' like I'm a colonel in the shah's Imperial Guard."

Tara grabbed her uncle's arm. "Dayi, his name is Hooman, too. On his birth certificate."

"What? You have a glorious name like Hooman, and they

call you Henry? Why? Did you know Hooman means *good person, benevolent* in Farsi?"

Samira could feel Henry's cheeks grow warm.

"It's an American nickname, I guess," he said with an awkward smile.

"He didn't grow up around any Persians, either." Tara pouted.

"How are you, my beauty?" Uncle Hooman said to Samira with great concern.

She summoned a chomper. "I'm good, Uncle Hooman."

He cast her a skeptical look.

Had Tara told him about Kamron since Uncle Hooman was also in recovery?

Both of Tara's great-aunts rose from the couch to kiss them on each cheek. They spoke very little English. Honestly, Samira didn't even know their names. She called them "khale," like Tara, or "auntie" in Farsi.

Tara's grandmother came out of the kitchen. "Mamani," Tara called her; she called Tara "little mouse" in Farsi. She was small and plump with wiry, dark hair and gnarled hands from cooking mounds of Persian food every day of her life. Tara's father was picking up the kabobs, but her grandmother had made all the side dishes.

She kissed Samira on each cheek and grasped Henry's hand. "Khoshbakhtam, Henry-jon. Khoshbakhtam."

"She says she's happy to meet you," Tara translated.

After the introductions, they all retreated to the great room. Mrs. Asghari had laid out pistachios, flatbread crackers, and feta cheese plus a pitcher of water infused with mint and cucumber as well as a pitcher of doogh, Tara's favorite yogurt-mint soda, which sounded like something Gran would have concocted. The adults drifted back into speaking Farsi.

"I still get goosies when I think about the pictures you both have of your dad," said Tara. She smiled proudly. "Samira might not have taken her DNA test if it weren't for me."

"Maybe not," Samira admitted. She piled some feta on a cracker.

Henry cracked a couple pistachios. "My girlfriend talked me into taking mine."

"You mean Linh?" Tara said.

Henry gave her a friendly sideways glance.

"I saw her on Instagram," Tara rushed to clarify. "We looked you up. It's not like I'm stalking you or anything."

"No, no. It's okay." Henry chuckled. "Yes, Linh."

"That reminds me," said Tara. She whipped out her phone and got into selfie formation between Henry and Samira.

"Don't tag me," Henry said with a sheepish grin. "No one knows where I am."

"I won't." She snapped the picture and, as she was uploading it, lowered her voice and said, "Samira told me about your dad."

Samira threw her a look. Before she could say anything, her phone buzzed with a text.

The room went silent while the air whooshed out of Samira's lungs.

sami call me please i need you

Why, *why* had she allowed herself to believe Kamron would make it through treatment when it was *always* better to expect the worst and be pleasantly surprised if it didn't happen?

"That one didn't turn out. One more," Tara coaxed and got back into selfie formation.

"Not now, Tara," Samira said sharply.

Dammit. She was not going to let him ruin her first night with Henry.

"I . . . sorry."

"It's okay." Tara held up her doogh. "Wanna try some? It's yogurt-mint soda."

"Uh . . ." Henry looked like a terrified smile emoji.

Tara took a sip and laughed. "Samira hates it, too. So, what do you think of Sonoma? Do you like it here?"

Henry marveled at the terrace of vineyards right outside the floor-to-ceiling windows. "It's beautiful. I've been here before for a tournament at the Snoopy ice rink."

Samira's phone buzzed again. can't take it, gotta get out of here.

She tapped the Do Not Disturb crescent moon icon.

"Every middle school birthday party was at Snoopy's Home Ice. The hot cocoa there is the *best*, right, Sami?" Tara said with a dreamy sigh.

Samira was too distracted by Kamron's texts to respond.

Anyway, it wasn't her problem. Sunrise Acres was supposed to ensure each new day dawned with hope. She wasn't even going to think about him again until Family Week.

"Right, Samira?" Tara was looking at her expectantly.

She had lost track of the conversation. "Right . . . what?"

"We should start going to San Jose Sharks games since we have those box seats."

"Oh, man. Box seats would be amazing," Henry said.

"Yeah," Samira said. "Um, excuse me." She stood up and made her way down the main hall, past the formal dining room and gym, to the bathroom. The minute she stepped inside and took her phone off Do Not Disturb, she was bombarded with a whole slew of texts from Kamron.

Maybe it was the excitement over Henry, or her desire to believe Kamron was better, but the levee broke. Samira could not stop the flood of tears that followed.

What the *hell* was she supposed to do? She couldn't call the admissions director again. He would laugh in her face. She couldn't take another nineteen days of Kamron texting like this. Why didn't he text Mom or Gran? The invisible mosquitos were devouring her alive.

Maybe she could talk to Henry about it.

But if he turned out to be an underfunctioner like Tara, who needed reassurance when Samira was sad because it made *her* sad, that would only make matters worse.

She picked up one of Mrs. Asghari's fancy napkins that matched the gold-leaf faucets and dabbed her eyes. She had to pull herself together and get back out there before anyone noticed she was—

"Ah!"

Uncle Hooman was standing right outside the bathroom door with that same look of concern as when she and Henry had first arrived.

"Samira-joon, I wish to speak with you privately," he said in a soft voice. He put his hand on her arm. "Tara told me about your brother." He managed a laugh. "She probably told you about me, too. It took too long, I know, but now I can say I am on the sober path, and I can help your brother if he needs it. Talk to him, encourage him. Would you like that?"

Samira would like more than anything in the world for a capable adult to step in.

She nodded. She didn't trust herself to speak.

Uncle Hooman put his arm around her shoulder. "Then you will text me his number, and I will call him as soon as he gets out. Anyway, the food is here: kabob. Cherry rice. You like cherry rice, yes?"

"It's my favorite," Samira said, wiping her eyes.

"Then let's go have a nice dinner. We won't worry about anything, just for tonight, okay?"

"Okay," she said with a sniffle.

He escorted her back to the ten-foot, hand-hewn, reclaimed oak table, whereupon she texted Gran: battery dying, if you need me, text Henry @ 555–437–2406 and turned off her phone. She wasn't going to worry about anything for the rest of the night.

There would be plenty of time to worry the next day.

CHAPTER TWENTY-SIX

Henry

The cherry rice was sweet, and the kabob was savory, but they were, like, perfect together." Henry replayed every detail of the evening with Samira as they drove back down Alexander Valley Road toward the freeway. "And the tahdig, that crispy rice with the stew on top? I've never had anything like it."

In fact, Persian food might be his new favorite. He didn't like the doogh—too salty and sour—but everything else was delicious. For dessert, Mrs. Asghari served what looked like funnel cakes soaked in honey, with tea and sugar cubes she said to let dissolve under his tongue.

She kept refilling his plate while Uncle Hooman told him all about the Safavid Empire that ruled Iran for over two hundred years. He said maybe Henry and Samira were descended from royalty, which annoyed Tara since she thought *she* was related to the queen of England.

Mr. Asghari even invited him and Daniel to see the Sharks in his box seats the next time they were in town for a tournament. The aunties and Tara's grandmother kept telling him, "You are a nice boy, Hooman-jon."

It had been one of the best nights of his life, a real Persian family dinner with his new sister.

"Mr. Asghari said Daniel and I could come up to watch the Stanley Cup Playoffs in his private screening room," he gushed.

"That'd be great," Samira said. She sounded distracted.

She had been quiet during dinner, too. And she scratched a lot, like she was allergic to something.

"You okay?" he asked.

"Yeah. Fine."

"You sure?"

"Yes," she insisted.

Maybe she was thinking about their dad. "I can figure out the best way to contact our dad when I get home. I'll have a lot of time on my hands. Once I'm, you know, grounded for life."

Samira barely cracked a smile. Something *was* wrong. "I'm toast, I'm going straight to bed," she said as soon as they walked through the front door.

Henry brushed her arm and tried to stop her. "Hey. Are you sure you're okay? You were really quiet during dinner."

"I told you, everything's fine." She flashed one of those big, broad smiles, but it wobbled.

Henry followed her through the living room and down the hall. He didn't want to push.

She paused in front of the bathroom. "Um, those are fresh towels," she said.

"Thanks," he said with a wan smile. The after-dinner high was rapidly receding.

"All right then, good night," she said, and continued on to her bedroom.

"Samira," he said before she disappeared. "I'm really glad I came."

"Me, too," she said with a grim smile and closed the door.

Henry couldn't help feeling uneasy.

After he showered and FaceTimed Linh—who assured Henry that Samira was probably just processing—it was almost midnight. He climbed into Kamron's bed. The room smelled faintly of weed. The pixie-ish anime characters whose mouths opened in horror were gaping at him. Henry pulled a pillow over his head. He shouldn't have had so much sugar and caffeine. He wasn't even tired.

Dad was going to crucify him when he got home. He would have to go on the attack and demand to know why he and Mom had kept him from his real father. This strategy might not get him acquitted but could result in a lighter sentence.

And what was up with Samira? Everything seemed fine until dinner.

There wasn't much he could do about either one of them now. He would talk to Samira over cheddar pancakes the next morning and be ready to face Robert's wrath when he got home.

A bright overhead light flipped on, and Henry shielded his eyes in the split second before someone screamed, "WHAT THE FUCK ARE YOU DOING IN MY BED?"

He bolted upright and squinted, trying to get his bearings. A figure was standing over him, but he couldn't see clearly. His eyes hadn't adjusted.

"Who the *fuck* are you and what the *fuck* are you doing in my bed?" he yelled again, and everything came into focus.

It was Kamron.

Shit. What was Kamron doing there?

"Get the *fuck* out of my bed, who are you?" he kept shouting. His words were slurred, his eyes bloodshot. He wore a black hoodie and sweatpants.

Henry scrambled out of bed with his hand out in front of him. "It's cool, man. It's cool. I'm your brother."

Shit. He shouldn't have said that. Kamron was in no place to hear it. He should have said he was a friend of Samira's. She could have explained everything later.

Kamron's face wrenched with confusion. "What are you talking about? I don't have a brother. I'm calling nine-one-one." He reached for his pocket.

"No, no, no, don't do that!" Henry yelled. The police would *not* be good for him or Kamron.

Jesus. He was only wearing his boxer shorts. He scrambled for his duffel bag on Kamron's desk chair. "I'm your brother, I swear." He nearly fell over trying to jump into his Levi's. "Our dad is Mohammed Safavi. I . . . I found Samira through a DNA test."

Before he could even get the Levi's buttoned, Kamron charged him.

He shoved Henry into the floor lamp, which came crashing to the ground. Henry faltered and tried to maneuver around Kamron when Samira came bursting in.

"I *knew* it!" she shrieked when she saw him. "I knew you wouldn't make it! I ruined my whole fucking future for you, and I *knew* you wouldn't make it." She broke down sobbing.

"I told you I wanted out. I told you I could do it from home," Kamron shouted back. Then *he* broke down. "You didn't want to hear it, I—"

"—begged the judge for recovery, you're gonna go to jail—"

"—told you I didn't feel safe. The counselors were *harsh,* always yelling at us. Every minute we had to be somewhere. I had panic attacks, like, every day!"

Henry stood there, frozen, next to the broken lamp. His twin impulses were to defend Samira and get in his truck and go.

"And who the fuck is this guy?" He nearly spit at Henry. "Get out of my room," he roared.

"He's our brother," Samira cried, as Henry slowly began to back out of the room. "He has nothing to do with whatever Dad did to you."

Henry bumped into Gran, who put her hand to her forehead as soon as she saw Kamron. "Oh, Kamron. Oh, honey. What did you do?" She tried to get him to sit on the bed.

"I didn't feel safe in there. I told her." He pointed an accusatory finger at Samira.

Gran turned to Samira. "Is that true? Did he tell you he didn't feel safe?"

Samira gasped. "Are you *kidding* me? Are you fucking kidding me, Gran?" she sobbed. "He's making excuses because treatment is hard and he's *weak*. And I'm sick of it! Grandad made me assume all this responsibility. Well, I don't want it! I'm done. I'm so fucking done!"

She stormed out of the room.

Henry grabbed his duffel bag and followed her, leaving Gran to calm down Kamron. "Samira," he called out to her.

She slammed her bedroom door in his face.

He stood in the hallway in front of her room, at a loss. She was crying. He wanted to comfort her, but clearly, she didn't want it. Linh was confusing at times but nothing like this.

He waited and waited, unsure what to do, then lightly rapped on the door. "Samira. I'm going to my truck. I'll sleep there tonight and leave first thing in the morning." He paused. "I'm sorry it worked out like this," he said, and he meant it.

It was freezing outside. He jumped in his truck and blasted the heat, rubbing his hands in front of the vent. Jesus. Everything was going great. How did it all turn to shit?

It was 2:30 a.m. Maybe he should just go. He would be home early. Dad would be happy.

The fight between Kamron and Samira was as bad as anything he had ever seen between Mom and Mama. Kamron was in bad shape. Poor Samira. There wasn't much he *could* do, though. His mere presence angered Kamron.

He decided to head home—he was not falling asleep anytime soon—when, suddenly, the passenger door flew open.

Samira tossed in her overnight bag, jumped in, and shouted, "Drive!"

CHAPTER TWENTY-SEVEN

Samira

D-drive where?" Henry stammered.

Now was not the time for questions.

"Just *go*," Samira commanded. Her throat was scratchy, her eyes red, and her nose stuffy. Jesus Christ, she hated crying.

Henry's tires screeched away from the curb.

"Turn left here," Samira said. Her tears were slowly diminishing to sniffles. "Now turn right. Get on 101 South."

"But . . . why?" Henry asked as gingerly as possible.

"Just do it," Samira snapped.

She pulled out the Benadryl she had thrown in her overnight bag and chewed it straight since she had forgotten a bottled water, then tapped Uncle Chris's contact on her phone.

"What's wrong? Is it Gran?" he said with the groggy panic of half sleep.

"It's Kamron," Samira said. She broke down again. "He escaped, Uncle Chris. Quit, left, whatever. He's home. He's been drinking. And I'm done. I'm *done.*"

Uncle Chris grunted and rustled around. "What are you *talking* about?"

"Kamron *quit* treatment. He came home. He was freaking

out, screaming at me because . . ." She stopped herself from mentioning Henry. ". . . because I wouldn't help bust him out."

Gran could tell Uncle Chris about Henry.

"What do you mean you're 'done'?"

She exhaled with exhaustion. "I mean I'm going to my friend Tara's for a couple of days. I need a break. And Gran needs you."

"Goddammit," he muttered under his breath. "Maybe your mom needs to come down and deal with her son."

"She's also not my problem and, seriously, Gran needs you." Samira hung up, laid her head back, and closed her eyes. She would not have left Gran, but if she had stayed, she would only have made things worse.

"Um, if we're going to Tara's, how come we got on the 101 South? Isn't she north of here?" Henry asked, treading very lightly.

Samira looked straight at him. "Because we're not going to Tara's. We're going to the Oregon State Penitentiary. To see our dad."

Henry's lips parted. No words came out.

Samira put her hand to her heart. "I want to know what happened to my family. *You* want to know what happened with you. *You* said, 'Absent parents are still around,' or whatever. Twenty years from now, neither one of us wants to be in some therapist's office asking those same questions. Let's find out now."

Henry stared straight ahead, probably in shock.

"Don't you want to go? I thought you wanted to fill in that 'big hole' in the center of your life?" Samira said with a tinge of annoyance.

"No, no. It's just, my dad said I *had* to be home today. If I'm not . . ." He trailed off.

She knew it. Samira *knew* he was a UF who asked for permission instead of forgiveness.

She crossed her arms. "Then turn around at the casino exit and drop me off at Tara's. She'll take me to see him."

She didn't want Tara, who would talk nonstop and Instagram the entire trip, to take her. She wanted to confront her father with Henry. Maybe she shouldn't have issued an ultimatum.

He had a pained look on his face, as if he were weighing the consequences.

Samira held her breath.

Casino exit in two miles. Henry was completely poker-faced. She chewed another Benadryl.

Casino exit in one mile. Samira wouldn't blame him for ditching her. After all, he had no idea what he was getting himself into.

The casino came into view; exit in half a mile. Grandad could spend all day there for his Texas Hold'em tournaments. *Play the blinds if you have money in the pot,* he always said.

They were speeding toward the exit. Samira sat perfectly still.

They passed the exit.

Samira was overwhelmed with relief. Henry was on her side.

And they were going to meet their father. Together.

"Take 116 to 37 East," she said in a small voice. "Here. I'll put the address in your phone." She laid her head back on the headrest again. "Kamron was texting me all night long. I should have answered."

Henry finally spoke. "Is that why you were quiet at dinner?"

She nodded.

He reflected on this. "What could you have said that would have made a difference?"

Samira shrugged. She had put on the cape. It would have been nice to have the superpowers.

"He hated me." Henry attempted a laugh.

Samira could hear the hurt. She stared out the passenger window as they merged onto Highway 37. The dark expanse of San Pablo Bay stretched out before them. "He doesn't even know you."

Henry had this habit of chewing the inside of his cheek before he spoke. "How could he just walk out? Don't they have security guards there?"

"The director said there are no inside locks on the doors. They can't make them stay."

"Going into a program like that probably *is* hard," Henry said.

"I know," Samira grudgingly admitted. What if a judge made her give up Benadryl when she had no other way to vanquish the mosquitoes?

Her eyelids were getting heavy. "We're taking 80 to 505 to 5 North."

"Right," he said, nodding to his map app.

Her eyelids fluttered. She fought to stay awake. There was something she had meant to do, but she couldn't remember what. Before long, the rhythm of the road—and the double shot of Benadryl—lulled her to sleep.

Samira squinted and blinked several times, then lifted her arm to shield her eyes from the sunlight streaming into the passenger side window. She tapped her phone: 6:42 a.m.

"Where are we?" she croaked. Her throat was dry. She needed water.

Henry yawned. "Just past Redding. About halfway to the Oregon border."

Suddenly, Samira remembered.

"Shit, Henry! I haven't checked the prison website for visiting hours and instructions." Henry drew a breath as if to say something but must have thought better of it. Her phone was teeming with notifications: texts and messages from Gran and Uncle Chris. She would respond later. She logged into the website. "We have to fill out an application first."

"Right. Same as Soledad," he said. "Can you do it online?"

Samira read the application instructions intently. "Yes. I can do it right now for both of us. I just need your name and address, driver's license number, and . . . oh God, Henry." She turned to him with a look of panic. "Our dad has to approve us." Samira could only imagine their father being told that two of his three children were there to see him, and could he please approve them?

"I know. What if he says no?" Henry worried.

Samira would not allow herself to entertain the possibility since this whole mess was her idea. "He won't. We'll submit the applications online. He could approve us by the time we get there. If not, we'll wait. We should be there by one. Visiting hours are until four. We can spend the night in the truck and see him tomorrow if we have to."

She glanced at Henry to gauge his reaction. Not good. His eyebrows were converging in the middle of his forehead.

She forged ahead. "All I need is his prison ID number." She typed their father's first and last name into the Oregon Offender Search box.

Nothing could have prepared her for the wallop of her father staring her right in the face from his prison ID photo, hair graying, face lined with deep creases and crevices. In a matter of hours they could be face-to-face with this man, this stranger who was also their father.

Samira braced herself and scrolled down to the List of Offenses right beneath his photo. "Oh God," she gasped.

"What?" Henry looked at her with wide-eyed alarm.

"Our dad," she said, voice cracking. She thrust her phone at him. "Henry. Our dad killed someone."

CHAPTER TWENTY-EIGHT

Henry

A loud honk startled Henry back into his lane after he had veered into the next. "*What?* Are you saying our dad is a murderer?"

"No, no," Samira quickly clarified. "Vehicular manslaughter. DUI."

Christ. Big difference.

"But someone *died*. Someone with a family who loved them," she said.

After two nights of very little sleep, a headache was blooming in the middle of Henry's skull. His better judgment had told him to drop Samira off at Tara's. Hopefully, Gran and Samira's uncle could get Kamron back into treatment. He could follow up on their father from the comfort of his own bedroom with his memory-foam mattress and matching pillows, which he would give anything to sink into right now.

He went against it because Samira would have been disappointed if he hadn't—even though he was going to be in a shit ton of trouble when he got home. And now she was wavering.

They passed a freeway sign: DUNSMUIR—15 MILES. "We can stop in Dunsmuir, gas up, and turn around if you want," he said, irritated. They had come too far to give up now.

"I don't know," Samira said. She was scratching like crazy. "I mean, I guess I thought his crime would be less serious, which sounds ridiculous, I know."

Henry had not wanted to think about his crime. "What about the therapist's office twenty years from now?"

"I'll probably be there anyway, one way or the other," Samira deadpanned.

Henry tried another tack. "What if Kamron hit someone? Would you cut *him* off?"

Samira paused for a moment before finally admitting, "No."

"Okay, then. I think we should—"

Henry was cut off by the buzzing of his phone.

"It's your dad," Samira said solemnly.

"I can *see* that." Henry sucked in a deep breath and tapped the green button. "Hey," Henry said. He didn't feel like calling him "Dad."

"Son," Robert said. "Are you on your way home?"

Henry could lie, but his brain was too foggy to concoct an elaborate cover story. "No."

Robert went silent. "We had an agreement."

Henry exhaled with frustration. "I know. I need some time. Another day."

Why couldn't they just *trust* him?

Robert's voice got quieter. "You said you'd be home *today*. You made a commitment."

His calm belied the vengeance Henry would surely face for his defiance. He would have liked to say that he was on his way to see his bio-dad, who was in an Oregon state prison for vehicular manslaughter, that Henry still wanted to meet him because he had blown a big black hole in the center of Henry's life, and Henry didn't want to end up in a therapist's office twenty years from now, and did he mention that he had found his half sister?

"I know," Henry said. His stomach knotted up while he awaited Robert's reply. Samira's eyes were so wide and round, Henry half expected her to hoot.

"Remember, this was your decision, Henry," Robert said with frightening calm and hung up.

"Oh, fuck. You're dead," Samira declared.

Henry knew it. He knew this day would come. Robert and Jeannie would probably have his bags packed and on the porch by the time he got home. Well, he wasn't going to let Robert bully him into submission. "If I'm already dead," he said, "then let's go see our dad in prison."

Samira slipped her sunglasses back on and said, "Let's go."

"We need gas." Henry took the next exit to the Valero, pulled up to a pump, and jumped out.

Samira slid out of the passenger seat. "I need some water, and I have to pee."

"Can you get me a 5-Hour Energy? I'll Venmo you."

He inserted his debit card into the pump. Robert's words kept ringing in his ears: *Remember, this was your decision.* On the surface, a simple statement of fact. Underneath, much more ominous. And whatever the consequence, Henry would have brought it on himself.

He entered his PIN for the third time. Jesus. He kept getting the *See cashier* error message. He grabbed his phone and headed inside.

Samira browsed the bottled water case while he got in line. A sketchy older dude in a MAGA hat—who the hell still wore those?—was ogling her from behind. Henry kept an eye on her until she joined him in line. "I'll pay for this, you get the bathroom key," he said.

The cashier handed her the key. "It's outside, around the corner."

"I'll wait for you if you need to go, too," Samira said.

The sketchy dude was following her outside.

Henry stepped up and handed the cashier his card while trying to keep track of Samira. "I think you have to reset pump number nine. Keeps telling me to see the cashier."

"How much you want?" the cashier asked.

"Make it fifty," Henry said. "And these."

He couldn't see Samira. She must have gone inside the bathroom. The sketchy dude was standing nearby in the parking lot checking his phone. A powerful sense of protectiveness rose up in his chest. He had to pay up and get out there.

The cashier tapped several buttons. The register kept beeping. He handed Henry's debit card back to him. "Got another card? This one's been declined."

That didn't compute. Henry had just deposited his birthday checks. When he last looked, his balance was over $400. "Can you try again? I know there's enough in the account." Jesus. He had to get outside.

The woman behind him in line with a sleeve tattoo cleared her throat. The cashier tried one more time while Henry kept glancing outside. Where was Samira?

The cashier handed him back his card. "Still declined. Call your bank. Sometimes they think out-of-area gas purchases are fraudulent. Let 'em know the charge is legit."

Henry stepped aside and quickly launched his banking app

to confirm his balance. When his home screen came up, his jaw hit the ground.

What the *hell*?

His balance was zero. He couldn't have spent more than a hundred dollars over the past two days. The cashier was right, there must be fraud on the card. He scanned his recent transactions and was ready to call the bank when—

Henry may as well have taken a slap shot to the head: his dad had cleared out their joint account! Transferred every penny back to his. How was Henry even supposed to get back home without any money?

He barreled out the double doors to find Samira and tell her they were screwed. He rounded the corner toward the restroom.

MAGA Hat was standing right outside.

"*Hey*. What are you doing?" Henry shouted just as Samira came out.

Henry barreled toward MAGA Hat and grabbed him by the shoulder. "What are you doing?" He would pound the shit out of this asshole, who seemed to think he could overpower anyone he thought was weaker than him.

"Henry," Samira said sharply.

MAGA Hat jerked away. "Waiting for the bathroom key."

"Here, *here*." Samira shoved the key into his hand. "Sorry."

She led Henry back to the truck by the elbow. "What are you *doing*? You're *eighteen*. If you hit him, you could get arrested for *assault*. We'd be in even more trouble if you got arrested."

She was right. His shoulders crumpled. "My dad cleared out my bank account," he said, near tears.

"*What?*"

"Every penny. We're screwed."

Samira threw her hands up. "What a shitty thing to do to your own son."

That was the point. Henry *wasn't* his son.

She pulled out her phone and launched her banking app. "Okay, okay. I have . . . eighty-six dollars and forty-two cents in my account. How much do we need for gas?"

"At least fifty." His voice rang with discouragement. "Probably closer to seventy." Robert was such a fucking bully.

"That would leave us . . . eleven dollars and forty-two cents for food."

"What about parking?" They may as well admit that Robert had won. He always did.

After a defeated beat, Samira perked up. "Wait, I can ask Tara to Venmo me a hundred bucks. Can you ask Linh to Venmo you?"

He could, but . . . "I didn't want to involve her in case my parents try to contact her."

"I haven't told Tara where we are, either. I could swear her to secrecy, and she'd spill her guts the second Gran called."

They stood in frustrated silence for a moment.

"Henry, we don't have a choice," Samira finally said. "If we want to make this trip, you get a hundred dollars from Linh; I'll get the same from Tara. That should be enough." She gestured to the pump. "I'll put fifty on pump nine and call Tara while you call Linh." Before she went inside, she put her hand on his arm. "Hey. Thanks. For defending me."

"Yeah. Sure," Henry said, but he was quickly losing faith that they would make it all the way to the penitentiary—and they hadn't even made it across the state line.

CHAPTER TWENTY-NINE
Samira

Tara was bummed Samira hadn't asked her to go with them to Oregon but thrilled she could still play a role in the whole adventure. "I am *totally* down to be part of this operation," she said in a hushed voice as if Samira were recruiting her for a high-level CIA mission.

Samira stood in a shady part of the parking lot while Henry was on the phone with Linh in his truck. She had debated whether to tell Tara about Henry coming to her rescue, but there wasn't time for all the details.

"What's my cover story if Gran calls?" Tara asked with breathless excitement.

"She's probably not going to call. If she does—"

"I'll say you're in the bathroom. Or no! The shower. That takes longer. *Ooh.* I could say we're about to watch a movie in the screening room, and you'll call her after. Then I text you and you call her. Or—"

"*Tara,*" Samira said firmly. "All I need you to do *right now* is Venmo me a hundred bucks. If Gran calls, tell her that you'll give me the message and I'll call her back as soon as I can. Okay?"

"Okay," Tara said with an audible pout. Right before they

hung up, she said, "Sami, should I tell Mrs. Sandoval you're absent because Kamron busted out of his treatment program?"

Another unexcused absence probably meant Samira wouldn't walk at graduation. She did *not* want to tell Mrs. Sandoval about Kamron. It was too private.

"No. I'll say I was sick."

She dreaded calling Gran next. She had unleashed absolute chaos back home.

As soon as Gran answered, Samira talked quickly before she could interrupt. "Gran, it's me, I'm at Tara's, I'm fine, I needed to get away, I'll be back tomorrow, how's everything there?"

"Oh, Sami. Samira, thank God you're safe."

Samira could just see Gran with a worried hand to her forehead. An avalanche of guilt nearly buried her heart. She had abandoned Gran.

"How is Kamron?" she asked while urgently scratching her neck.

"He's asleep. He fell asleep before your uncle got here. Chris is going to call the attorney. And Sunrise Acres. We're hoping to get him readmitted."

Samira had *completely* abdicated her duties. And she should have told Kamron about Henry so he wouldn't have been blindsided. Maybe they *should* turn around and head home.

No. *No.* Like Henry, she had to figure out the origin of that big black hole at the center of *her* life, too, before it sucked her in like Kamron.

"I'll be back tomorrow," Samira said. Her voice cracked. "I love you."

She hung up before Gran's tears could trigger her own and climbed into the passenger seat. "Let's go." They had to make good time, or they would miss the visiting window.

She launched the prison portal on her phone. "Give me your address and your driver's license number for our applications."

Henry recited his information while they merged onto the freeway. Brown fields extended all the way to the horizon, framed by foothills and mountains that still had snow on their caps.

Once Samira pressed *send,* she dug around in her purse for a Benadryl and popped one with a water chaser.

"You eat those things like candy," Henry remarked.

Was it that noticeable?

"Why do you take them?" he said, his face filling with concern.

Because I itch, she could have said, and left it at that. But after everything they had been through in the last twenty-four hours alone, she felt like she should tell him the truth. "I have this autoimmune disorder where I'm, like, swarmed by invisible mosquitoes that leave little red welts all over my body when I'm stressed. They itch like crazy. The doctor told me I need to do a better job 'managing my anxiety,'" she said with a half laugh.

Henry scratched his chin; he seemed to weigh what he was about to say. "I, uh, I was diagnosed with depression a few years back. They put me on Prozac, but it messed up my game. So I went off it, and sometimes . . . sometimes I feel this nothingness." He allowed a smile. "Finding you, searching for Dad—I definitely feel something."

"We're feeling *all* the feels," Samira concurred.

They drove in silence for a while—comfortable silence—through the Shasta-Trinity National Forest and all the hippie mountain towns until they finally reached the WELCOME TO OREGON sign.

"This is where my mom lives," Samira said offhandedly.

Henry did a double take. "*Here?* Where?"

"In Ashland."

"You wanna stop and see her?" Henry asked.

Samira shook her head. "No. We have to get there by one." The last time she and Kamron drove up together, she woke up to Kamron screaming and Mom crying and put the pillow back over her head. "Maybe on the way back," she said.

"Lewis & Clark is up here, right?" Henry asked.

"Ugh, don't remind me." Samira reclined her seat and closed her eyes. "Tomorrow is Decision Day. I have to officially decline admission."

Her escape hatch had closed. There was no back support coming from her father. She would be stuck at home for the next two years, at least, while Kamron struggled to stay in recovery, and Gran struggled to pay the bills.

"Wait, I thought you said you were going?"

Samira's face grew unexpectedly hot. Henry's truck must have cost $30,000; his house was probably much fancier than theirs. He would not have to decline admission to help pay for his brother's court-ordered treatment program.

There was no point in lying. "I had to use the savings bond my grandad left me for tuition to help pay for Kamron's treatment."

"Oh, man. I'm sorry. That *sucks*." His face twisted. "If tomorrow is Decision Day, I have to officially *accept* admission." He didn't look happy about it.

Samira side-eyed him. "You haven't accepted admission yet? Why not?"

He hesitated. "I want to slow down. Maybe take a gap year."

"Why don't you? Take a gap year. Tara is."

"My parents would freak. Robert wants me to go to U of D because of the partial scholarship." He let out a bitter laugh.

"Probably not going now. No way he's paying for anything after this."

Samira sat up, alarmed. "Once you explain everything to them, won't they understand?" If she had blown his admission to the University of Denver by jumping in his truck and insisting they visit their dad, she would never forgive herself.

"They never understand," Henry said. "In sophomore year, I asked if I could quit hockey. They said no. I said I wanted to go to Cal State with Daniel, undeclared, instead of U of D as an accounting major because how am I supposed to know what I want to do for the rest of my life? They said no. And when I was in Fresno one time for a hockey tournament," Henry said bitterly, "I asked my dad if we could look for him, you know, Mohammed. He said no."

Samira's face wrenched with apology. "Henry, if searching for our dad got you in trouble with yours, it's all my fault," she said.

"It's not," Henry said. "I want to see him, too."

Samira left it at that. Besides, it was too late to turn back now. Google Maps said they would arrive at the Oregon State Penitentiary in less than four hours.

CHAPTER THIRTY

Henry

"You know you're getting on 22 West, right?" Samira said.

"*Yes*," Henry said, once again nodding to his phone. She didn't seem to believe he was capable of reading a map app. Or as capable as she was.

He chalked it up to nerves. They were less than twelve minutes away.

He followed the directions to the prison entrance, which was dotted with willow and pine trees. "This place is a lot nicer than the one in California," he said. That sounded weird. "I mean, Soledad was all dry and dusty."

"Five stars on Yelp," Samira said, drumming her fingers on her knee.

The visitor lot had all the same warning signs: WARNING: VE-HICLES SUBJECT TO SEARCH and so on. He pulled into a parking space at 1:18 p.m. "There should be lockers, but whatever you bring inside will have to fit in a clear plastic bag," he said. He would take the lead since he knew what to expect.

"I know, I read the instructions on the website," said Samira, who downed the rest of her bottled water and kept taking things in and out of her purse.

"Don't bring your Benadryl," Henry warned. "You mainly need your license."

"I *know*," Samira said.

She was touchy under pressure. He would be the one to keep it together. He collected his keys and wallet, put their overnight bags on the floor in the back seat, and waited for Samira to finish fiddling with her purse. "Ready?"

"Yes."

Green grass and flowering bushes lined the walkway. The prison itself was pale yellow with brown awnings and trim. Two staircases flanked the OREGON STATE PENITENTIARY sign, which was shaped like a police badge. From a distance, it could have been a hotel lobby entrance.

"There's the reception area." It felt good to know what he was doing this time. Henry pointed to two walk-up windows, each of which had a line ten people deep. "There are the lockers and vending machines." He pointed behind an already full seating area.

"God. It's like the DMV, only sadder," Samira said with dismay. "It's so crowded."

Henry tapped his phone: 1:30 p.m. They could wait until 4 p.m. that day, like Samira said, and spend the night in his truck if they had to.

Samira frowned at him. "I thought we weren't supposed to bring our phones inside."

"I'll put it in a locker before we go through security." He tapped his home screen again. The lack of text or voice messages from Robert was unnerving.

Samira got quiet while they stood in line. She must have been taking in all the families and kids clutching their juice boxes and teddy bears and thinking what Henry had been thinking in Soledad: that could have been them.

"What do you think he'll say when they tell him, 'Your kids are here to see you'?" Her face was pinched with worry.

Henry considered this. "'It's about time . . .'?"

She allowed a half smile.

That was what he hoped, at least. He nodded to the vending machines. "You want something?" He still had the dollar bills that Robert had given him to tip the valet at the Westlake Lodge.

"Not hungry," said Samira.

Neither was Henry, although his stomach was growling.

Finally, it was their turn to check in. Samira stepped up to the bulletproof window before Henry could. Jesus. She *always* had to be in control. He stood to the side and let her. It must have made her feel less nervous to take charge.

"We're here to see Mohammed Safavi," she said.

"Did you complete the visitor application?" the clerk asked with the same slightly distracted manner as the clerk at Soledad. Must be a job requirement.

"We did." She pointed at Henry. "We're his kids: Samira Murphy and Henry Owen."

Henry leaned in and raised his hand.

"How do you spell it, your father's name?"

Samira spelled out their father's first and last names. "We submitted our applications this morning. On the website."

The clerk clicked away on her computer. "Did you make an appointment?"

"No, but . . . the website said walk-ins were okay. We drove all the way up from California," Samira hurriedly added, as if that would make a difference.

Without glancing up from her screen, the clerk said, "Mr. Safe-uh . . . Mr. Soff-uh . . . the inmate in question has approved your application. I can give you a tentative two-thirty appointment."

Henry's heart nearly burst. They had done it. After a lifetime without him, they were going to see their dad!

"I need your government-issued ID."

Henry quickly dug into his wallet while Samira retrieved hers from her back pocket. The clerk scanned their IDs.

"Have a seat in the waiting area until you're called to security. Put your phone, other valuables, and anything metal in a locker. If you're wearing an underwire bra, take it off."

"I'm not," Samira said defensively.

"Anything you bring into the visiting area must fit in a small plastic bag. Keep your ID with you at all times."

Samira found a seat in the waiting area first. Henry was able to join her once a mother, who was trying to feed her crying baby a bottle, stood up to go through security.

Samira looked after her. "Can you imagine our moms bringing us here?"

Henry watched her juggle the baby and her belongings. "I guess if they had to."

Samira's face flickered with sadness. "We've lost so much time, Henry. I don't know if we can ever make it up."

"Let's not lose any more," he said gently but insistently.

After twenty long minutes, they were summoned through security. Henry stashed his phone, wallet, and keys in a locker—everything except his ID. They were lightly patted down, then screened with a metal-detecting wand. A guard escorted them down a dank hall to the first of two prison gates. They paused at the second gate, which wouldn't open till the first gate had closed.

Neither one of them uttered a sound. Henry's heart was pounding rapid-fire, and his mouth was dry.

Once they got through the second gate, they were technically outside, but *inside* a twenty-foot prison wall covered in barbed wire that towered over the prison yard.

This was dead serious, definitely *not* a hotel.

Before Henry and Samira could enter the visiting area, their hands were stamped with special ink, visible only under a black light, then were led into the visiting room. Family members sat across from inmates at rows of small individual tables arranged like a school cafeteria.

"These chairs must be left in the original position," the security guard ordered as if they had already tried to move them. He pointed to the back wall. "You may purchase items for the inmate from the vending machine. You may not share *anything* with the inmate, including food or cash. Visitor restrooms are along the east wall. Inmate Safavi should be out shortly."

Inmate Safavi.

Samira's face went pale. "I think I'm going to throw up," she squeaked as soon as the guard walked away.

Henry's head was spinning. He had only eaten some kettle chips, cashews, and a Slim Jim.

Worse still, their dad would be out any minute, and he seemed to have forgotten every single thing he wanted to ask or say to him. And what if their dad didn't want to answer any of his questions anyway? What if they sat across from each other in awkward silence the entire time? The whole trip would have been for nothing.

And now Henry felt as if he were going to be sick, too.

CHAPTER THIRTY-ONE
Samira

As soon as they walked into the visiting area, it hit Samira with the force of an asteroid: Kamron could be an inmate sitting opposite her and Gran. She felt nauseous, feverish, and faint.

Gran was probably a nervous wreck, and Kamron had called *her* for help. She should be home with them instead of here, waiting for a perfect stranger.

The hundreds of prison reunions she had seen on *Law & Order* marathons with Grandad did not prepare her for this. Two armed guards sat on a raised platform monitoring the room. The inmates wore blue denim jeans and shirts with their ID numbers embroidered like a ghastly brand logo. They were all wolfing down food from the vending machine heated in the microwave like it was their last meal.

She could not look at Henry. He seemed to think they had arrived in Oz and were waiting to see the wizard, who would magically fix all their problems.

She had said she wanted to find their father for the back child support. Then for Kamron's sake. But deep down, it was clear: she wanted the father who had once loved her as wide and as far and as high as he could reach to love her that way again, which was now looking impossible.

"Deatherage," a guard called out from the far side of the room. An inmate and his family were guided to a large fading backdrop of a waterfall hanging from the prison wall. They posed in front of it. The guard gave them the wet Polaroids to bring back to their seats.

The sadness, the grief of the place overwhelmed her. Samira's instinct was to run. And she would if she weren't too scared to move.

The minutes ticked by. The seat across from them remained empty. "Where is he?" Samira harshly whispered. "Should we ask someone?" The clock above the platform said 2:51 p.m.

Henry was starting to look as pale as she felt. "I don't know," he said. "Maybe we give it ten more minutes?"

Samira fixated on the clock as the second hand swept slowly around the dial.

Finally, a guard came out. "You here to see Safavi?"

"Yes," Samira and Henry said in unison.

"Yeah, he's not feeling well and won't be able to make today's appointment."

Samira froze with her mouth open like she had been turned into a statue.

"He . . . he doesn't want to see us?" Henry stammered.

"I didn't say that. I said he's not feeling well. And you'll need to clear the visiting area." He held his arm out toward the exit. Samira stood up in a daze. They followed the guard to the door.

"Can we . . . can we leave a message for him?" Henry sounded desperate.

"You can send him a letter. Or set up an account with ICS to text. It's on the website."

They walked back through the prison yard in shock, through the two gates that wouldn't open until the other had closed.

As soon as they got safely to the waiting area, Samira spun around. "Who the *fuck* does he think he is, denying his own children a visit after we came all this way?"

Henry reared back. "I don't know. Maybe he got nervous or—"

"Or he doesn't give a *shit* about us. Why should we give a shit about him?" She tamped down the gusher that was about to burst, pushed past Henry, and headed for the double doors.

Henry scrambled after her. "Where are you going? The guard said we could text him. We can come back tomorrow, we can car camp if we have to!"

She charged right through the double doors and down the stairs. Henry followed. "I have to get home, Henry. I have to get back to Gran and Kamron."

"I thought you were *doing* this for Kamron," Henry cried.

Samira stopped abruptly. "We tried. We *failed*. And I'm tired." Too tired to fight back the tears. "I want to go home," she said, her voice breaking.

Henry didn't seem to know what to do. "But we're *here*," he said weakly.

"We have to accept it, Henry," she insisted. "He doesn't care about us. He never has."

Henry looked away. He didn't want to hear it.

She exhaled forcefully. "Think about it. My mom has the same cell phone number since before I was born. He could have contacted her anytime. Yours, too, probably."

Henry's face fell at the realization.

"I shouldn't have left in the first place," she said sadly and continued on to the truck.

"You can't make him stop drinking. You know that, don't you?" Henry called after her.

She spun around. "There's nothing he can say that will fill that big black hole in the center of your heart. You know *that,* don't you?"

Henry looked as if she had shot him with a pellet gun.

God. Why did she say that? She walked back to him. "I'm sorry he doesn't want to see us, but can't we just go home?" She was overcome with exhaustion and hunger.

Henry's face was wrenched with indecision. He kept chewing his cheek and glancing back at the guard tower. Finally, he muttered, "Okay," and they walked back to the truck in silence.

Samira ignored all the text and voice messages from Mom, Gran, and Uncle Chris until she could summon the energy to return them. Anyway, they would be home before midnight. She could talk to Gran in person.

CHAPTER THIRTY-TWO

Henry

Henry and Samira drove back down Interstate 5 and made it past the Oregon border by 7 p.m. Henry's stomach burned as if he had drunk battery acid, but he had no appetite.

He understood why Samira wanted to get home, but still . . . It was *her* idea to come. An extra day might not make that much difference for Kamron, but it could have made a world of difference for him.

Plus, he kept turning over what Samira had said in his head. His father *could* have contacted Mama if he had wanted.

They passed the WELCOME TO CALIFORNIA sign.

The bleak thoughts kept coming. Now that he had defied Robert, he would never pay for college. In fact, they would probably kick him out, and their worst fears about him would come true: he would end up like Mama with a series of odd jobs and no future. Like Mohammed Safavi.

"Henry," Samira said sharply.

He snapped to. *Oh shit.* There were flashing red lights in his rearview.

"Were you speeding?"

"*No,*" Henry insisted. He pulled over into the exit lane. "I set the cruise control to sixty-five." His chest tightened. This was not good.

He took the next exit and rolled to a stop in front of a Chevron station. The patrol car pulled up behind him. An officer got out and approached the driver's side window, standing a foot or so behind it, visible in the side-view mirror. "Do you know why I pulled you over?"

"No, sir," Henry said, staring straight ahead, gripping the wheel. Robert had told him he damn well better keep his hands where the cops could see them if he ever got stopped. He had only been pulled over once before for doing fifty in a thirty-five.

The officer aimed his flashlight in the car. "License and registration, please." Henry fumbled in the center console for the car's registration and pulled his license out of his wallet. The officer took them and returned to his patrol car.

"He didn't say why he pulled you over," Samira said in a low voice.

"It doesn't matter," Henry said. Robert said never to challenge the police.

"But he has to tell you why he pulled you over. He can't just—"

"*Samira.*" Henry shut her down. He was in enough trouble.

The officer's boots crunched on the gravel as he walked back to the truck. "What is your relationship to the registered owner of this vehicle?"

Relationship? "He's my dad, I mean, my uncle, technically my uncle, but he's my dad," Henry stumbled over himself.

The officer wiped the edges of his mouth with his thumb and forefinger. "Well. This vehicle has been reported stolen."

Henry's heart stopped. Robert had reported his truck as *stolen*?

The officer leaned down. DIXON was embroidered above his right pocket.

"Miss, I need to see your ID, too," he said to Samira, who quickly sifted through her purse.

"*Stolen?*" she whispered as he walked back to his patrol car.

Henry was still in shock. Was he being *arrested*?

After a tense beat, Officer Dixon returned to the truck. "Is this your girlfriend?"

"She's my sister," Henry said. Officer Dixon glanced back and forth between them. "Half sister. We just found each other through a DNA test. We were looking for our dad. We've never met him," he rambled.

Officer Dixon studied them for a beat. "You'll have to come with me, both of you. The vehicle will be impounded and put in storage until the owner can retrieve it. Can you exit the vehicle and give me the keys, please?"

"Y-yes, sir," Henry said. "Can we, uh, get our bags out of the back?"

"You can. They will be subject to search and seizure."

Henry quickly grabbed his phone and duffel bag. Samira gathered up her purse and overnight bag.

They slid into the back seat of the Yreka Highway Patrol car. "I'm sorry," Henry choked.

"Fucking Yreka," Samira said. "Did no one know how to spell 'Eureka'?"

The back seat was hard; the roof was so low that Henry had to hunch down so his head didn't bump. They faced a steel mesh divider with bulletproof glass.

And it was all Henry's fault, like Robert had said. His heart sank into his stomach.

Officer Dixon merged onto the road and glanced at Henry in the rearview. "You a runaway?"

Henry squirmed. "I, um, wanted to get away for a few days. I'm eighteen. It's my car. I mean, the car my parents gave me."

"Thought so. Kid gets mad, takes car registered to parent. Doesn't respond to calls or texts. Parent reports the vehicle as stolen under section ten-oh-eight-five-one of the vehicle code: joyriding. A way to find the kid and recover the vehicle."

"Will I go to prison?" Henry croaked.

"It's possible."

Henry looked at Samira with alarm.

"All depends on the judge. And your attorney."

What the *hell* was Robert thinking? Why would he want this to go on Henry's record?

"How does he expect us to get home?" Samira murmured.

"Don't worry," Henry promised. "I'll figure out a way." Somehow. "Daniel will pick us up. Or Linh."

The patrol car pulled into the Yreka Highway Patrol station: an older, single-story building with a wood-shingled overhang. Officer Dixon allowed Henry and Samira to carry their bags inside and pointed to the lobby. "Have a seat. I'll call you back shortly," he said to Henry.

They were the only two people there. After a moment of exhausted silence, Samira said, "God, I'm starving."

"I . . . I have cash if you want something from the vending machine," Henry said distractedly. He was so far beyond hungry, he wasn't hungry anymore.

"I'd rather have real food," Samira said. "Once they let you go, we can sit down somewhere and figure out whether we're taking the bus back or hitchhiking." She let out a dark laugh. "Did your dad text you, like, 'Heads up, you're about to be arrested'?"

Henry shook his head.

"That's hella fucked up that he didn't give you any advance warning," Samira pronounced, and it was.

He wouldn't even give Robert and Jeannie the *satisfaction* of kicking him out. He would leave before they could and stay on Mama's couch until he found a job and a roommate since Daniel would be in a dorm.

Daniel. Damnit. He had missed a playoff game.

Just then, Officer Dixon motioned for Henry; Henry followed him to a cubicle in the booking room. "Sit tight while we contact the plaintiff."

The plaintiff. His dad. Jesus.

Henry nervously glanced around, then slid his phone just outside of his pocket to launch the website for the inmate texting service the guard had mentioned. He and Samira deserved to know why their dad was a no-show.

He kept looking up. He probably wasn't supposed to be on his phone. The site required payment, and Venmo was taking forever to go through. Finally, his payment was authorized. But now he had to wait for his father to approve him as a contact.

A queasiness came over him. What if he didn't? After all, he hadn't shown up for their appointment.

Officer Dixon reappeared with an official-looking document in his hand. "DA is charging this as misdemeanor joyriding. Worst case: a year in county jail and a five-thousand-dollar fine."

All the air got stuck in Henry's lungs. "Are you *kidding*?"

"If the plaintiff drops the charges, all of this disappears."

Great. Another threat for Robert to hold over his head.

"This is your copy of the citation. Your arraignment is on May thirtieth."

Perfect. Same day as graduation.

Officer Dixon stood up. "For now, you're free to go."

On his way back to the lobby, Henry texted Daniel, won't be back Monday, tell coach sorry. And a text finally came through from Robert: On 10 AM flight f/LAX to Medford. Booked you a room @ Yreka Motel. Will pick you & truck up tomorrow.

They had passed the Yreka Motel on their way to the station. It looked sketchier than a two-star Motel 6, but at least he and Samira wouldn't have to hang out at a twenty-four-hour Denny's all night long waiting for Linh or Daniel.

He collapsed into the chair next to her. "Misdemeanor joyriding. Hopefully, Robert will drop the charges after he's sure I've 'learned my lesson,'" he said bitterly and reread the text. "He's flying into Medford tomorrow. He booked me a room at the Yreka Motel down the street. I can ask for a double. We can drop you off in Santa Rosa on the way home." He took out his phone. "There are a couple of restaurants around here that we—"

"Henry, I'm not going with you," Samira interrupted.

Henry's face contorted, and the rug was ripped out from under him when she added, "My mom's on the way."

CHAPTER THIRTY-THREE

Samira

As soon as Henry went off with Officer Dixon, Samira sifted through Tara's texts: did you see him?? did you cry? did Henry?? 😭 now I'M crying!!!! 😩

And: reading about prison labor ⚙ boycotting everything from victorias secret! throwing out thongs and bras 😡 And seconds later: except for pink lace underwire, makes my boobs look so big!! 😳

Right when she was about to text Tara that their dad was a no-show, her mom called.

"Samira, I know you're at Tara's. I talked to Gran." Her tone was soft and somber like Grandad's funeral director at the veterans' cemetery. "Are you okay?"

Samira exhaled as if she were blowing out the candles on a birthday cake. She had not intended to ask her mother to pick them up. Generally, OFs did not rely on UFs—and there were simply too many land mines with Mom. But she lived less than an hour away, and Samira and Henry could stay with her until Linh or Daniel could come pick them up.

"I'm not at Tara's," Samira admitted. "Henry came to stay the night, and we . . . we drove up to Oregon to see our dad. He was transferred from Soledad to the Oregon State Penitentiary."

Her mother had either fainted or was speechless.

"We didn't get to see him. It's a long story. Anyway, Henry's dad—the dad who's raising him—got pissed Henry took off without telling him. He reported Henry's truck stolen. Henry got pulled over for joyriding. They impounded the truck, and now we're stranded at the California Highway Patrol station in Yreka."

"I'll come get you," Mom said right away. Samira didn't even have to ask.

∞

She thought Henry would be happy that her mother was coming to pick them up. But now he was looking at her like a lamb she was throwing to the wolves.

"I didn't know you had made other arrangements." She cringed. "I mean, that other arrangements were being made for you." His dad was the last person she was expecting to be on his way. And now her back was itching in that spot that was hard to reach.

He ran his fingers through his hair. "Yeah, no. It's okay."

It didn't sound okay. And it didn't feel right ending their search this way: in the lobby of the California Highway Patrol station. But she was not staying at the Yreka Motel and driving all the way to Santa Rosa with Henry's asshole dad.

"I'm glad we came," she said in a tone that was meant to be convincing.

His face turned red. He attempted a laugh. "Big waste of time."

"No, it wasn't," Samira insisted. At least now she knew the truth about her father: he would never love her again the way she needed to be loved.

"I'm gonna try and text him," Henry said, "to see what happened, why he didn't show up."

Samira nodded. She would *not* be texting him. Or calling.

After a melancholy beat, Henry peered past her out the double doors. "Is that your mom?"

Mom's aging blue Subaru was out front. Samira stood up. "That's her." She picked up her purse and bag. God, she hated awkward goodbyes. "Oh." She brightened. "Let us at least give you a ride to the motel so you won't have to lug your bag."

"Yeah, okay." Henry sounded like a deflated accordion. "Thanks."

Mom stood with her arm draped on the driver's side window. "Hello, Henry," she said with a bittersweet smile. Her wispy brown hair was swept up in a messy bun; her delicate features were dwarfed by chunky, square-frame glasses Samira had picked out for her.

"Hello, Mrs. . . . uh—"

"Call her Erin," Samira said. "Mom, we're dropping Henry off at the Yreka Motel." She tossed her overnight bag in the back seat. "His dad's coming tomorrow to get him and the truck. He's staying there tonight. I said we could give him a ride."

"Yes, of course, Henry. Get in."

He threw his duffel bag on the back seat. Mom secured herself in the driver's seat and put her hand on Samira's wrist. "Hi, baby."

"Hi, Mom," Samira said with a weary smile. Hunger and fatigue were again overtaking her, but she was determined to keep calm and carry on, as Tara's many pillows decreed, until she could get to the safety and privacy of the guest room at Mom's apartment.

"It's off of Main Street," Henry said.

"I passed it on my way here," Mom said. She locked eyes with Henry in the rearview. "You look just like him, don't you? And Kamron."

"I guess," Henry said glumly.

"Do you want to drive through somewhere before we drop you off, Henry?"

"No, ma'am. I'll get something after I check in."

He sounded dejected, like a kid who had been sent to his room. Samira was filled with guilt. She had abandoned Kamron and Gran, and now she was abandoning Henry. But she had to get home.

As soon as her mother made the turn from Main Street into the parking lot of the Yreka Motel, a pall fell over them. The motel was decrepit: peeling paint on the salmon-pink doors. Sagging roof. Cracked windows. The kind of place where bodies were buried under the floorboards—and no one noticed.

"You can't stay here." Samira turned around to face Henry. "You have to stay with us."

Henry was fixated on the people around the pool, which had been drained of water and was littered with beer bottles. "I—I can't," he said. "My dad's expecting me here."

"Samira's right," Erin said, her face full of worry. "It's not safe."

Suddenly, a door on the second floor flew open. A mangy dude with matted hair and flailing arms spilled out shouting, "I *paid* for that shit, it's my stash."

Erin put both hands up. "All right. Go get the key so your dad knows you checked in. You'll stay with us tonight. I'll run you back in the morning."

Henry hesitated.

"What time is your father's flight?" Erin pressed.

"Ten a.m."

"Direct or connection?"

"Connection. Through San Francisco."

"His flight won't get in till three at the earliest. And he still has to pick up a rental car and drive to Yreka," she added.

Who had invaded Samira's mother? This was the most OF thing she had ever heard Mom say. "*Go*," Samira commanded.

Finally, he climbed out of the car. They kept watch on him as he crossed to the lobby and approached the front desk. "He's very well-mannered," Mom observed.

"His dad's an ex-Marine. And an asshole," Samira said dryly.

Mom turned to face her; her big, sad eyes magnified by the frames. "So, you didn't get to see your dad?"

Samira closed her eyes and shook her head. "I don't want to talk about it right now, Mom."

Henry popped into the back seat and held up the key. "Got it," he said.

"Take a picture and text it to your dad," Samira said, gaining steam. "We can stop at Big Al's on the way home," she told her mother. Henry would appreciate a good burger, and she was dying for their chili cheese fries and a banana shake.

⚭

They sat around the dining room table in Mom's two-bedroom apartment inhaling their burgers, fries, and shakes. Ordinarily, Samira would have been embarrassed her mother's furniture was mostly castoffs. She would take her and her mother's castoffs over Henry's asshole dad any day.

"This is great, thank you," Henry said around a mouthful of tater tots. "And thank you for having me."

"You're welcome," Mom said, picking at her fish and chips.

Samira could tell she wanted to ask about what had happened. "He was a no-show," she said simply and demolished the last chili fry.

"Do you know why?" her mother asked, tentative.

Samira stood up and collected her trash. "No. We waited. A guard came out and told us he wasn't coming."

"The guard said he wasn't feeling well," Henry interjected.

"Which was *bullshit*." Samira crunched up her wrappers and stuffed them in the trash under the kitchen sink. She paused to take in her mother's refrigerator, which featured a rotating gallery of her kindergarteners' self-portraits made with crayons, glitter, and macaroni: a sea of happy faces with round heads and almond eyes and two red circles for cheeks. Except for one kid's self-portrait, which was just two black lines for the eyes and an angry red slash for the mouth.

"We're his *kids*," Samira huffed. "We haven't seen him since we were babies. He doesn't care about us. Never has."

"That's not true," Mom said insistently.

"It is," Samira snapped. She turned on the tap to wash her hands. "If he was so great, why is Kamron so fucked up?"

"Please don't speak about your brother like that," Mom pleaded.

Henry's shoulders were hunched, but Samira wasn't backing down.

"Why? Because it's the truth." She wiped up the countertop furiously. "You and Gran—Kamron, too—can't handle the truth. Me and Grandad could." In an instant, tears were cascading down her cheeks. "That's why he put *me* in charge of the funeral. He knew you and Gran couldn't handle it."

"Thank you for taking on that responsibility," her mother said delicately. "You handled everything with such grace."

Samira scrubbed harder. "Like it wasn't hard on *me* when the doctor said his aneurysm was inoperable because he wouldn't survive the anesthesia? Or when I came home to find the ambulance in front of the house?"

She was not keeping calm and carrying on. She was breaking down again. *God.* She was worse than Tara, whose emotions were always *right there* beneath the surface.

"Or when I had to find an attorney for Kamron, pray the judge would give him treatment, then she does, and he *leaves*? I blew up my college admission for him, and he doesn't even care! No one does." She aimed her ire at Henry. "And if you think our dad cares about us, you're as delusional as they are."

With that, she ran off to her bedroom and threw herself on the bed, clutching Oatie, the ratty oatmeal teddy bear she had been holding in the Facebook video. At least he still loved her.

She couldn't stop crying. It was so fucking UF.

She could hear her mother's and Henry's murmurs of concern drifting in from the dining room and gave Oatie a squeeze.

Slowly, as she began to calm down, embarrassment eclipsed the anger. She should go back out and apologize for her childish outburst, but she couldn't bring herself to budge from her bed.

After a while, her mother knocked lightly on the door. "Samira?"

"What?" she said. Her voice was all phlegmy.

Mom opened the door. "Are you okay?"

Samira kept her arms folded. "I guess."

"Then I'd like you to come out," Mom said. "There's something I need to tell you and Henry. About your father."

Samira almost said, *I don't want to hear it.* Something about the look on Mom's face told her she had no choice.

CHAPTER THIRTY-FOUR
Henry

In the time Henry had known Samira, which was less than two weeks, she had never acted like this—not even on her blind date from hell. Linh had had a similar reaction when she didn't get into Stanford. Mama had had her Mother's Day meltdown. For the most part, Henry was not used to these extreme displays of emotion. He was left smiling awkwardly at Samira's mother when Samira ran to her room.

"Here, let me . . ." he said, and began to gather up the trash.

Erin waved a hand at him. "I'll get it, Henry. Please. Sit."

He did as he was told.

She took off her glasses and massaged the outer corner of her eyes with her thumb and forefinger. "She's been deeply wounded by her father, you know, and is still grieving her grandfather."

"She worries a lot about Kamron, too," Henry said. Maybe he shouldn't have.

"She does," Erin acknowledged. "And that's my fault."

"I . . . I didn't mean it that way, I—"

"No. It's true." She held up her right hand as if swearing on a Bible. "Without me there, a lot of responsibility falls on her. Papa put pressure on her to do very adult things." She stared off into the distance, then found her way back. "I think it's good you're trying to connect with your father. I hope you don't give up on him."

Henry fished his phone out of his pocket. "I'm setting up an account so I can text him once he approves me." Henry hoped with all of his heart that he would.

Erin put her hand on his. "He was a good man, you know. In so many ways."

"That's the thing," Henry said. "We *don't* know. All we know are the bad things everyone says about him."

Erin seemed to think about this for a moment, then suddenly stood up. "Go get yourself something to drink. There's water and kombucha in the fridge. Have a seat in the living room," she said, and disappeared down the hallway.

Henry had no idea what was happening but got himself a Mystic Mango kombucha and proceeded to the living room. He sat on the futon across from a bamboo swivel chair. All of Erin's furniture looked secondhand, but she tied it together with funky artwork: wooden sculptures, impressionistic prints, and hand-dyed fabric swatches on the walls. It was cool.

She was cool. She'd welcomed Henry without hesitation and gotten them banana shakes and let Samira say "fuck." If Henry ever spoke to Mom that way, Robert would flatten him.

After a couple of minutes, Samira came out of the bedroom clutching an old teddy bear and sat next to him on the futon. "I'm five," she said with a sardonic smile.

"I'm not here to judge," Henry said, relieved that there was at least a moment of connection between them.

Erin made a detour to the kitchen.

"You okay?" he asked.

Samira shrugged and hugged her bear.

When Erin returned and sat opposite them on the bamboo swivel, Henry decided he better not get in the middle of her and Samira. He would simply listen to whatever Erin had to say.

She set her lemon ginger kombucha on the side table. "This conversation is long overdue." She closed her eyes and murmured what must have been a prayer or meditation. Then she opened them and said, "I met your father at Cal State Fresno in 2002. A ceramics class, of all things." A dreamy smile surfaced. "He could *not* master the pottery wheel. I helped him. I knew he was a veteran, one of the first to enlist in the army after 9/11. I respected that. He showered me with flowers and cards. Took me to see Coldplay."

"Oh God, Mom, *Coldplay*?" Samira sputtered.

"Read me poetry by Hafez."

"I have a book of his poetry, too," Henry said excitedly. "Our dad's. My mom gave it to me."

Erin smiled warmly at him. "Anyway, it was a real *90-Day Fiancé* kind of thing. We met in September, we were married by Christmas. I was pregnant with Kamron by New Year's." An invisible force pulled down the corners of her mouth. "After a few months, I realized something was wrong. He could be moody and withdrawn. Something had happened in Afghanistan; I still don't know what. I begged him to see a therapist. He wouldn't."

She picked up her kombucha and put it back down without a sip. "By the time Kamron came along, your father had started drinking. He had these . . . episodes. He would lock himself in the bedroom, howl in Farsi like a wounded animal. I couldn't understand him. All I knew was that it had something to do with his experience in the army. His patriotism was constantly questioned, even though he was born here."

"You're making excuses for him," Samira said defiantly.

Erin's eyes welled with tears. "I know it was frightening for Kamron: his father was screaming. I was crying and banging on the door. I left him when I got pregnant with you." She nodded to Samira. "Moved back in with Gran and Grandad. That must be when he got involved with your mother, Henry."

That was what Mama had said. The timeline synced up.

Tears rolled down Erin's cheeks. "I felt like such a failure. I thought, if only I had been a better wife, I could have helped him."

"Why are you taking responsibility for him?" Samira demanded, which Henry found ironic when she was always taking responsibility for Kamron. "Samira," he said. "Let her talk."

"He was a good man in so many ways," Erin said. "He worked hard as a security guard. Made Persian food for his parents every Sunday. Nursed your grandfather through cancer."

"Our *grandfather*?" Henry said. His throat caught. He hadn't even thought about the possibility of Persian grandparents. "Where is he?"

"Your grandfather passed," Erin said sadly. "Your grandmother is still in Fresno, I think. She wouldn't speak to me after I left." She paused like she was unsure whether to continue. Finally, she closed her eyes and took a deep breath. "He begged me to come back. Eventually, I did."

"You went *back* to him?" Samira cried.

Erin's voice broke. "He was good for a few months. He never got the help he needed. He started drinking again." She took off her glasses and wiped her eyes. "But he loved you and Kamron, I swear."

"Sure he did," Samira said.

"And you, too, Henry. I'm sure of it."

He desperately wanted to believe her.

"He taught Kamron how to play soccer, practiced with him in the backyard for hours. And you were such a fussy baby," she said to Samira, laugh-crying, "the only thing that calmed you down was that teddy bear. He would sit in the recliner and read to you both for hours at a time."

Samira held the bear out in front of her as if she wasn't sure whether to hug it or throw it across the room. "Why wouldn't you ever talk about him? Why was it all a big secret?"

Erin's face crumpled. "Everyone told me to leave him: Uncle Chris, your grandparents. My friends. I wouldn't listen."

"Pfft. Figures." Samira rolled her eyes.

"Samira," Henry said sharply. He couldn't help it. "Let her *speak*." He wanted to hear Erin's story, to know more about their father.

Samira huffed and crossed her arms. The teddy bear stayed tucked between them.

Erin studied Samira and Henry for a beat and pursed her lips. "I thought maybe . . . if we took a vacation, got away for a few days as a family, that would help. It's so hot in Fresno during the summer. Dusty. Dry. We drove to Cambria, you know, along the Central Coast, where it would be cooler. You kids could play at the beach.

"At first, everything seemed okay. The drive was fine. We stopped for lunch at a little café along the way." Her expression soured. "By the time we got to the motel, I don't know how, but he was drunk. His mood got darker and darker. He started howling again. I was at my wit's end. I gathered you up, you and Kamron, got your things—his little suitcase, your diaper bag—put you in the car to take you home. But he saw, and he was *furious*. He ordered me to bring you back inside, and I did. I was *so* scared."

Henry did not exhale.

"Then he told *me* to get in the car. I didn't know what to do. You weren't even two. Kamron was six. I couldn't get to my phone. I had left it in the bathroom. There was no one around to help." She began to weep. "I thought you'd be better off locked in that motel room than in the car with us, so I got in. And left you there all alone. I should never have left you all alone."

She was shaking. Samira hugged her teddy bear tighter. Henry considered getting Erin a tissue but thought better of it.

"He was sure I was going to leave him; he was distraught, driving erratically, swerving in and out of lanes. He wouldn't listen to me. *I* was sure we were going to die." Her cheeks were streaked with tears. "I remember . . . I remember passing this church and looking out the window at a mom with two kids *exactly* your age: the little girl had on a red sun bonnet and the little boy a Curious George T-shirt. I could see them so clearly. At the very next stoplight, as soon as the light turned green, I pushed the door open and *ran* across two lanes of traffic. Cars were honking, I don't know how I survived. I ran into the church screaming, 'I need help! Someone call the police, please.'" She needed a moment to catch her breath. "When we got to the motel, you and Kamron were hysterical. The police stayed with me until Uncle Chris came to get us."

She broke down. "I was so ashamed. Ashamed I stayed as long as I did. Ashamed for what I put you through. Ashamed I couldn't help, even though I know it's not my job to 'fix him.' Every time I wanted to talk about his PTSD, everyone said I was making excuses for him, but he needed *help*." She let all the air out of her lungs. "I couldn't defend him, but I wouldn't badmouth him like everyone else. He was still your father."

"He sounds abusive," Samira said.

"He was *not* abusive. He was self-destructive. All of his shame and his anger were directed at himself." Her voice broke again. "We were the collateral damage."

"Is that why he never saw us again?" Samira asked in a hushed voice. "Did he get arrested?"

Erin nodded sadly. "Yes. For child endangerment. He pleaded guilty and was only allowed to see you and Kamron during the afternoon on supervised visits. By that time, we were three hours away. He was drinking again. He stopped coming. He fell behind on child support. I think he lost his job. And then . . ."

They all knew what happened then.

"I want to know what happened in Afghanistan," Henry said with quiet resolution.

Erin's face fell. "I should have told you all this sooner."

Samira held on to her teddy bear. "Now I understand why Kamron is the way he is."

For Henry, too, several missing pieces of a puzzle were falling into place.

Henry wanted to talk to Samira about everything Erin had told them, but she quickly retreated to her bedroom. Instead, he washed his face, brushed his teeth, and came back to the living room, where Erin was spreading out the futon.

"This is where Kamron usually sleeps," she said, fluffing the pillow. "It's pretty comfortable." She kept fluffing and smoothing and wouldn't look directly at Henry. "I hope what I said wasn't too upsetting."

Henry set down his duffel bag. "It made some things make sense."

She sat on the edge of the futon. "Did your mother have a . . . a similar experience?"

"She doesn't talk about him much. Neither do my mom and dad—I mean, my aunt and uncle, the ones who raised me."

"I wish you had grown up knowing he loved you," Erin said. "I'm sure he did." Her face was etched with regret. "I don't think Kamron would be struggling the way he is."

Henry offered a sympathetic nod.

She allowed a faint smile. "Sleep well. I'll run you back to the motel in the morning."

He settled in on the futon and texted Daniel did we win? Even if he had missed the game, he still wanted the Ice Devils to take the championship.

Afterward, he called Linh. "That's a serious betrayal, babe," she said when Henry told her what Robert had done. "Are you going to tell your mom and dad everything that's happened?"

"I don't know," Henry said. He hadn't even *begun* to formulate how he would explain it all.

"They can't fault you for wanting to find your father, can they?"

"They can and probably will," Henry said with a yawn. "I want to know what happened to him in—" He stopped short as his phone buzzed with a new text.

"Shit!" He bolted upright. "Oh *shit*."

"What is it? What's wrong?" Linh cried.

"I just got a notification," Henry said excitedly. "My dad approved me as a contact."

"Babe," Linh squealed.

His mind went blank. "What should I text him?"

"Tell him . . . tell him you drove all the way up from California and were disappointed you didn't get to see him," Linh said, sounding very much like her therapist.

Henry quickly tapped the message. "Then what?"

"You need a closing salutation. Something like, 'Hope you are well, Henry.'"

"Yeah, yeah," Henry said. "Got it."

"Oh my God, babe. You're now officially in contact with your father. I'm so happy for you!"

"*If* he writes back," Henry said, suddenly doubting he would.

Henry was awakened by a text notification the next morning. His heart catapulted into his throat. His father had replied: I'm sorry, son. If you're still in town, maybe you can try again.

Son.

Henry clambered out of bed. He had to tell Samira.

CHAPTER THIRTY-FIVE

Samira

Samira needed time to process her mother's revelations about their father before any discussion with Henry. She couldn't stop picturing her mother in the car with him; how scared she must have been. It made her angry. And itchy.

She had just taken a shower and gotten into bed when another text in a string of unanswered texts from Gran came through: how long are you staying at Tara's?

Samira had better call her and tell her everything.

"Well, where did Henry stay last night if you two drove up to visit your mother this morning?" Gran asked.

Well, not everything. Gran didn't need to know about their father just yet.

"Tara lives in a mansion, remember?"

"Oh yes, I remember," Gran said. "Can you imagine what I could make in that kitchen?"

"But Kamron's okay? And Uncle Chris talked to Beth Woolsey?"

"She's petitioning the judge to readmit Kamron to Sunrise Acres."

Wow. This was a first. Shit was getting done without Samira

there, which was somewhat disconcerting. She was used to being the problem solver.

"You'll be home tomorrow night, right, honey?"

"Yes, tomorrow," Samira said. Mom was driving her. "We should be home by dinner."

"I'll make my Spanish rice," Gran promised.

Samira didn't have the heart to tell Gran that actual Spanish rice was more than white rice with tomato sauce and a hunk of Velveeta on top. After she hung up with Gran, she called Tara.

"I saw that on a Lifetime movie, I *swear*," Tara said in hushed amazement after Samira relayed her mother's story. "Do you still want to meet him, your dad?"

"*No,*" Samira said, indignant. "I don't want anything to do with him."

"But what about your bear and the video?"

Samira held up Oatie with his missing eye and torn underarm seam.

"The army is hella fucked up for Iranian Americans, Sami. *All* Middle Easterners. Especially after 9/11. That's what Uncle Hooman said. He had friends who served."

"Now you're making excuses for him, too." Samira tapped her photo roll and brought up his portrait. There *was* something in her father's eyes—Kamron and Henry had it, too—a sadness. A fragility. He *had* suffered.

"I'm not making excuses. Don't you want to understand him?"

"No. I'm just tired, T." Samira yawned. "I feel like I've been up for days. I'll call you tomorrow on our way back, okay?"

"Okay." Tara's voice oozed disappointment. "I was going to wait for you to get back before telling you this news . . ."

Oh no. Samira couldn't take any more drama.

"The cashier at Mary's Pizza, the one with the tattoo of a lion, anyway, she asked if I wanted to hang out," Tara squeak-squealed.

"We'll talk about it tomorrow, T," Samira said, already half asleep.

◯│◯

"What the *hell*? Who is it?" Samira roused herself from her sleep coma. Someone was rapping on her bedroom door.

"It's me. Henry," he said with quiet urgency.

Samira grabbed her phone: 5:12 a.m. "What are you doing?" she groaned. "The sun's not even up yet."

"He texted me back, Samira."

"What?" His voice was muffled.

"Our dad," he said louder. "He texted me back."

WTF? "Just a *minute*," Samira said crossly. She tossed off her covers, slipped on an old sweatshirt from her closet that barely fit, and opened the door with her eyes still squinting. Her breath must be gross. "It's practically the middle of the night," she said, and got back in bed, pulling the covers around her legs.

Henry was bubbling over with the excitement of a first grader on a school bus bound for Disneyland. "He texted me back! Dad. He said if we're still in town, we should come back."

She crossed her arms. "He had his chance. If he wanted to see us, he could have."

"But he *does*. That's what he said in his text."

Of course he would throw a curve ball like this when Samira was ready to get home. "What did it say?"

"Here." Henry thrust his phone at her.

Samira read the text: I'm sorry, son. If you're still in town, maybe you can try again. Not exactly the engraved invitation Henry was making it out to be. "What if we drive all the way back and he's a no-show again?"

Henry deflated, as if the bus driver had said they were going to the dentist instead of the Happiest Place on Earth. "Why would he say that if he didn't mean it?"

"I don't know, Henry. And what about your dad? Robert, I mean," Samira said. "There's no way we could make it to the prison and back to Yreka by three."

This gave Henry pause. He seemed to do a series of mental calculations. "If we leave in the next half hour, we could make a ten o'clock appointment and be back in Yreka by four," Henry said, determined. "His flight doesn't get in until three. Your mom said he still has to pick up a rental car and drive to Yreka."

"What if you're *late*? What if your dad is *pissed* and doesn't drop the charges?"

He was *not* thinking clearly. Samira had to do it for him.

"Samira, we're *here*. And he wants to see us." After a frustrated beat, he implored her, "Whatever shit I'm in when I get home, I want it to have been *worth* it. I don't want to have come all this way for nothing. I can't do it without you. I wouldn't want to, even if I could."

Goddammit. He had discovered her kryptonite. She did not want to go. But he *needed* her. Above all else, OFs need to be needed. And then something Grandad had said popped into her head: *Play the blinds if you've got money in the pot.*

"Every minute counts," he murmured.

"Okay, *okay*." She threw the covers off again. "We're stopping at Dutch Brothers for a dirty chai latte on the way. Your treat."

"Deal," Henry said, and ran off to get ready.

❧

Samira mainlined her dirty chai latte and Henry his quadruple iced Americano while Samira drove. Mom made them peanut butter and jelly sandwiches so they wouldn't have to stop for lunch.

Samira had puttered around town in Gran's Kia but didn't have much experience with freeway driving, especially in Mom's old Subaru. She had difficulty merging—were you supposed to speed up or slow down?—but finally made it into the slow lane on I-5 North.

After a few minutes spent chugging along, Henry said, "What are you doing?"

"What do you mean, what am I doing?" Samira said, her eyes fixed on the road ahead.

Henry looked past her out the driver's side window. "Are you going to get in the fast lane?"

"No," she said stubbornly. "I'm fine here." The fast lane scared her; she wasn't admitting that to Henry.

He took a big gulp of his Americano, seemingly to avoid saying something he would regret. After another ten minutes, he couldn't help himself. "At this rate, we'll get there tomorrow."

"Do you want to drive?" she snapped. She would prefer it.

"Yes," he said emphatically. "Get off at the next exit."

They got back on the road with Henry behind the wheel. Samira closed her eyes. Car rides made her sleepy.

They passed the Medford Airport. "Did your dad—I mean, Robert—text you this morning?"

"Yep. His flight number. Delta flight two-oh-seven departing at ten fifteen, arriving at three eleven, routing through San Francisco. That's it."

God, he was an asshole.

"We better be back at my mom's house by three. You *have* to get to Yreka before he does." Samira pulled one of the peanut butter sandwiches Mom had made out of the brown paper bag. "What are you going to tell him?"

"No idea."

She gave Henry half. "You could try the truth."

"He won't understand." Henry polished his half off in a few bites. "So, what did you think about what your mom told us?"

Samira swished her chai latte to dislodge the peanut butter that had gotten stuck to the roof of her mouth. "I knew he was bad, I guess. I just didn't know how bad."

Henry's eyebrows immediately converged over the bridge of his nose. "'Bad'? That's how you see him? He had PTSD. Don't you want to hear about what happened in Afghanistan? You should see the shit Robert posts to Facebook about Muslims. He was a Marine."

"It doesn't change anything."

Henry bristled. "Why not? He's our dad, like your mom said."

Another one who couldn't handle the truth. "He's a stranger, Henry. That's all Mohammed Safavi will ever be to me." Her heart squeezed with regret as she said it, but it was true.

"He doesn't have to be," Henry argued. "Your mom said he loved us, she said—"

"God! You're so gullible," she said with a bitter laugh. "What was she supposed to say? 'Sorry, kids, he never cared about you'?"

"He *does* care. He wanted us to come today."

"He sends *one* half-assed text saying, 'Come if you want,' and we come running."

Immediately, Henry clammed up.

Which was just as well. She was tired of talking. They drove for another hour in silence.

Once they got near Eugene, Henry merged into the exit lane for 99 West.

"What are you doing?" Samira demanded.

"Driving," Henry replied.

"I know." Samira clucked. "What are you *doing*? We're supposed to stay on Five North."

Henry flashed irritation. "There's an accident on Five North. Waze is redirecting. You're really bossy, you know, like my mom," he pronounced.

"Which one?" Samira said, oozing sarcasm.

"Both of 'em."

She harrumphed. "I'm only bossy when I feel like people don't know what they're doing."

"I *know* what I'm doing!"

They didn't speak the rest of the way.

Henry finally pulled into the visitor's lot at 9:45 a.m. and jumped out of the driver's side. Samira didn't move. "Aren't you coming?" he asked.

She shook her head. She had promised to drive with Henry; she hadn't said anything about going in—especially now that she was faced with that guard tower and barbed wire again.

He leaned back in. "Samira. C'mon." He tried to coax her. "We came all this way."

She didn't move. She could not give their father the opportunity to pull the rug out from under her again.

"Please?" he pleaded.

Samira said nothing. Why couldn't she just tell him she was scared their father wouldn't show?

When she didn't answer, he exhaled. "Okay." He headed toward the entrance.

Goddammit. She couldn't let Henry wait by himself, go through security by himself, walk through those gates by himself. And she couldn't let her brother face their father all by himself.

Holy shit. Her *brother*. Henry was *her brother*.

She jumped out of the car. "Henry," she called out to him. He paused and turned. "Should I, um, should I leave my phone in the car?" She held her breath.

"Yeah. I have mine."

She choked up. He didn't miss a beat or make a big deal out of her changing her mind.

They checked in and took a seat in the waiting area. A notice with the grim headline ATTENTION FAMILIES: INMATE SUICIDE AWARENESS was posted on a nearby bulletin board urging families to notify prison officials if they saw signs of severe mood changes in their loved ones.

Samira felt fluish again as soon as they were called to security. But she could do this. She *needed* to do this.

Henry took several dollar bills out of his wallet before closing the locker door. "I'm bringing some cash in case Dad is hungry."

Dad. They were about to meet their dad.

They followed the guard through the double gates, past the prison yard, and had their hands stamped with the invisible ink.

Samira's mind went blank as they sat down, and the guard recited his preamble about not touching the chairs or sharing their food. She kept watching the hallway out of which inmates came and went. Would she recognize him? Would he look like the man in the video?

Their appointment was for 10 a.m. The clock with the excruciatingly slow second hand said 10:05 a.m. Families were greeting other inmates.

Shit. He wasn't coming. Samira had jinxed it with her negativity, and Henry would be devastated, and—

"You have forty minutes," a guard said, and suddenly, a man who was much smaller than Samira had anticipated with brown skin, graying hair, green eyes, and a dimple in his chin, who wore denim jeans and a button-down and was holding several photographs, stood before them.

"Henry-jon, Samira-joon," he said softly. "Thank you for coming. I'm sorry I missed you yesterday."

Without warning, Samira burst into tears. All those years she had wanted to crawl through the video screen and into his lap, and he was *right there* in front of her.

Mohammed slowly lowered himself into the seat opposite them. "Samira-joon, shh, it's okay. Samira-joon," he said, and put his hand on her forearm.

"I can't believe it's you," she said, through convulsive sobs. "You're real, and you're here, you're finally here." Henry put his arm around her shoulders. She wiped her eyes with her sleeve.

"And you are here," her father said with a gentle smile. "Oh, Samira-joon. Henry-jon, look at you. You are a grown man."

He sounded *exactly* like he did in the video.

"Hi, Dad," Henry said. His voice caught. He cleared his throat.

"Well," their father said, nodding to his environment. "We have a lot to catch up on."

CHAPTER THIRTY-SIX

Henry

For Henry, the fact that his father was right before him in the flesh, admittedly shorter and more soft-spoken than he had imagined, did not diminish his mythic status. This was the man Henry had dreamed about since he was a little boy. He didn't even know where to begin with his questions—and didn't trust his voice if he did.

"I'm sorry I missed our appointment yesterday," Mohammed said. His eyes crinkled with remorse. "This is not where I would have wanted to meet you after all these years. To be honest, I didn't know what to say to you. And I was afraid of what you would say to me."

He waited for them to respond. Henry and Samira remained tongue-tied. He seemed to know their time was limited and forged ahead.

"You probably saw my offense on the website." He offered a grim smile. "My name is Mohammed Safavi, and I am an alcoholic." He glanced around. "I'm not sure I would have gotten into recovery if I weren't here. I met with the family of the young man who, uh . . . whose life I took." He bowed his head. "There's nothing I can do to make up for their loss except honor my commitment to recovery every day. Now I go to meetings every week. Group therapy."

He waited again for Henry or Samira to say something.

When they didn't, he spread out the photographs he was carrying. "I wanted to show you these. I've had them since I got here. And at Soledad before that."

Henry and Samira gasped.

They were pictures of Henry, Kamron, and Samira: Mohammed and baby Henry swimming in a pool; holding infant Samira with her teddy bear; with Kamron and the soccer ball.

"Oh," Samira said, and put her hand over her mouth.

"We have your picture, too," Henry finally spoke. "Your military portrait."

Mohammed's eyes grew red. "I've missed you both, and Kamron, so much."

"Then why didn't you write or call us?" Samira had finally found her voice. "Our moms have had the same cell phone numbers since . . . since, you know."

Mohammed looked down at the baby pictures and lightly touched each one. "Samira-joon, by the time I came here, I had done so many bad things. Why would you—or your mothers—want anything to do with me?"

"Samira's mother said you had PTSD," Henry said softly.

Mohammed rested his fingertips on the photo of him and Kamron. He was silent for a moment. "War is traumatic for everyone, Henry-jon. Soldiers and civilians alike."

"Casey." An inmate and his family were called for their Polaroid against the fading waterfall backdrop.

"But she said something terrible happened to you there,"

Henry pressed because it would help explain everything that had happened since.

"Henry-jon," Mohammed said warmly, "I want to hear about *you*, your lives. You are both in high school, yes? Are you going to college, are you—"

"Kamron is a mess right now because of what he went through with you," Samira asserted.

Their father flinched as if she had slapped him, which broke Henry's heart.

"If you can tell us something that would help him understand—help *us* understand. *Please*."

"Kamron is a mess?" their father asked, barely audible.

"Yes," Samira said. "What happened over there?" she beseeched him.

He glanced up and back down at their baby pictures. After another long beat, he said, "I . . . I enlisted in the army after 9/11. Afghans speak Dari. It's like Farsi. I thought I could help. I wanted to help. We came to this country when I was a little boy, after the revolution. Everything I had—my job, my education—was thanks to this country."

He pursed his lips and reluctantly continued. "I went to base camp in Georgia and was shipped out two months later. Some of the guys in my platoon, we became friends. Williams, he shared the oatmeal-raisin cookies his mother baked for him every week. Thompson, he was a Christian. We had long conversations about God."

Deep lines materialized on his face. These were painful memories for him, Henry could tell.

"I was everything we were fighting against: Middle Eastern. Muslim. I started getting hassled. They kept teasing that I was

Al-Qaeda, I was going to join the Taliban. Someone stole my Koran and wrote . . . nasty things in it."

Henry's chest squeezed with sympathy. He could picture Robert doing just that.

"Couldn't you say anything?" Samira interjected.

Henry knew the answer to that one. If he tattled to Coach about another player, he'd only make it ten times worse for himself.

His father's eyes were worn and sad. "No, Samira-joon. It wouldn't help. I said, 'I'll keep my head down.' We went on patrols through the cornfields; I took my shift in the guard tower every night." He glanced up at the guards on the platform and grimaced. "One morning, we were on patrol. We stopped at a local village to talk with the elder. They usually told us if they had information. He said he didn't but asked if we wanted warm bread and chai with milk and sugar." He had to smile. "You would not believe the luxury real chai with milk and sugar is over there. We all sat and ate our bread and drank our tea, and I was happy because many of the guys had called the Afghans 'savages' and 'animals.' I was happy this elder had shown us kindness."

His face contorted. "As soon as we got outside the village, we were ambushed. He had set us up, this elder who had served us bread and tea. We took two casualties: one of them was Thompson." He choked up. "His limbs were blown off."

"Oh, God," Samira cried.

Henry was speechless.

Mohammed's voice broke. "We waited for the helicopter to come. Everyone was in shock. We had lost two of our *brothers*. They started calling me 'traitor'—even Williams—accused me of setting them up. They said I was Taliban. They tried to convince the CO, our commanding officer, to court-martial me."

"They wanted you *arrested*? For what?" Henry asked.

"Nielson." The family at the next table was called for their photo.

Mohammed waited for their chatter to subside before continuing. "It didn't matter. They wanted someone to pay. Everyone in my platoon thought I was guilty. I *felt* guilty. It was my fault. How stupid I was to trust the elder, to ask others to trust him; to stop for bread and tea. Every night, as soon as I closed my eyes, all I could see was Thompson's body, blown to bits."

Samira wiped her eyes again with her sleeve.

A storm cloud rolled across Mohammed's face. "I started to derail. I was late. Sloppy. I disobeyed my CO. I *was* court-martialed. My JAG—my attorney—negotiated an early discharge." He shook his head sadly. "I wish I could tell you everything got better after that. It got worse. I got angrier and angrier. Angry at the way I was treated, angry at everyone's ignorance, angry I wasn't allowed to pray when I was called to prayer, and I—"

"Haywood," the voice said over the PA as another inmate was called for his portrait.

Mohammed closed his eyes again. "There is never a moment of peace in here." He centered himself and continued. "Anger was easier to express than guilt. The anger was outward." He tapped his chest. "The guilt was in here." He brushed the photograph of him and Kamron again. "That must be what Kamron remembers. The anger. The drinking."

"And the motel incident," Samira murmured.

Mohammed's face sank. "Yes. The motel incident. I was out

of my mind, Samira. If she were here, I would beg your mother for forgiveness. She cut off all contact with me. I don't blame her."

He turned to Henry. "I was not in a good place when I met your mother, Henry-jon. I felt . . . liberated with her. But I was drinking too much." He looked down at the photograph of the two of them. "When Robert and Jeannie took custody of you, I moved back to Fresno. I thought . . ." His voice caught, his eyes watered. "I thought, I'm losing another child. I wanted to take you for the weekend, but I didn't have visitation." His eyes bored into Henry. "I took you anyway. I wasn't prepared. I didn't have a car seat. A high chair. Baby food, enough diapers. And I was drinking too much." He squeezed his eyes shut. "Your mother refused to call the authorities on me. Robert and Jeannie came to get you."

Henry's face twisted. He had never heard this story before.

"It's a good thing," Mohammed assured him. "CPS might have put you in foster care if they had found you with me. Please thank them for that."

Mom and Dad had not *stolen* him. They had *rescued* him? Henry would need more time to process that revelation.

"Fresno. Is that where our, um, our grandmother lives?" Henry asked.

Their father lit up. "Yes, yes. Your maman bozorg, your grandmother, is in Fresno. And your Amme Daria, your auntie. She's in San Francisco. They miss you—and Kamron—every day. *I* miss you every day. And I hope, Samira-joon, Henry-jon, one day you—and your mothers—can forgive me, and I can be your father, your babah, again."

"I want to get to *know* you," Henry declared.

Samira said nothing. She seemed overwhelmed.

Their father's face softened. "We can get to know each other."

Just then, the scent of a microwave cheeseburger reminded Henry. "Oh, Dad. Are you hungry? Can I get you something from the vending machines?"

"Henry-jon, I . . . I . . ." Mohammed wiped his eyes with a shaky hand. "When you call me Dad, it . . . it's poetry to me."

"I have your book of poems by Hafez," Henry said excitedly. "Mama gave it to me. The highlighted passages were like messages from you."

His father smiled warmly at him and glanced upward, as if he were trying to remember something. Then, in a very soft voice he said:

> *"Your love*
> *Should never be offered to the mouth of a*
> *Stranger,*
> *Only to someone*
> *Who has the valor and daring*
> *To cut pieces of their soul off with a knife*
> *Then weave them into a blanket*
> *To protect you."*

His eyes welled with tears. "Samira-joon, Henry-jon. I don't want to be a stranger to you. I want to be a father who will cut off a piece of my *soul* and weave it into a blanket to protect you, I promise."

Henry swallowed hard to block the tsunami that was coming. Samira squeezed his hand.

Mohammed lightly touched the photographs again. "Now, please. Tell me about *you*."

Henry and Samira looked at each other. Henry was at a loss for where to begin.

Samira piped up, "Henry got a hockey scholarship to the University of Denver."

"Samira," Henry muttered under his breath. Who knew whether he was still going?

"Hockey." Mohammed nodded. "I don't know much about the game, but I think it's something like soccer. You must be very, very good, Henry-jon."

"And Samira is deferring enrollment to Lewis & Clark," Henry said.

Samira flashed him a look of confusion over "deferring" instead of "declining."

"I'm very proud of both of you. I—"

"Safavi," the guard called. It was their turn for the Polaroid portrait.

"Oh," Mohammed said with a tinge of embarrassment, "we don't have to."

Samira stood up. "Yes, we do."

Their father broke into a wide smile. "Yes, Samira-joon."

They made their way to the photographer, who gestured to the X's on the floor in front of the waterfall backdrop. Henry and Samira stood on either side of their father.

"And who do we have here?" the photographer asked as he looked through the viewfinder.

Keeping his hands clasped in front of him so as not to touch Henry or Samira—as the signs instructed—Mohammed beamed and announced, "We are the Safavis."

Henry was grinning from ear to ear.

CHAPTER THIRTY-SEVEN

Samira

Hold on." Samira laugh-cried as she wiped her eyes with her sleeve again.

"Of course, your mothers raised you," Mohammed rushed to correct himself. He pointed to Samira and Henry. "You are Samira Murphy, and you are Henry Owen, but we . . ." He motioned in a circle to the three of them. "We are . . ." He trailed off, embarrassed.

"We are the Safavis," she said. There *was* something about her connection with Henry and her father that was different—not better, just different—from what she had with Mom and Gran.

Hopefully, one day Kamron would feel the same way.

The photographer snapped the first shot and waved the Polaroid around to dry while the image of Samira, Henry, and their father slowly revealed itself.

"Have you ever seen one of these before?" their father teased. "It's before your time."

Time. The minute the photographer snapped the second shot, Samira turned to him and said, "When do you get out of here?"

Mohammed nodded to the photographer. "Let him get the last shot, Samira-joon. Other families are waiting."

After he did, Samira begged for one more. "I need it for my

brother." Wait till she told Kamron everything she had learned about their father.

"Sorry, one per person," the photographer said, and handed them their prints.

Samira wilted.

"Here, he can have mine," Henry said during their walk back to their table. "You can text me a picture of yours."

"Five more minutes, Safavi," the guard said as soon as they sat down.

"Five minutes?" Samira cried. It had gone by so quickly. "When do you get out?"

Mohammed rubbed his eyes. "I was sentenced to ten years on August 31, 2017. I've been up for parole twice. They don't even meet with me, the parole board. They look at my priors, and . . ." He trailed off, then forced a smile. "I'll be out on August 31, 2027."

"That's not that long," Henry said.

"All right, Inmate Safavi. Say your goodbyes," the guard said, and stood behind him.

Once again, the grief and sadness of the place overtook Samira. This time it was personal. They had only just begun to cram a lifetime into less than an hour.

They all stood up. Samira looked past her father at the guard. "Are we allowed to . . . ?"

The guard nodded.

She wrapped her arms around her father and nestled into his neck to recreate the father/daughter moment from the video she had so desperately needed.

"Dokhtar, Samira eshgham," her father said gently. "Dooset daram, I love you." He took her face in his hands. "Please tell Kamron his father loves him and thinks about him every day."

"I will," she said, tears running down her face.

He kissed her on each cheek, then pulled Henry in for an embrace. He put a hand to Henry's face and said, "Henry-jon, my beloved son. I thank God, praise be to Allah, you found me. And each other."

"Time," the guard said. "Let's go, Safavi."

Their father was ushered away to be searched before returning to his cell. He looked stricken. "Please write," he said with an urgency that cut Samira's heart in two.

"We will," she vowed.

Henry couldn't speak.

∞

They didn't say much on their walk back to the waiting area. Henry must have been replaying every moment of their visit, too. While he retrieved his phone and wallet from the locker, Samira took in the families spread out on the hard plastic chairs, some of whom must have driven for days to see their loved ones. This place was going to become very familiar.

Once they got to the parking lot, she glanced back at the prison. The barbed wire and guard tower still made her nauseous. She took the Polaroid out of her back pocket. Her father's smile comforted her.

When they climbed into the Subaru, Henry turned to Samira and said, "Thank you."

She fastened her seat belt and pulled her phone out of the glove box. "What did I do?" There were several texts from Tara and Gran and Mom. She would answer them all later. She closed her eyes. She needed a nap.

"We wouldn't have been able to come if it weren't for you." He rolled out of the lot and headed back to the freeway.

Samira opened one eye. "You're the one who found him."

"You're the one who jumped in my truck and said, 'Drive.'"

Now it was a game. "You're the one who drove." Samira giggled.

"You're the one who said the thing about the therapist's office," Henry countered.

"You're the one who sent the text." Samira laughed, determined to one-up him.

"We make a great team," Henry pronounced.

Suddenly, she noticed the time. "Henry! We've got to get home by three. It's almost eleven."

"Mmmm-hmm, I know," Henry said.

"Then what are you doing?" she said with alarm. "I'm not trying to be bossy or anything, I swear, but we're supposed to be getting on Five South. You just got on Five North."

"We're making a stop," Henry said. A little smile played at his lips.

Samira looked behind them as the on-ramp for the correct freeway receded farther into the distance. "Your dad is going to shit."

What was Henry doing? What could possibly be worth making the harsh sentence his asshole dad would hand down even worse? Just as she was about to tell him he was an idiot, her jaw hit the floor. "Henry, no," she said. Her eyes stung. How were there any more tears left to cry?

They were driving through the gates of Lewis & Clark College.

"It's May first," Henry said, guiding them to the visitor lot. "And *I* care that you blew up your college admission. You're going to go in there and tell them you'll be back in two years."

Samira gaped at the verdant grounds and stately Frank

Manor House she'd fallen in love with on the college tour. "You're smart, Samira," Henry said. "You'll get another scholarship. You'll only need two years of expenses instead of four. You have two years to save."

"Henry," she said, laughing through her tears. "You're going to be in so much trouble."

He put the car in park. "What can he do, kill me?"

She stared out the windshield at students crisscrossing the campus and grabbed his hand. "Will you come with me?"

"Of course."

She pulled down the passenger visor and frowned at her reflection in the mini vanity mirror. "Oh God. I look awful. Why didn't I listen to Tara about the concealer and the mascara?"

"You look fine." Henry laughed. "C'mon."

He put his arm around her shoulder and accompanied her to the admissions office.

"I think my long speech about why I had to decline enrollment but would be back in two years was wasted on that admissions clerk," Samira said with a laugh as they made their way back to the car. In response, the clerk had said simply, *Sure, hon. Come back when you're ready.*

"At least you made the commitment to yourself." Henry climbed into the driver's seat and navigated out of the lot.

Samira yawned. "You can go to Dubai with Tara for your gap year." She closed her eyes. She really needed a nap. They neared Salem and passed the exit for the prison. "He was . . . shorter than I expected," Samira said.

"Yeah, shorter," Henry agreed. "And his voice was softer."

When the prison was well in the rearview, she said, "Did this change anything for you?"

Without hesitation, Henry said, "It changed everything."

Samira reflected on this for a moment. "Yeah. For me, too."

The open road rushing toward them hypnotized her for the next hundred miles until Henry's phone started buzzing with texts. "Your dad is on the ground in Medford," she reported. "We're at least forty minutes from Medford."

Henry chewed the inside of his cheek. "Can we go straight to Yreka? It'd be faster if we didn't have to pick up your mom. Only if you feel comfortable driving back to Ashland."

"Yes, Dad. I'll be fine," she said with mock exasperation. Another text came through from Henry's dad. "He's at the rental car counter," Samira said.

Henry nodded. He was really going to town on that cheek, which reminded Samira: time for another Benadryl. She rummaged around in her purse for the pink packet. Only, she wasn't that itchy. Something had shifted. The anxiety that had gnawed at her all her life was lifting. And anyway, even if it weren't, she had to find a better coping mechanism. How could she expect Kamron not to drink when she was popping pink pills all day?

"When can we come back up to visit?" Henry sounded anxious to lock down a date.

"This summer, I think," Samira said. "We can stay with my mom."

"I can pick you up again," Henry said. His shoulders sagged. "If I still have my truck."

His phone buzzed with another text. "He just got on the freeway," Samira said. "He's—"

"*Okay*," Henry said. "I don't need a play-by-play." He exhaled and made a bumblebee sound. "Sorry. I already know what's coming."

Sure enough, at 4:37 p.m. Robert texted, Here in Yreka, where are you?

At 4:45 p.m.: Hotel said you never occupied your room.

At 4:50 p.m.: goddammit Henry you better have a good explanation.

Finally, at 5:03 p.m., he called. "Where in the hell are you?" he said as soon as Henry answered.

"I'm almost there," Henry replied.

"You better have a good goddamn explanation when you get here."

"Yes, sir," Henry said with remarkable calm. "I do have a good explanation."

They hung up.

Samira restrained herself from saying, *What an asshole.*

"Listen," Henry said. "No matter what happens, I'm glad I came."

"Me, too, Henry," Samira said as fervently as she had ever said anything. "Me, too."

CHAPTER THIRTY-EIGHT

Henry

Is that him?" Samira asked of the man sitting in the bright blue Chevy Cruze rental car parked in front of what would have been Henry's room at the Yreka Motel. He had backed into the space to spot Henry on arrival.

"That's him," Henry said. He pulled up perpendicular to Robert so Samira could drive straight out of the lot. "He looks mean," she whispered.

Robert did not move from the driver's seat. He stared, almost unblinking, at Henry, who formulated his strategy. "We're going to get out at the same time," he said quietly. "I'm going to introduce you as my half sister." This would throw him off guard. "When I move away from the driver's side, you climb in and go."

Samira's eyes were wide with worry. "Don't you think I should stay in case I need to, like, call the police or something?"

"He's not going to beat me." Henry half laughed. "I don't think."

"He called the police on you." Samira scowled.

He grabbed her hand. "Hey. I'll be okay. I'll call you as soon as I can." He gave her hand a squeeze. "Ready?"

She gulped. "Ready."

They opened their doors in a synchronized fashion. As soon as they got out, Robert did the same. He leaned his elbows on the driver's side window and roof of the car, nodded to Samira, and said, "You want to tell me who this is?"

Clearly, he thought Samira was some girl Henry had picked up along the way, as Henry had anticipated. Loudly—and proudly—he said, "This is Samira. She's my half sister. We found each other through a DNA test."

Robert registered the combination of shock and recognition Henry knew he would. He slowly took his elbows off the driver's side door and closed it.

"We went looking for our father," Henry said with a tinge of defiance. "And found him."

Robert turned the whitest shade of pale Henry had ever seen. His strategy of shock and awe was working.

"It's nice to meet you, Mr. Owen," Samira called out. She scurried around to the driver's side when Henry moved away from it. He handed her the keys. "Are you sure you don't want me to stay?" she said under her breath.

"No, it's fine. Go."

She threw her arms around him and, through tears, whispered, *"Remember, we are the Safavis."*

Henry choked up and whispered back, *"We are."*

He waited for her to get safely in the driver's seat before grabbing his duffel bag and patting the roof twice to signal all clear. "Jesus," he muttered when she nearly sideswiped a Prius pulling out of the lot.

Henry climbed into the passenger seat. Robert stood outside working on an apology for calling the cops on him, hopefully, now that he understood why Henry had needed more time.

When he finally got in the car, he put the keys in the ignition, then took them back out. He paused as if there were something he wanted to say.

Henry had rattled him. Good.

He put the keys back in and started the car. "Let's get the truck."

That was *it*? Not a word about Henry's revelation? Or Robert having him arrested?

Robert was tight-lipped during their drive to the station. When an officer drove the truck out of storage, Robert instructed Henry to get in the truck and follow him to the Budget rental agency in Redding, where they would return the Chevy Cruze. "I'll drive the rest of the way," he said.

Henry climbed into his truck now deeply unnerved. Robert expected—no, *demanded*—respect. He must think Henry had disrespected him by searching for Mohammed Safavi. *After everything your mother and I have done for you,* he would say.

His mind raced as he followed Robert to Redding. *Dammit.* He had a right to search for his biological father, didn't he? If he hadn't, he never would have found Samira.

Robert probably wasn't happy about *her,* either.

After they arrived at Budget, Henry switched to the passenger side of the truck and braced himself for a lecture about how ungrateful he had been and how hurt his mother would be when she found out what he had done.

Instead, Robert climbed into the driver's side and headed back to the freeway without a word. Nearly an hour ticked by. Henry stared out the passenger-side window. A growing sense of dread was spreading from the center of his abdomen outward. He may have miscalculated. Badly. How could he have thought reuniting with Mohammed Safavi would be anything but a slap in the face to them?

"Are you hungry?" Robert asked as they drove through Chico. He sounded mad.

How the hell could he be mad after everything Henry had told him?

"No," Henry said without looking at him.

"We're stopping in Stockton for the night. The halfway point," Robert said. "You can get something there."

His phone buzzed with a text from Samira: the Polaroid of the two of them with their father.

Fine. If Robert and Jeannie were going to disown him—as he had always feared they would—let them. An entirely new family was forming anyway.

They sat in stone-cold silence for the rest of the drive and pulled into the Stockton Marriot just before 10 p.m. As soon as they got to the room, Henry threw his duffel bag on the bed next to the door in case he wanted to escape. Daniel could come pick him up. Henry could stay with him for a few days until he figured out what to do next.

Robert put his bag on the bed next to the bathroom and disappeared inside.

He hadn't said *one word* about Henry having found Moham-med.

Henry googled closest In-N-Out and found one a mile away. Open till eleven. He would walk there to get some fresh air and distance from Robert.

As soon as Robert came out of the bathroom, Henry stood up. "There's an In-N-Out down the street. I'll walk."

Before he got to the door, in a voice so quiet Henry could hardly hear him, Robert said, "Your mom couldn't have children, you know. Jeannie. Had several miscarriages. The last one was when she was seven months along. Broke her heart."

Henry froze.

"When she told me, 'Nancy's really struggling with her baby. We have to help,' I didn't want to. The miscarriage was too painful. But your mother insisted." Henry turned back toward Robert, whose face was twisted with sorrow. "As soon as I saw you, I knew I was meant to raise you. I'm not saying I was there to replace your father, but I knew you were my boy."

Henry stood there, speechless.

Robert rubbed his chin and stared past Henry. "When I was little, my brother, Earl, and I—your uncle Earl, you met him once—we'd play with Matchbox cars for hours," he said with a faint smile. "We really thought we were race car drivers. In our own little world." The smile quickly receded. "My dad would come home from the Chevy plant every day at five-thirty sharp. Clock out at five, home by five-thirty. First thing he'd do was pour himself a shot of Jack Daniel's. Then another. Get good and drunk before dinner. Every night."

Henry did not move or utter a sound. His dad had never opened up to him like this before.

"We were two little boys. You knew we were going to do something stupid: throw peas at each other. Laugh until milk came out of our nose." His eyes watered. "He'd yank one of us right out of our seat—usually my brother, which made me feel guilty as hell since I was older—take us out to his gym in the garage, and give us a whipping with the pulleys from his rower."

Henry flinched.

"Your father, Mohammed, he drank a lot. He lost his temper. A *lot*. I felt like it was my duty to protect you from him. From *becoming* him." He looked away; he was struggling to find the right words. "The Marines taught me how to be a man, but . . . Goddammit, no, they didn't. They taught me how to follow orders. *No one* ever taught me how to be a dad, and if I was too hard on you, I . . . I never . . ." He closed his eyes to stop the tears that seeped out anyway. "Henry, I never thought about how hard it would be for you to lose your dad because I thought, 'Well, *I'm* his dad.'"

Henry had never, *ever* seen his dad cry. In fact, he had thought him incapable of it. And now his dad was crying *over him*.

"But you . . . you called *the police* on me," Henry said, trying to reconcile the man who did that with the man standing in front of him, weeping.

"I wasn't going to press charges, Henry. I swear," he said with his right hand up. "We didn't know how else to find you. We were desperate. Your mother was worried . . ." He choked up again. "Your mother was worried, you know, you might do something . . . drastic."

Because of his depression.

Everything Mom and Dad had done for him was being cast in a new light. All his life, Henry had thought Robert barely tolerated him, when the truth was he was trying to protect Henry the best way he knew how.

And just as Henry's heart was softening, it hardened again. The Facebook posts.

"He had PTSD from his time in the army, Mohammed did. As a Muslim," Henry said pointedly. "It was hard. He took a lot of shit for it." He swallowed nervously. Was he really going to say it?

He was. "I've seen your Facebook posts."

Robert's face reddened with embarrassment. "I . . . my friends post stuff, and I . . ." He trailed off, seemed to recognize that he had no defense. "I'm sorry about that, Henry." He looked Henry right in the eye. "I'm *really* sorry. I . . . I'm going to delete that account."

They held a look.

Henry had never been able to talk to his dad like this. To confide in him, confront him, even.

After a long, contemplative beat, he motioned to the door. "You hungry?"

Robert's face relaxed into the hint of a smile. "Uh, yeah. I am. Let me wash up."

During their walk to In-N-Out, Henry filled in his dad on how he had found Samira, and how they had found Mohammed. "He's in recovery now," Henry said. "He . . . he said I might have wound up in foster care if you and Mom hadn't rescued me in Fresno. He said to thank you for that."

There would be a day when Robert and Mohammed would meet again, and Henry might as well start to smooth things over for when that day came.

Robert took it all in, listening intently, saying very little.

When they sat down at a table to wait for their order, it hit Henry. "Jesus. I have forty-two minutes to accept admission at U of D."

"Oh?" Robert said with a raised brow. Of course, he thought Henry had already accepted.

There was one way to find out if Robert really *had* changed, or if he was going to lecture Henry about getting off track and losing his scholarship. "I'd like to defer enrollment, Dad. Maybe take a gap year," he said, and waited to exhale.

"Okay, son," Robert said, even if it was with some disappointment.

Henry quickly changed the subject before Robert could

change his mind. As they wolfed down their burgers, he told his dad about the prison, the double gates, and the invisible ink.

When they walked back to the hotel, Henry felt compelled to tell him, "I'll call Mohammed 'babah.' It's Farsi for father. You're still my dad."

Robert draped an arm around Henry's shoulder. "I'll always be your dad, Henry," he said.

For the first time since he could remember, Henry didn't feel as if he were on probation. The heaviness, the nothingness was lifting. His biological father loved him. And so did his dad.

Later, when Henry was updating Linh on everything that had elapsed over the previous forty-eight hours, Mama texted, you okay?

By now, Dad had told Mom about Mohammed, and she must have told Mama. Henry texted back: yes, found my half sister through dna test & we found dad. not a millionaire 😔.

Little dots swirled for several minutes as she read his message and seemed to be composing a lengthy reply. But all Mama texted back was, I know . . . I wanted you to be proud of him.

Henry tapped his camera roll and brought up the image of him and Samira with their father, a man who had taken responsibility for his actions and was in recovery, who had defended his country and cared for his dad. A man who loved poetry. A true patriot.

A powerful warmth filled Henry's chest, and he replied simply, I am.

CHAPTER THIRTY-NINE
Samira

Since Mom didn't drink coffee, Samira sipped the tea she had steeped for fifteen minutes—it still wasn't strong enough—while waiting for her. They needed to get an early start home.

They had agreed that Samira would tell Kamron about their father, and Mom would tell Gran and Uncle Chris. They had the entire drive to figure out how.

Tea spilled over Samira's commuter mug when Mom came out of her bedroom lugging the large Samsonite suitcase that matched the one Kamron had taken to Sunrise Acres.

"Overkill for overnight," Samira said. Her mother never stayed longer than a day or two.

"I know. I got someone to sub for me these last two weeks of the year. I'm going to stay until after Kam gets out of recovery," she said with a hopeful smile.

"Oh. Oh good," Samira said, as hope blossomed inside her, too.

They piled everything into the Subaru. Mom drove; Samira spent the drive texting Henry and Tara and writing a long email to Mrs. Sandoval explaining the events of the past several weeks.

To her surprise, Mrs. Sandoval replied: Thanks for sharing,

Huh. Tara was right about asking for help. She had been right about Henry, too. And, of course, the Glossier concealer. Maybe Samira needed to listen to her—and ask for help—more often.

Before she knew it, they were within an hour of Santa Rosa. Samira had not thought *at all* about what to tell Kamron about their father. How could she when Kamron could barely stand the mention of his name?

She would show him the Polaroid and try to explain why he was not the monster Kamron remembered.

Of course, Gran was waiting for them on the front porch when they arrived. Samira nearly collapsed into her arms. "I'm sorry for leaving you with Kamron," she said, her voice breaking.

Gran hugged her tight. "We got along fine. I'm glad your mother got to meet Henry." She took Samira's face in her hands. "Are you okay, honey?"

Samira nodded. Except for the tears sliding down her cheeks, she was.

Gran beamed. "Well, Kamron is in his room, and the Spanish rice is in the oven." She turned to Mom as Samira headed inside. "Here, honey, let me help you with that."

"Thanks, Mom. Listen, I need to talk to you," her mother said, and she and Gran headed into the kitchen.

Samira went straight to her bedroom and tossed her bag on the bed. She caught a glimpse of herself in the mirror. Dark circles and tangles aside, something about her was different. So much had happened over the last three days. She had to tell Kamron. Somehow, the words would come. She made her way down the hall and knocked lightly on his door.

No answer.

She knocked again, louder. "Kamron?" she called out.

Still no answer.

Shit. Had he escaped?

She burst the door open.

He was in bed with his headphones on playing *Doom*. He pulled the headphones down around his neck. "Hey," he said sheepishly.

"Hey," she said. She took a few more steps inside.

He made a hissing sound as he exhaled. "I'm sorry. For the freakout and that I left."

She sat on the edge of his bed. "It's okay."

He set his laptop aside. "They're, um, letting me back in. I don't know if you heard."

"I heard."

It was weird. She looked at him differently now, too. Not as a UF but as someone who had known the love and the light of their father—and, yes, the darkness—and then it was suddenly extinguished, which must have been devastating.

She touched his forearm. "Kam, I'm sorry for saying I knew you wouldn't make it. I haven't been very understanding of . . . of everything you've gone through."

He offered her a grateful smile; they sat for a second in silence as Samira mentally rehearsed what to say and how to say it.

"But Kam, we found him," she said simply. "Our father. Me and Henry. In Oregon."

Kamron's whole face furrowed with confusion.

"He's in prison. For a DUI. He hit someone. He told us all about it: the drinking, the rage. He had PTSD, but he's in recovery."

Kamron stared at her for a long beat before pulling his headphones back up. "I don't care."

"Kamron, listen." She pulled his headphones back down. "The army, they blamed him for something that was not his fault. He was on patrol with his platoon. He was the only one who spoke Dari. He was talking to a village elder one day and—"

"I don't *care*," Kamron said, scrambling out of bed as if the monster had burst out of the closet and come roaring back to life.

Samira spoke louder and faster. "The village elder, he served them bread and tea. But it was a setup. They were ambushed. Two soldiers *died*. One of them was his friend."

Kamron started pacing back and forth. "I don't care, I don't care," he said with his hands over his ears.

"Kamron, listen to me, *please*." Samira stood up. "Everyone called him a traitor. He was court-martialed. It wasn't fair. That's why he was so angry. He started drinking, and—"

"You don't remember!" Kamron pointed an accusatory finger at her. Hot, angry tears rolled down his cheeks. "I do. He scared the *fuck* out of me and Mom. She was always crying."

She took his other hand. "I know, I *know*. But Kamron, he's sorry for what he did. He loves you; I swear. He loves all three of us: you, me, Henry."

He jerked his hand away. "No, he doesn't."

She struggled to stay calm. If only he would listen. "He has all our baby pictures, the one with you playing soccer. He said they're the only thing that's gotten him through."

"It's bullshit," he said, his face wrenched with pain and anger.

"He attends twelve-step meetings in prison, he's in counseling for the PTSD. He's *changed*." She shoved the Polaroid in Kamron's face. "Look," she begged him.

He reared back.

"Kamron." She closed her eyes. "You don't have to write him or visit or even talk to him if you don't want to. I just want you to know we were *loved*. Our father *loved* us. He loved *you*. He still does. And that . . . that changes everything."

Slowly, reluctantly, Kamron accepted the Polaroid. Samira remained perfectly still while he reckoned with it. He sat down on the bed clutching the image.

He held up the Polaroid. "Is this mine?" She nodded.

She gazed at him a moment before retreating to her room. Samira could only imagine what it was like for him to see their father in a whole new light, as she had; for Kamron to realize he was not the monster in the closet. Only a man who had been terribly, tragically misunderstood.

Kamron had the most family members at Family Week: Samira, Mom, and Gran. They sat in a large open room with their chairs arranged in a semicircle around a brick fireplace, above which hung a portrait of a Sonoma sunrise glinting across the vineyards.

Samira kept careful watch on Kamron, who seemed fragile and raw, but was no longer trying to scam his way out of the place.

As it turned out, Hartford Blakey, the admissions director, was also their counselor. He started by asking each family member to introduce themselves and share why they had come. For Samira, that was simple: "I'm here for my brother," she said, smiling at Kamron.

Hartford clasped his hands behind his head. "You're here for *him* when you should be here for *you*. Kamron has learned he is here for himself."

Samira bristled. Clearly, Hartford did not understand the situation. "I know, but my grandfather asked me to help him, you know . . . with this. It was his dying wish."

Kamron looked down.

Hartford nodded thoughtfully. "How old are you, Samira?"

She glanced uneasily at Gran. Clearly, a trick question. "Seventeen."

He leaned toward her and rested his arms on his thighs. "You're still a kid. If the adults in your life asked you to stand in for them, they *failed* you."

Samira's face turned red hot. "No, they didn't."

"They did. If your grandfather was asking *you* to do adult things like manage your alcoholic brother's recovery, he *failed* you." He turned to Mom and Gran. "And, sorry, Mom and Gran, but if you allowed her to take on that responsibility, you failed her, too."

Samira was speechless. Also, weren't they supposed to be talking about Kamron?

Her mother's eyes filled with tears. "I'm so sorry, baby," she said.

Gran's eyes flashed red with anger. She pointed an accusing finger at Hartford. "You don't know my husband. He was a good man. And Samira is a *very* capable young woman." She stood up and collected her purse. "I need the ladies' room," she said, indignant, and left.

Mom flashed Samira a look of apology and followed her. "I'll be back."

Kamron mouthed "sorry."

Hartford seemed energized by the defection. "It's not a successful Family Week unless someone walks out. She'll be back. Families, take note," he said. "We're going to learn a lot about what you *own* this week. Spoiler alert: it's not your family member's recovery."

Over the next couple of days, Hartford chided Samira for arranging Kamron's AA meetings and urged *her* to attend Al-Anon for her co-dependence. He instructed Gran to set firmer boundaries, and for all of them to make a plan for when Kamron eventually relapsed—because he *would* relapse.

On the third day, Samira began to accept that he might be right. While she wouldn't be a UF anytime soon, she was developing a clearer sense of what was her responsibility and, more important, what wasn't, which was like cutting an anchor loose that had weighed her down for years.

The week concluded with the ninth of the Twelve Steps: amends. "You'll each sit opposite your loved one, who will read a prepared statement to you," Hartford explained. "All you need to do is listen without judgment and maintain eye contact."

Kamron went last, after a middle-aged man apologized to his wife for blowing their retirement savings on his coke habit.

Mom sat across from Kamron. Their knees touched. His hands shook as they had during his arraignment. He acknowledged how badly he had behaved over the last several years. "I didn't understand Dad's struggle with PTSD," he said. "I was hurt and scared and took things personally that weren't personal at all."

Samira could say the same.

"Here are the amends I want to make to you, Mom: I

apologize for shutting you out. I apologize for saying I hated you. I apologize for directing all my anger and hurt over Dad toward you. The truth is . . ." He paused. He couldn't speak.

"Baby," Mom said gently.

"The truth is, I love you, Mom." His face was wet with tears. "I miss you. I want you back in my life."

Mom took his hand. "I want the same."

Gran went next. Kamron apologized for yelling at her, for being disrespectful, for taking the keys to the Kia without her permission, for driving drunk and making her bail him out. Gran murmured, "It's okay, honey," "I know," and "I understand" after every amend. If Kamron were a serial killer, Gran would find a way to forgive him. That's what grandmothers do.

Samira had the most difficulty maintaining eye contact. She was working on her co-dependence; she was. Kamron's raw vulnerability made it hard.

"I'm sorry for yelling at you," he read from his prepared statement, "for being an asshole about AA. And Henry. And our dad. For driving drunk and making you come to county jail. And most of all, for making you give up your college dream so I could be here."

Samira stopped herself from saying "It's okay" and let him take responsibility.

"I . . . I promise I'll pay you back." Then Kamron put down his handwritten note and spoke straight from the heart. "Sami, you're my little sister and I've failed you. I want to be someone you look up to. Someone you come to for advice. Someone who has your back." Kamron wiped his eyes with a trembling hand. "I want to be your big brother again."

Samira threw her arms around Kamron and held on as if

they had just been rescued from a desert island. In a way, they had.

She had come to Family Week believing she was there to support Kamron. She left knowing she had come for herself—and with a referral from Hartford Blakey to a local chapter of Al-Anon.

◐◑

"Woo! Go, Henry! Go, Daniel," Tara, Linh, and Nancy shouted when Henry and Daniel skated onto the ice for the opening ceremony of the Labor Day weekend tournament at Snoopy's Home Ice in Santa Rosa.

Samira's enthusiasm was more muted. She was sitting with Henry's parents. She felt obligated since they had agreed to pay for Henry to fly home (instead of driving back with Linh) so he could stay two extra nights with her and two more in Ashland to visit their father.

Tara and Linh snapped together like two magnets and spent the entire game gabbing about Tara's trip abroad (she was leaving in two weeks), Glossier makeup, and double dating with the cashier from Mary's Pizza (the one with the lion tattoo) the next time Linh and Henry visited.

Henry had warned Samira his parents weren't too sociable, and they didn't talk much at first. Then, out of nowhere, in the middle of the second period, his mother said, "Henry is allergic to cats, you know."

"Is he?" Samira said, unsure what to do with this information.

"Oh yes," Jeannie said, eyes on Henry the entire time. "We had a beautiful Russian Blue when he was little. It made his eyes water and his nose run. I said, get rid of it. He begged us not to." Her face toggled from anxious to proud. "He had to get allergy shots every week. He would turn his little head and have this stoic look on his face. But he never cried." She let out a little sigh. "We did our best," she said, almost to herself as much as to Samira.

"It shows," Samira said with a warm smile. "He's great."

Apparently, that was the icebreaker Jeannie needed. She spent the rest of the game sharing sweet anecdotes about Henry, like the time he slept on the floor next to his hamster's cage for a month so he wouldn't be lonely.

Samira was so caught up in her conversation with Jeannie, she didn't notice the game had ended: Ice Devils on top, 4–1. Henry had gotten a goal and two assists.

Everyone gathered in the Warm Puppy Café for snacks and hot cocoa afterward, where Henry excitedly introduced Samira to Daniel, Coach Nielson, and the other players.

Afterward, Tara and Linh came marching over, arms wrapped around each other's shoulders. "We're here to remind you," Tara boomed. She giggled at Linh. "Tell 'em."

"You have *us* to thank for meeting each other," Linh boasted.

Henry turned to Samira. "That's true," he said.

"And we thank you both," Samira said with a deep curtsy.

"This calls for another round of hot chocolate," Tara pronounced as if by royal proclamation. She and Linh went skipping off to the counter arm in arm.

Henry had to laugh. "They must have gotten high in Linh's Lexus between periods," he whispered so his parents wouldn't hear him.

Daniel drifted over. "Dude, Linh's gonna leave your ass for Tara," he teased.

"She might," Henry said, playing along.

Samira nodded to Jeannie, who was standing off to the side

with Robert. "Your mom told me about your incredible act of bravery in the face of your life-threatening cat allergy."

Henry shook his head. "She loves that story."

"She really loves you, you know."

Henry regarded her with compassion. "I know."

When the coach called Henry and Daniel over, Nancy made her way to Samira. "How'd you like the game?" she asked.

"Very exciting," Samira said. Jeannie was watching them. This was the first time Samira had met his moms and she was already feeling the tension Henry must feel trying to satisfy them both.

Nancy stood there for a moment. Before the silence became too awkward, she said, "I didn't know about her, you know. Your mom."

Samira nodded. What else could she do?

"If I had, I wouldn't have . . ." Like Jeannie, her eyes remained fixed on Henry. "Or I don't know. Maybe I would have. That's how we got Henry."

Samira allowed a smile.

"He said you're going to see Daria tomorrow?"

Their Amme Daria was throwing a luncheon in their honor the next day in San Francisco with their cousins and assorted aunties and uncles. Their grandmother was driving up from Fresno. "Don't eat for a week," Samira's father had told them during their last video chat. "Maman will be cooking the whole month."

He was right.

There must have been twenty people stuffed into Daria's tiny apartment. Everyone hugged and kissed Samira and Henry on each cheek and gushed over them in Farsi. Amme Daria, who was impossibly chic like Tara's mother, cried the minute she saw them. Their grandmother kept telling Samira how beautiful she was ("Shoma ziba hasti," she said over and over) and Henry how much he looked like their father. Her hair was wiry and gray, but she covered it with a brightly colored mosaic silk scarf.

She made tahchin, a huge rice cake stuffed with chicken and yogurt (which also sounded like a Gran thing but was actually delicious) and rice layered with tart cherries because Samira's father had told her grandmother that cherry rice was Samira's favorite, plus bowls of pickled vegetables and yogurt with mint and cucumber. And doogh.

During dinner, Amme Daria stood in the dining room with Samira and Henry and tapped her glass to get the attention of all the aunts and uncles and cousins balancing plastic plates on their laps. "Thank you, everyone, khale merci, for coming today to see our beloved Mohammed's precious son and daughter." She turned to them. "Henry-jon and Samira-joon, the days you came into our lives as babies were the brightest. The days we lost you—and our Mohammed—were the darkest."

Samira winced at how painful it must have been for their grandmother and aunt to lose her and Kamron and Henry.

Daria raised her glass. "The sun is shining on us again; praise be to Allah." A chorus of cheers erupted. "Henry-jon, Samira-joon, the Safavis welcome you back—and this time, we're never letting you go." She hugged them both as everyone applauded.

The whole experience would have been even more dizzying without Henry.

For dessert, their grandmother served honey-soaked Persian pastries and tea while their aunt shared a childhood photo album. Daria laughed at a picture of her and her prom date: Mohammed was in the background, scowling at her date.

"Your father was very protective of me," she said with deep sorrow in her voice. "Of everyone around him. That's why he joined the army." She flipped to the last page of the album: an eight-by-ten of their father's military portrait. "That's why he was so devastated by what happened."

Their grandmother teared up. Amme Daria comforted her in Farsi.

When Samira and Henry finally caught a private moment together on the balcony, he gazed in amazement through the sliding glass door at all the relatives who had come out to greet them. "Can you believe all these people were strangers a few months ago?"

Samira followed his gaze. "Well, they still are."

"No, they're not," he said sincerely. "They're family."

"You're right," Samira acknowledged. They *were* family, whom she would get to know better and better as time went by.

When they finally said their goodbyes around midnight, Amme Daria hugged them tight and their grandmother pleaded, "Please, please come to visit me," in halting English.

"We will," they promised.

Henry drove them back over the Golden Gate Bridge to Santa Rosa in Gran's Kia since Samira had never mastered the city's one-way streets. As the fog swirled down from the mountain, they vowed to visit their aunt and grandmother every couple of months if they could. And drive up to see their father as often as they could. And talk and text and FaceTime with each other and Kamron now that he had completed treatment and was living in Ashland with Mom, who had gotten him a job running the school's tech lab. *The kids love him,* she said proudly.

Since he had been able to visit their father once a week,

Kamron was as excited as anyone to plan his homecoming party in 2027. They all vowed to be there for him when their father got out.

Because they were his children. They were family.

And now that they had found each other, they were never letting go.

Acknowledgments

My husband, Wayne, was raised as an only child by his aunt and uncle. His bio-mom remained in the picture, but he never knew his biological father, who seemed to have disappeared. Several years ago, I got him a DNA test to see if he had inherited any health risks from his dad. To our utter shock, he got an email from the genetic testing company with the subject line: *Closest Possible Match—Sibling.* Wayne was matched with his younger half sister, Mitzi! As it turned out, they grew up in Southern California less than twenty-five miles apart.

Suddenly, my husband was not an only child anymore. He and Mitzi became close. He's tickled by the notion that he's now a big brother. Immediately, I began thinking about what their lives would have been like if they had connected as teenagers. That's why, first and foremost, I must acknowledge and thank Wayne and Mitzi Deatherage Linscott for inspiring me and for allowing me to incorporate some real-life details into this book (yes, my husband played hockey and had two moms; yes, they were rivals for his affection).

The story they inspired would not be an actual, published book without my agent, superwoman Laura Bradford, the most capable and unflappable person I know (unflappability being a key trait in an agent). Thank you for your excellent editorial instincts, Laura, and for your continued faith in me.

I am so monstrously proud of this book thanks to my editor, Alexandra Sehulster, who pushed me to find its deepest emotional depths with her usual kindness and sensitivity. Thank you, Alex, for being such a wonderful champion for me at Wednesday Books. I will forever be grateful to you for making my lifelong dream come true.

And thank you to Alexandra's assistant, Cassidy Graham, who stepped up in a big way on this book! I'm so lucky that you were there to keep things running smoothly.

This gorgeous cover is thanks to the incredible artistry of designer Olga Grlic and illustrator Petra Braun. And thank you to designer Donna Noetzel for the beautiful book interior!

Publishing is a team sport, and I could not be more grateful to the Wednesday Books team of superstars who put their whole hearts into supporting this book, including Rivka Holler, Brant Janeway, Melanie Sanders, Eric Meyer, Diane Dilluvio, and my publicist, Meghan Harrington.

I was fortunate to have had quinn b. rodriguez as a sensitivity reader for alcohol addiction. It was humbling to realize how little I actually knew about the subject from the perspective of a person in recovery considering that I drew on my lived experience with a family member. quinn made me look at Kamron with much more compassion, and for that, I am deeply grateful.

Thank you to my dearest friends in the world and beta readers (often of multiple drafts!) Kitty Schaller, Jena Ellis, Benita Shaw, and Carol Pearce, whose early-stage input is always invaluable.

Shout-out to my critique partners Lynn Q. Yu, Jason "J Bae"

Nadeau, and Clifton Tibbetts, who gave such thorough and thoughtful notes that were critical in the shaping of this story.

I'm super lucky to have a sister like Shirin Donoghue who reads—and unquestioningly loves—everything I write! And thanks to my brother-in-law, Kevin Donoghue, as well as my stepbrother, Mohammed Mohajer, who acted as advisors on several key areas.

I wish my mom, Sharan McNerney, and my grandmother Jenny were here to celebrate this book's release with me, but I know they are cheering me on from above.

I'm very thankful that my dad, Iraj Azimzadeh, and my step-mother, Mitra Mohajer, *are* here. As Henry and Samira learn, family means everything, and I am very grateful to have mine around.

Thank you to my sweet baby, Teddy, who's always my most constant companion while drafting and editing, and to my son, Alec Boyer, whose intellect, humor, courage, and passion inspire me. I love you, babe!

And I do need to thank my wonderful husband, Wayne Boyer, again because I could not write without the unconditional love, stability, encouragement, and support he provides. You have made every single one of my dreams come true! What a treat it was to create Henry in your image. I love you, honey.